Dead Meat: Day 1-3
Copyright © 2021 Nick Clausen

Edited by Diana Cox
Cover by CreativeParamita.com
Created with Atticus

The author asserts his moral rights to this work.
Please respect the hard work of the author.
No zombies were harmed in the making of this book.

DAY 1

The following takes place on
Saturday, July 26

ONE

Thomas tries to block out the sounds. Tries to keep his head clear. To think straight. But it's difficult. Jennie is complaining about the pain. Dan is sobbing. And from the other side of the door comes the relentless sounds of scraping nails and low moaning.

"It really hurts," Jennie moans. "I think I need to go to the ER. Could you try calling them again, Thomas?"

"I tried calling a hundred times already," Thomas mutters without looking up at her. "I keep telling you: there is no signal down here."

The basement is stiflingly warm and stuffy. Cobwebs are hanging in threads from the ceiling. The room is crammed full of old furniture, cardboard boxes, worn-out books, and cast-off clothes. The windows are sitting high and are too narrow for a person to pass through—not even Dan is able to squeeze out. A few rays of dusty, orange sunlight are streaming through, reminding them of the scorching hot summer day outside. The heat wave is going on its third week.

In the middle of the room hangs a naked lightbulb. Thomas wonders how much light it will provide if they're still here come nightfall.

Another low moan from the other side of the door.

Dan wipes his nose on his sleeve. "Do you … do you think we should put more stuff in front of the door, Thomas? That box doesn't look very heavy."

Why do I have to make every little decision? Thomas thinks. Who the hell named me captain? He bites back the anger and says in a moderately calm voice: "The box is heavy enough—it's full of porcelain. I almost couldn't drag it over there. She won't be able to move it."

"But—"

"But it doesn't really matter," Thomas interrupts, "since the door is locked and the key is on our side. She's been out there for"—he checks his watch—"forty-five minutes now, and so far, she hasn't tried to pick the lock. She hasn't even grabbed the knob. I don't think she has much brains left, so don't worry about the door."

Jennie gives off another groan of pain. "What the hell's even happened to her?"

"She's a fucking zombie, that's what's happened to her," Thomas grunts. "Haven't you ever seen a zombie movie? Dawn of the Dead? World War Z? Ring any bells?"

"Zombies aren't real," Jennie sneers. "And don't talk to me like I'm stupid, just because I don't watch the same nasty movies as you do."

"Can't believe you two are dating," Dan mutters.

Thomas sends him a look, but can't help but smile despite himself. He likes Dan. And Dan is right. In fact, Thomas and Jennie probably would have broken up this morning, if the day hadn't turned to shit. Thomas had set his mind: He was going to tell her straight up that he didn't want to go out with her anymore. That was the reason he agreed to go on the paper route with her in the first place. He didn't know she had also talked Dan into coming along.

"Jesus, it's still bleeding," Jennie complains. "How can it still be bleeding? It's just a scratch."

Thomas looks over at her and sees her uncoiling the towel from around her arm. "What are you doing?" he says. "You need to keep it tight."

She darts him a sour look. Her mascara has left dark traces down her cheeks. "So, you're suddenly a doctor, are you?"

Thomas is very close to being fed up. He tries to find a way to get them out of this basement, tries to think, but he keeps getting interrupted. And the noises from the door are starting to get on his nerves. A drop of sweat rolls down his nose. He blows it away, thinking: Of all the ways I could have spent my Saturday ...

"Hello?" Jennie says loudly, waving at him. "I'm talking to you."

"What?" Thomas asks through gritted teeth.

"I don't think this stupid towel is working. We need to find some bandages or something. There has to be a first aid kit around here somewhere. Check those shelves over there, Dan." She drops the towel on the concrete floor and points.

Dan gets up.

"Sit down, Dan," Thomas says. "There is no first aid kit. I already checked."

Dan hesitates, unsure whom to obey.

Jennie rounds on Thomas. "And what if you missed it? You didn't really look, did you? You're not the one bleeding, after all, so why would you even give a fuck?"

Thomas is on his feet and strides to Jennie in three long paces. He bends down, grabs the towel and wraps it around her arm. "Put that thing back on," he sneers.

Jennie begins to struggle. "Don't! Let go of me!"

Thomas manages to tie a knot, tightening it fiercely. "There! That's how tight it should be. Got it?"

Jennie gives off a cry and tries to pull her arm away, while taking a swing at him with the other hand. Thomas catches her wrist and is just about to twist it, when Dan shouts: "Stop it! Both of you! Stop!"

The struggle stops. For a moment, Thomas and Jennie just scowl at each other. Then Thomas turns to walk away—but then he notices something. "What the hell? What's wrong with your skin?"

Jennie turns her back to him. "Mind your own business."

"Jennie," he says. "Show me your arm."

Apparently, she picks up on something in his voice, because she turns back and holds out her arm hesitantly. "It's still bleeding," she mutters.

And it's true: a thin stream of pink blood runs from the cut in Jennie's forearm and drips to the floor. But the blood doesn't concern Thomas—he's looking at her skin. Jennie is tan all year round, as she regularly goes to tanning salons. But around the cut the color seems to be draining from the skin, leaving a pale, greyish hue.

"I hadn't noticed till now," she says uncertainly. "You think it could be … blood poisoning or something?"

"I don't think blood poisoning sets in that fast. What did you say she cut you with?"

"A knife."

"Are you sure?"

"Well, it all happened so quickly, I didn't really get a chance to …"

"What kind of knife? Did you see it?"

"Yes. I mean, no. I didn't see it, but I felt it. When she attacked me."

"What did you feel, exactly?"

"Why? Does it matter?" Jennie shakes her head in annoyed confusion. "What's wrong? Why are you both staring at me like that?"

Dan has joined them, and like Thomas, he looks at his sister with wide, knowing eyes. "I don't think she had a knife," he says stiffly. "Why would she use a knife? She's a zombie. Zombies don't use weapons."

It's so obvious, Thomas should have seen it earlier. But the situation is so surreal he didn't give it a second thought.

"Tell us what happened, Jennie," he says, and for the first time in a long time, his voice is soft, almost loving.

Jennie's lip starts to quiver. "It happened just as we entered the living room. I ... I heard her come from behind, so I spun around. She tried stabbing me, but she tripped over something ... like, an ottoman, I think. And when she fell down, that's when the knife cut me."

"But you didn't actually see the knife?" Thomas asks.

"No, but ..."

"Her fingernails were long," Dan whispers. "I noticed."

Jennie looks at the cut on her arm. "All right, maybe it was her nail and not a knife. What difference does that make?"

What difference? Thomas thinks. What difference?

Jennie wasn't lying; she really hasn't watched any zombie flicks. If she had, she would have known right away what a cut from a fingernail means.

But Dan knows—Thomas can tell from the look of terror and disbelief on his face, as he turns his head and stares blankly at Thomas. It's like an unspoken question passes between the boys in that moment. Two small words.

How long?

"What is it?" Jennie asks, audible fear in her voice now. "Why are you just staring at each other? Hello? Talk to me!"

TWO

The temperature in the basement steadily rises, as does the pain in Jennie's arm—and not a minute passes without her telling them so. The skin on her forearm gradually changes color. It's starting to take on a greenish tone.

Dan just sits by the wall, staring at nothing. Thomas can see his lips moving, like he's silently talking to himself.

Thomas glances at Jennie, who keeps checking her phone for a signal. Of course she didn't believe him when he explained to her how serious the situation is. That the infection will probably become fatal within a few hours. That she will most likely end up like the lady outside the door. Jennie kept stubbornly saying it was only blood poisoning and that she just needed to go to the hospital.

But Thomas knows her too well. He can tell she's scared.

He hides his face in his sweaty palms. How did they end up here? Less than an hour ago they were in his car, driving down the road, sweating and listening to music.

They're almost at the end of the route, only four stops left.

Dan is in the backseat next to the box of newspapers.

Jennie has tilted back her seat and put her feet up on the dashboard. "I can't believe you bought a car without air-conditioning. Honestly! What's the point in having a car if it doesn't have air-con? We're burning up!"

Thomas pretends not to hear her and concentrates on the GPS. They're a few miles outside town. The house appears at the end of the long, dusty gravel road. He parks in the courtyard.

"It's your turn, Dan," Jennie says. "If she doesn't come to the door, just go inside and put it on the table in the scullery. That's what I usually do."

Dan obediently leaves the car and trudges to the front door, a rolled-up newspaper in his hand.

Thomas turns down the radio slightly and looks sideways at Jennie. She's wearing sunglasses, so he can't see her eyes. Good. That'll make it easier. He's just about to say it. The words are on his lips.

"I don't think it's working out between us anymore."

But he can't get them out. He just can't. The moment is not right. Instead, he says: "Who lives here?"

"Some older lady," she yawns. "She's kind of weird. I think she suffers from dementia or something."

"Does she live alone?"

"Yeah, can you believe it? I mean, who the hell wants to live out here in the middle of nowhere all by themselves?"

At that moment, Dan screams from inside the house.

Thomas and Jennie look at each other for a brief second. Then they each open their doors and jump out. They run to the front door.

As soon as Thomas enters the house, time seems to speed up tenfold. He briefly notices the weird décor: colorful stones and crystals everywhere, faces cut out of wood, a large bamboo flute, dried flowers dangling from strings in the ceiling. He also registers a bad smell. But there's no time to think before the woman steps out a few feet in front of him.

Thomas has played a lot of Resident Evil and watched every episode of The Walking Dead—he knows what a zombie looks like. Her eyes are pale yet piercing, her mouth contorted into a snarl, the grimace made even more pronounced because of the missing piece of her lower lip. It looks like it might have been torn off, revealing the grey teeth and pink gums. Blood has run down her chin and stained the front of the dress, which once was white but now looks more like a butcher's apron. Her long, silver hair hangs in a thin, whiplike braid.

She reaches out her arms and staggers towards him on boney, wobbly legs, while producing a low rumbling growl from deep down her throat.

Then, everything turns to chaos. Tipped over furniture, yells and screams, grabbing and pushing.

Jennie screaming: "She cut me! She cut me!"

Thomas tries to get to the front door, but is cut off, and suddenly they're all cornered. A door behind them. Thomas yanks it open, revealing a dim staircase leading down to the basement. They have no other choice. They flee down into the darkness.

And now, here they are. In the dim, dusty heat. The zombie lady has followed them down the stairs and is now waiting on the other side of the door. Scraping and moaning, scraping and moaning.

Jennie gives off a tortured sound. She wipes her forehead. "Christ, I'm sweating buckets. I think I might have a fever. I really need to see a doctor." She glances at the door. "Doesn't she ever leave?"

Thomas just shakes his head.

"Well, she has to leave sometime," Jennie persists. "Doesn't she get sleepy or something?"

"Nope. She'll keep at it until she rots."

Jennie wrinkles her nose. "Don't say stuff like that. The smell down here is bad enough." She gets up and goes to the door. "Hello? Can you hear me? Could you please move away from the door? I need to get out. But please don't try to hurt me, okay?"

The scraping noises grow louder, more eager. Like the zombie can sense Jennie standing right on the other side.

Thomas gets up. "Don't open the door."

Jennie rolls her eyes. "I'm not going to open the door as long as she's out there. Do you think I'm a complete moron?"

"Actually, yeah, I do think that, since only a moron would try talking sense into a zombie." He jabs himself with a finger in the temple. "She's not a person anymore. She's a walking corpse. How many times do I need to tell you? The only thing on her mind is fresh meat. She wants to—"

"Yeah, I know, she wants to eat us all alive," Jennie sneers. "Right, whatever." She goes back to the chair and slumps down. Then, she lights up. "Hey, what if we're completely quiet?"

"You're the only one still talking," Thomas remarks as he sits back down.

Jennie pretends not to hear him. "Maybe she'll forget about us if she can't hear us. Maybe she'll go back upstairs. You know, to look for someone else to ... eat."

The idea has actually crossed Thomas's mind. "It depends on whether her senses are still working, or if she's driven by instincts. Maybe she doesn't need to hear us, maybe she can simply sense we're here." He looks at Dan. "What do you think?"

Dan blinks, obviously surprised to be asked for his opinion. "Well ... I don't know. I guess it's worth a try."

"Right," Jennie says. "From now on, no one makes a sound."

They all fall silent. All except for the zombie. It goes on scraping, moaning.

Tirelessly. Insatiable.

THREE

Half an hour passes by.

Dan looks briefly in a box of books before lying down on a blanket, curled up like a dog. Thomas is slumped over on his seat, almost nodding off despite the heat. His clothes are sticking damply to his skin, his mouth is dry. Both of the two narrow windows are open wide, but only a warm, lazy breeze seeps in.

Jennie is the first one to break the silence. "Right, it's obviously not working," she snaps. "She's not going to leave." She sighs. "I'm just … so … fucking … thirsty! Honestly, I'm going to die if I don't get something to drink soon."

We're all going to die if we don't get something to drink soon, Thomas thinks, wiping a dangling drop of sweat from his brow.

"Look," Dan says, getting up. "I found this in one of the boxes." He comes over, holding out an old photo album for the others to see.

"It must be her when she was young," Jennie says, as Dan flips through the pages, pointing to a slim woman with long, blonde hair.

The photos tell a story of the woman going on a journey to somewhere warm and tropical. The locals are black.

"Where is it?" Jennie asks. "Africa or something?"

Dan slips out one of the photos and checks the backside. "Haiti, it says."

The photos show a wedding. Not a traditional one in a church with a bride in a white dress. Instead, the woman is standing with her black husband under the open sky on a beach at sunset. All around them, the guests are dressed and painted in what seems to be the traditional local outfits.

"She married one of them," Jennie says. "How sweet."

Dan flips through the pages. Pictures of the woman and her husband in this house. A picture of the woman with a large, pregnant belly. A family photo: the woman, her husband, and a half-black boy. The woman's hair grows silvery, her skin starts to wrinkle, and her son becomes a man. Him kissing a redhaired woman. The last of the photos shows a small, bi-racial girl, smiling between her mom and dad.

As they reach the end of the album, the spell is broken, and Thomas gets to his feet. "Listen, I think I know how we can get out of here."

Jennie gives off a tiny exclamation of excitement, and Dan straightens up.

"We can't contact anyone outside. We can't even hope for someone to come by. She lived alone out here, so it could be days before she has a visitor."

"I thought of the mailman," Dan interjects. "Don't they usually come on the weekends too?"

"Maybe," Thomas says. "But that wouldn't make a difference. The mailbox is up by the road—I noticed it when we came. The mailman won't come anywhere near the house."

Dan bows his head.

Thomas nods towards the door. "It doesn't seem like she ... like it ... is planning to give up anytime soon. Which means we need to find a way out ourselves, and the sooner, the better. If we just keep sitting here, we'll lose strength. And Jennie's arm ..." He glances at her. "We need to get her to the hospital, so they can treat her."

He avoids Dan's eyes, yet he can hear the lie in his own voice. If zombie movies taught him anything, it's that once you get bitten or scratched, the show's over. There is no vaccine, no cure, no nothing. The victim can only wait for fever, coma, death.

And then: life once more.

"Sounds fine with me," Jennie says, sounding a bit more optimistic. "But how do we do it? As soon as we open the door, she'll come barging in."

"That's right, and I can't think of a way to lure her away from the door. That's why we need to let her in."

Dan lets out a gasp. "We can't!"

"There's no other way. As far as I can tell, we have three options once we open the door. One: We can try and slip past her and get up the stairs. It'll be difficult, though, since there's three of us, and there isn't a lot of room to move around. I think there's a big risk not all three of us will make it out of here unharmed. Two: We can try and lure her into a trap. It doesn't have to be anything fancy. If we can make her trip or throw a blanket over her head—just confuse her for a few seconds, that might be all we need to get past her."

"That sounds dangerous," Dan says. "We need to get pretty close to her if we're going to trip her or throw something over her head."

"I know. That's why I'm partial to the third option." Thomas gets up and makes his way through the basement. Against the wall in the corner leans a piece of rusty iron pipe. Thomas grabs it and weighs it in his grasp. It feels heavy and cold and assuring. He looks at Jennie and Dan. "The third option is fighting our way past her."

Jennie raises her brow. "You're not serious, are you? You want to hit her with that thing? That's assault! And she's old—what if you kill her?"

"That's the idea," Thomas says dryly.

Jennie stares at him in disbelief. "Are you insane?"

"She's already dead," Dan reminds his sister. "Killing her again would actually be kind. Like, an act of mercy. That's what they always say in the movies, anyway."

Jennie shakes her head. "You two need to get a grip. This is not a movie. And it's not some crazy monster on the other side of that door. She might be sick or something, but she's still just an old lady. Did you forget about the photos already? She has kids and grandkids and everything. We can't just ... kill her with a pipe!"

"We can," Thomas says, but he doesn't feel quite as convinced as he sounds. Because it's going to be him doing the killing. Jennie is obviously out of the picture—she couldn't hit the floor if she fell down, especially not with her wounded arm. And Dan isn't strong enough. Thomas grips the pipe firmer. He used to play rounders when he was little, and he's confident he can put the zombie to rest with one good swing—providing he doesn't miss.

"You'll only get one try," Dan says darkly. "If you miss, she'll get you instead."

"I might have time for two, maybe three tries," Thomas says. "Look." He swings the pipe swiftly. It's heavier than he expects, and it slips out of his grip, whooshes through the air and hits the wall with a bang.

Jennie screams. "Watch it! Are you out of your mind? You could have hit me!"

On the other side of the door, the zombie scratches more eagerly, apparently sensing the commotion.

Thomas picks up the pipe. His palms are reddish brown. "It was because of the rust," he mutters. He gives it another go, more carefully this time. But he still has trouble swinging the pipe hard enough without losing his grip. It seems Dan is right. He'll only get one shot.

"I vote for the second option," Jennie says. "One of you guys get behind the door with the blanket, and as soon as she enters, you throw it over her head and push her down. When she falls, we all make a run for it."

Thomas considers the idea. "What if one of us doesn't make it out before she gets back up? Then that person would be seriously fucked." He shakes his head. "No, I still think eliminating the threat is our best course of action."

"Eliminating the threat," Jennie repeats. "Just listen to yourself, would you? You think you're some kind of soldier? You couldn't even swing that thing without dropping it."

"I told you, that was because of the rust. Now I'm prepared for it, it won't happen again."

"And what if it does? Then we're all fucked!"

Thomas scoffs at her. He turns to Dan. "What do you think? We need a deciding vote."

Dan doesn't answer; he seems to be studying the place where the pipe hit the wall. Then, he says: "I vote for a fourth solution." He points, revealing a hole in the wall.

Thomas comes closer. "What the hell? I thought it was a brick wall."

"No, it's something much more smoldery. Plaster, I think. And it's not very thick, either. There seems to be another room on the other side!"

Thomas bends down and looks through the hole. It's too dark to see anything, but an unpleasant smell seeps through.

"Phew," he says, pulling away. "Something stinks really bad in there."

"Who cares?" Jennie exclaims. "Just hurry up and break down that wall, will you?"

Thomas pushes Dan aside, raises the iron pipe and starts swinging.

FOUR

The wall proves surprisingly easy to break down. For every swing of the pipe, large, crumbling pieces come off. Soon the air is filled with white dust.

Thomas is panting and sweating, as he pulls back and swings, pulls back and swings. The putrid smell gets more and more poignant as the hole in the wall grows larger.

Within five minutes he has made an opening wide enough for them to pass through. He puts aside the pipe and just stands there for a moment, heaving for breath and feeling faint from the heat.

"Right," Dan says, looking from Thomas to Jennie. "Who's first?"

"Let me just catch my breath," Thomas says. "Then I'll go."

Jennie gets up resolutely. "Sorry, but I'm getting out of here right now." She manages two steps before she starts wobbling. It looks like her legs simply give way, and she stumbles into an old dresser.

Dan jumps forward to catch her. "Are you all right?"

"Yeah, sure," she mumbles. "I just got a little dizzy, that's all."

Dan helps her to sit back down. Thomas studies her face closely. Her cheeks have turned feverish red, the sweat is beading on her forehead. The skin on her wounded arm has turned alarmingly dark.

It's going a lot faster than I thought, Thomas thinks, swallowing a lump tasting like drywall. Really hope we find a way out through the next room ... or Dan and I will soon have a much bigger problem on our hands.

He pushes the thought aside, turns to the hole in the wall. The stench is really bad now. He can also hear something buzzing in there. He holds his nose as he gets out his cell phone and activates the flashlight.

The next room has no windows. It seems larger than the one they're in right now, but that might only be because it's not stuffed with junk.

The only pieces of furniture are an oblong dining table in the corner and in the center something which reminds him of a small altar. It's only knee-high and covered in a red tablecloth. Around the altar, in a circle on the floor, are six wooden stools all facing the center. As though someone recently held a small round table conference.

"What's in there?" Dan asks, coming closer. "Yuk, what's that horrid smell?"

"I don't know, but look!" Thomas points the light into the corner. A wooden ladder leads to a hatch in the ceiling. Thin beams of daylight are streaming through the cracks.

"It's a way out!" Dan gasps.

"What's in there?" Jennie asks from behind them.

Thomas steps in through the hole. He moves carefully along the wall until he reaches the ladder. He crawls up a few steps, so he can reach the hatch. He gives it a push, but it doesn't give. He pushes harder and hears the clinging of metal.

"Goddamnit. It's locked from the other side."

Dan lets out a moan.

Thomas steps back down and notices a switch on the wall. He flips it. A big lightbulb turns on reluctantly.

A loud gasp from Dan makes Thomas turn around.

So that's where the smell is coming from …

On each stool sits a small pile of furry mess. They are gutted animals: cats, rabbits, even a tiny dog. They have all been flayed and their skin nailed to the seats. The bared flesh is dark with rot, and an army of flies is buzzing around the feast. Blood has trickled down the legs of the stools and produced small puddles on the floor. Thomas looks around and notices strange symbols drawn on the walls with chalk. From the ceiling hangs a variety of objects in strings, such as large, black feathers, dried branches and thin bones.

"Holy shit," Dan whispers. "She's made some sort of crazy ritual down here."

Thomas runs his forearm across his cheeks and realizes he's sweating even more profusely now. The temperature is even higher in this room. The stench from the rotting animals has made its way into his sinuses—he can almost taste it.

"We gotta get out of here," Jennie says, as she steps tentatively through the wall. "We need to ... we need ..." Her voice trails off, as her eyes go blank. "Dan ... would you please ...? I'm a little ... dizzy ..."

Dan tries to catch her, but this time she collapses, slipping through his arms and on to the floor, her eyes halfway open, her mouth still trying to speak.

"Jennie? Jennie!" Dan calls out her name and shakes her gently, but he doesn't get any comprehensive response from Jennie, so he looks up at Thomas. "She's fainted."

Thomas waves off a fly. "I could tell she was getting worse. I guess we'll have to carry her when we—"

A bump from upstairs.

Both of them look up at the ceiling.

"Was that her?" Dan whispers. "The zombie lady, I mean."

Thomas goes back to the hole in the wall, sticks his head through and listens for a moment. He can still hear the sound of scraping nails from the door. He turns to Dan. "It wasn't her; she's still by the door."

"The door ..." Jennie mutters without opening her eyes.

Another bump from above. The ceiling gives off a low creak.

Thomas and Dan stare at each other.

"Someone else is in the house," Dan croaks.

FIVE

Thomas has been standing on the ladder with his ear pressed against the hatch for two minutes, when Dan no longer can take the silence.

"Do you hear anything?" he whispers.

Thomas steps back down onto the floor, shaking his head in mild confusion. "It doesn't sound like a big person. The steps are very light. Perhaps it's a child. But as far as I can tell, whoever is up there is just wandering about in circles."

Dan bites his lip. "Do you think it's a zombie?"

"That's the million-dollar question, I guess," Thomas says, shrugging.

"Should we try and call out for them?"

Thomas runs a hand through his hair, which is greasy from sweat and dust. "If it is a zombie, we don't want to draw its attention."

"But if it's a living person, they might be able to open the hatch and let us out."

"Zombie," Jennie echoes in a faint mutter.

Thomas darts a glance at her. Although he has come to more or less hate her over the last few months, it still pains him to see her like this. Dan has taken the blanket from the other room, rolled it up and put it under her head. Her wounded arm is resting on her stomach. The sweat is pouring from her face, the eyes are rolling around beneath the lids. Her legs twitch now and then.

She's going into a coma, Thomas thinks. Eventually, she'll die. After that, it's only a matter of time before she opens her eyes again. He shivers violently despite the stifling heat.

"I think we should call out," Dan says, licking the sweat from his upper lip. "If it is a zombie, we can't get out that way anyway. It makes no difference whether it knows we're here or not."

Thomas takes a deep breath. "You're right. We might as well try."

"Call for him, Thomas!" Jennie exclaims suddenly. "Just call for him!"

They both look at the sweating, fevered girl on the floor. It's almost like she has been following the conversation, but it's obvious to Thomas that she's merely delirious.

Dan starts sniveling.

Thomas reaches out and squeezes his shoulder. "We can still get her to the hospital. As soon as we get out of here, we run straight to the car, and ..."

Dan looks up at him, tears in his eyes. "I know the rules, you know."

Thomas can't think of anything else to say.

Jennie twitches again.

"Are we just supposed to ... leave her?" Dan asks, blinking as a fly lands on his cheek. "If we get out of here, I mean."

"I think we might have to. For now, anyway. Once we get a hold of the police, they'll have to come and get her."

"You think there's still police?"

"Why shouldn't there be?"

Dan shrugs. "Because the world is probably ending."

Thomas's mouth glides open. The thought hasn't even crossed his mind. What if Dan is right? What if this is the zombie apocalypse? Even if they make it out of here, they just might meet a world where everything is falling apart, where the zombies are rapidly taking over and where the remaining survivors are struggling to keep alive. His tongue suddenly feels way too big and sticky.

What about Dad? Or Mom? Or Christian? Or all the guys from work? Are they walking around as zombies right now?

"We'd better not think about that right now," he manages to say, shoving aside the images. "First we need to focus on getting out of this fucking basement."

"All right, but ..." Dan glances at his sister. "What if we can't get the hatch open?"

Thomas catches his drift. "Then we'll have to tie her up."

Dan looks ill just thinking about it, but he nods bravely.

Thomas goes to the ladder and looks up at the hatch. Then, he calls out: "Hello? Can you hear us up there?"

They listen.

Jennie mutters something.

Thomas can hear the steps coming across the floor. They stop right above the hatch. A few seconds of dead silence follow.

"We're down here!" Thomas yells. "In the basement! Right below you!"

They listen again. Another second or two passes by in silence.

Then, there's the sounds of two muffled bumps. Thomas imagines how the person drops down on his knees. He prays that whoever is up there will answer him within the next second or two, or at least begin to work the lock.

But it's a completely different sound that comes from the hatch.

The sound of scraping nails.

Thomas feels his heart sink. He turns his head to look at Dan.

The hopeful expression on Dan's face slowly crumbles. "Oh, no," he breathes. "It's another zombie …"

SIX

Dan looks around. "What do you think happened here?"

Thomas tries not to look at the gutted animals. "Something really fucked up."

"It almost looks like a sacrifice," Dan goes on.

Thomas shrugs. He has almost gotten used to the stench and the flies constantly landing on him by now. "Maybe she was a witch or something."

Dan approaches the table. It has a wide range of jars and pots, stones, crystals and wooden figurines. There's a row of bird skulls and an old, thick book. Dan opens it and leafs through the pages.

"What does it say?" Thomas asks.

"I don't know—it's not written in Danish."

"Is it English?"

"No, it's not a language I've ever seen. But it has some pretty sick illustrations."

Thomas tries to say something, but starts coughing instead. "Christ, I could really use a glass of water right now. My throat is dry as sand."

"Check this out," Dan mutters, still leafing through the book. "I think she used this when she did the ritual."

Thomas goes to see. Dan stops at a page with a single, large drawing which resembles the lineup in the room. A lot of incomprehensible words are written around the illustration.

"What do you think was the point of the ritual?" Dan asks.

"No idea. I didn't go to Hogwarts."

Dan doesn't seem to hear the joke. He just starts turning pages again.

Thomas goes to check on Jennie. She's fallen still, and it's almost like she's just sleeping normally. But as he crouches down to feel her cheek, he finds it glowing hot. Her arm is dark and swollen, the skin abnormally distended and shiny. The infection obviously already reached the fingers, which are thick like sausages.

A memory comes to him. That night they met at the disco. He recalls the tingling sensation in his stomach when Jennie slid her fingers in between his. He feels a deep stab of pain and sympathy.

Don't think about that now.

He straightens up and takes a deep breath. Suddenly, he just wants to get out of here. Right now. "We need to choose one of the ways, Dan," he says firmly. "I vote for the hatch. If it's only a kid up there, it'll be easier for us to get past it. Plus, if we break open the hatch, it'll probably fall through. If we're lucky, it'll break its legs."

Dan nods. "You're right. Let's try."

"Maybe we need to look for something to use as a weapon …"

"How about this?" Dan takes something from the table which Thomas didn't notice till now. It's a huge knife, the blade black with dried-up blood.

"Holy shit! That's the biggest knife I've ever seen."

"I know, it was just lying here, next to the book. I think she used it to flay the animals."

"Right, now we only need something to punch our way through the hatch. I guess this is our best option." He picks up the iron pipe and goes to the ladder. He darts a look at Dan. "Would you keep an eye on your sister?"

Dan nods, his face solemn.

Thomas takes a few steps up the ladder and starts punching the pipe up into the hatch. It's made of wood, and it'll take quite some time to break through; his punches only leave small marks.

After a minute or so, he takes a break and rests his arm. From the other side of the hatch he can hear the scratching has grown faster and louder.

It's helping me, he thinks and almost bursts into laughter. It's trying to break through from the other side.

Dan has brought the book and is now sitting next to Jennie studying it.

"Dan?"

He looks up. "Yeah?"

"Maybe you shouldn't … you know, be that close to her."

Dan glances at his sister, then moves a few yards away.

SEVEN

Thomas has been banging away at the hatch for some minutes, when Dan speaks.

Thomas stops and looks down at him. "What's that?"

"She's written something in Danish," he says, pointing to a place in the book. "It's on the last few pages."

"Huh," Thomas says, not feeling particularly interested. Small chips have started coming off the hatch. He's about halfway through, and he's earned a short break, so he places the pipe under his arm and rests his hands. A couple of sore blisters have appeared on his palms.

"It's very confusing," Dan goes on, frowning. "But I think I figured out what the ritual was for. Listen to this …" He starts reading aloud. "Seven lives are needed. Their blood must flow from them and find its way to the new veins where it once flowed warmly but now has turned cold. Once more it will flow with warmth and life …" Dan looks up at this point, nodding towards the table. "I think the animals were sacrifices. She killed them to bring something else to life."

"But there's only six of them," Thomas points out. "Where is the seventh?"

Dan swallows audibly. "Get this. Farther down it says … Oh, my beloved darling. You most beautiful child. Your Little Good Angel is dead and gone, but your Big Good Angel can never die. It's my fault. Take my blood so you can once again live."

Silence falls over the basement, as Dan stops—except for the scratching noises from the hatch, and the ragged heaving of Jennie's breath.

"So there was a child," Thomas mutters. "And it died?"

"Yeah, I think so. Perhaps there was an accident. And then the woman used this ritual to bring the kid back to life. She needed seven sacrifices, and the seventh …"

"... was herself," Thomas concludes. "Fuck me. It's like something out of a horror movie."

"The last thing she wrote was: Awaken, my dearest. I guess that was right before she did it."

Thomas points to the hatch. "So that's the child up there?"

"I think so, yeah."

Thomas tries to process the information. "I guess that's good news, then."

Dan looks baffled. "How so?"

"Because this was where it started. It means the world hasn't ended. Only this house."

"But we don't know if they have been outside the house."

"If they had, why would they have returned? I think they've been trapped here until we came by. None of them were able to open a door or a window."

Dan doesn't exactly look thrilled. "So no one else but us knows about it. And if we die, there'll be three more zombies in this house. So when the next poor guy shows up ... they won't know until it's too late, and the zombies will get out."

Thomas thinks for a moment. "You're right. I guess it's up to us. We can't let them get away. We need to find a way to keep them here, until we can reach the police, and—"

He's interrupted as Jennie suddenly gives off a loud, rasping gasp. She doesn't open her eyes, but her face contorts into a painful grimace. The flies are crawling all over her.

"It won't be long," Thomas mutters. "We need to find something to tie her up with."

He steps down from the ladder and goes to the first room to look. The best he can find is a piece of cord. Back in the other room he finds an old, rusty electric heater mounted to the wall.

"Help me move her, Dan."

Together the boys gently drag Jennie across the floor. It's easy, since she has suddenly gone completely limp and quiet again. Her skin is no longer particularly warm, either. Thomas figures she has slipped into a coma. He's amazed at the speed of the infection.

He pulls the cord tightly to test its strength. It seems very strong, so he ties one end to the heater, making sure to do a few extra knots just to be sure.

This is where they always fuck up in the movies. Some fool doesn't tie the rope properly, so the knot unties itself once the zombie wakes up and starts tugging.

Thomas ties the other end of the cord around Jennie's ankle and makes it as tight as he can, with three strong knots.

Dan looks at his sister, a pained expression on his face. "How long do you think it'll be?"

Thomas reaches out to feel her pulse. It's very faint. "Not long," he whispers. "We better keep our distance from this point on. Do you ... uhm ... want to say goodbye?"

Dan squeezes his lips firmly together. He kneels down in front of Jennie. Thomas doesn't want to look, so he turns his back, but he can still hear Dan whisper.

"Jennie? I don't know if you can hear me, but ... I hope so. I'm really sorry this had to happen. I wish I could make it better. You ... you were a good big sister to me. Most of the time, anyway." He sniffs wetly. "And by the way ... I was the one who hid your phone that time you couldn't find it for three days. I did it because I was mad at you. I'm sorry."

Dan gets to his feet and wipes his eyes with the sleeve of his T-shirt.

"I'm sorry, Dan. She didn't deserve to die."

Dan nods and walks to the table.

Thomas stays with Jennie for a moment, looking at her, feeling like he needs to say something, but unsure what. "I love you," seems so tacky, so movie-like. Instead, he just whispers: "Bye, Jennie. Sorry we need to leave you like this."

He's just about to turn away, when he notices something different about her. He kneels down and puts a finger under her nose. No wind. Jennie isn't breathing anymore. He turns his head and looks at Dan.

Dan stares back at him, shifting his weight from foot to foot. "Is she ... is she dead?"

Thomas nods.

Dan breaks down into tears. He slumps to the floor and sobs into his palms. "Why is this happening? Why us? Couldn't it have been someone else who had to take out those stupid papers?"

Thomas feels a hard lump in his throat. The whole thing is still too surreal to take in. It's gone way too fast. He can't believe Jennie is gone—not really. It starts spinning behind his eyes. A sharp headache is throbbing right underneath his temples. He has never been this thirsty in his life.

He goes and picks up the pipe and starts banging away at the hatch once more. Then, Dan calls out his name.

Thomas turns around. Dan is standing a few feet away, stiff as a board, pointing to Jennie.

Jennie is lying in the exact same position; she hasn't moved an inch. But her eyes are open. They're staring up into the ceiling.

They're blank.

But alive.

EIGHT

Thomas bangs away faster and faster. He's no longer worried about the zombie child waiting on the other side of the hatch. He doesn't register the dust or the woodchips hitting his face and getting into his eyes. He doesn't even feel the blisters burning on his hands. He just wants to get out of here before Jennie comes back to life.

Dan has gone to the farthest corner. He's just standing there, staring across the room at his sister, who's still lying there, not moving, eyes open wide.

Almost through … almost through …

The muscles in his arms are aching. Between the blows he can hear the zombie scratching eagerly right above him.

And then it happens.

A piece the size of a fist breaks off. Thomas lowers the pipe, panting, and stares up through the hole. For a moment, nothing happens.

Then a milky-white eye appears on the other side. The dead gaze fastens on Thomas, as he feels his skin contracting all over his back. The eye disappears, and instead a tiny, greyish hand comes through the hole. Judging from the remains of sky-blue nail polish, the hand once belonged to a girl. The hand grabs and flails eagerly in empty air.

"I think it's her," Thomas says. "The girl from the photo album."

Dan doesn't reply.

Thomas turns to look at him, and immediately sees what Dan sees.

Jennie is sitting up. If he didn't know better, he could almost be tempted to think Jennie's body might have fought off the infection, that she's no longer ill.

But one good look at her face is enough to break that illusion. The seventeen-year-old girl who less than half an hour ago was Thomas's annoying girlfriend, is dead. The creature now sitting there, glaring around with an empty expression, has nothing to do with Jennie. It looks like her, but behind the eyes is nothing human; only hunger.

The Jennie zombie bares its tiny, white teeth and growls from deep in its throat. It starts getting to its feet with cumbersome movements, like an overgrown toddler.

Something flies across Thomas's brain at that moment. He has seen a lot of zombie movies. In some of them, the zombies run around like people on speed. They can sprint, jump and even climb fences. But in other movies, they are slow and wobbly and move around like sleepwalkers. Those movies have always been his favorites, because the zombies are a lot more terrifying when they move slowly.

Jennie obviously belongs to that category. It takes her half a minute to stand up. When she finally manages, she immediately reaches both arms out towards Thomas and takes two steps forward.

For a moment, Thomas is certain the cord won't hold. It will simply snap and Jennie will walk right over to him, put her arms around his neck, like she used to do back when they were still in love, but this time it wouldn't be to kiss him—instead, she would bury her fingernails in his neck and bite off his ear. He sees it all very clearly.

The cord holds.

The pull of it is almost enough to throw her off-balance. She stumbles and snarls. Regains her balance and tries for another step forward. The cord stops her once more. She tries again. And again. She doesn't look down, not even for a second. She's not at all concerned with finding out what is holding her back. Her eyes are only fixed on Thomas. Her first meal, waiting right there, a few yards in front of her. She steps forward again. Is stopped. Again. Stopped.

Thomas forces himself to regain focus, and he looks over at Dan, only to see a boy who has obviously left the situation mentally. His gaze is distant, his lips are trembling, and he is absentmindedly shaking his head.

"Dan? ... Dan! ... Dan!"

Dan turns his head and looks at Thomas, his eyes coming somewhat into focus again.

"I'm almost through the hatch now. As soon as it breaks, we need to be quick—so be ready, okay?"

Dan nods.

Thomas turns back to the hatch in the ceiling. The zombie girl's arm is still groping around for anything to grab. He directs another blow at the hatch. The zombie girl's fingers brush across the back of his hand.

"Fucking hell," he hisses and pulls away. "She almost scratched me ... Get away!" He hits the zombie across the hand, hard. It only makes her grope more vigorously.

"Thomas," Dan says, his voice is weirdly dreamlike. "I think the heater is coming loose."

Thomas turns his head. The cord around Jennie's leg still looks in pretty fine shape. But the electric heater, which he tied it to, has come off the wall at one end. Now it's dangling crookedly off the wall, threatening to come off entirely with every tug from Jennie's leg.

Fuck, fuck, fuck! Why didn't I think to check the stupid thing was securely attached to the wall?

Desperately, he turns to the hatch again, hitting it three time in a row, the woodwork rustling with every blow. The zombie girl grabs at the pipe, but catches Thomas's wrist instead.

He shrieks and pulls his hand away, staring at it. No scratch marks. But it was a really close call.

Jennie lets out a moan behind him. She pulls more eagerly now. As though she can sense she's almost free. The heater is hanging by one stubborn hinge now.

There is only one thing to do.

Thomas jumps down from the ladder and steps towards Jennie. "Turn away, Dan."

"What are you gonna do?" Dan croaks.

"Turn away!"

Dan turns away.

Thomas tightens his grip on the pipe. He looks down, not wanting to face Jennie. Come on. You can do it. It's not Jennie anymore. Don't look at it. It's not Jennie.

He counts to three. Then he steps forward and raises the pipe. Just as he swings it, his eyes lock with Jennie. It takes off some of the force of the blow. But he still hits his target with an audible slam.

Jennie stumbles sideways and falls to her knees. It doesn't seem to bother her, though. She simply gets back up and resumes her tireless effort to get to him.

Don't look at it!

But he can't help it. He stares at Jennie's face. It looks all wrong. Like her skull has been bent out of shape. Her cheekbone is pressed inwards, the skin under her eye is bulging, causing the eye to squeeze shut. Her mouth is contorted into a crooked snarl.

Holy shit ... what did I do?

Thomas feels the nausea come rolling up into his throat. He drops the pipe with a loud clanging. He can't hit her again. No way.

He squeezes his fingers into his temples. *What do we do? What the fuck do we do?*

He looks up at the hatch again, and an idea comes to mind. It's crazy. But it just might work. And he's pretty sure he can do it. After all, he didn't know the zombie girl like he knew Jennie. He hasn't even seen her face. It wouldn't feel personal. He hopes.

"Dan," he mutters. "Hand me the knife."

As Dan goes to the table to get the knife, Thomas uses the pipe to reach the towel that Jennie had been using as a pillow before she died. She reaches for him hungrily, but he makes sure to keep a safe distance.

"I need your help," he tells Dan. "I'll catch her arm with this towel, so she can't scratch us. Then you hold it while I cut."

"Cut?" Dan asks, looking puzzled for a moment, but then he catches on, and his expression turns to horror. Still, he nods bravely.

Thomas goes to the hatch and uses the towel to catch the flailing arm. The zombie child starts struggling, but Thomas manages to wrap the hand tightly.

"Here," he says over his shoulder. "Take it!"

Dan comes closer, reaches out hesitantly and grabs hold of the towel.

"Grip it firmly," Thomas demands. When he feels sure Dan has a confident grip, he lets go, bends down and grabs the knife. Stepping back up on the ladder, he mutters: "Right. Right, here we go."

He picks out a spot right below the elbow and puts the blade to the skin. He takes a breath. His stomach feels like it might turn itself inside out any moment. He tries not to think of the photos from the album.

Do it. Your own and Dan's lives depend on it. Do it now!

Thomas closes his eyes and cuts. The blade sinks into the arm way too easily. It cuts through the dead meat like it is butter. He feels the cool liquid spurting out, drenching his hand and dripping onto his T-shirt. There is no audible reaction from the zombie child, and she doesn't even try to pull back her arm. She just keeps struggling to get free of the towel so she can grab one of them.

Thomas cuts even deeper and feels the knife hit something hard. It's the bone. He bites down hard and pushes with all his strength, wriggling the knife back and forth in a sawing motion. It doesn't give, so he increases the pressure even further, grabbing the knife with both hands, leaning sideways, putting his whole body into the task.

"Come on, come on," someone snarls, and Thomas realizes it's him. His arms are shaking, his muscles are aching with the effort. The growling of the zombie child fills his ears.

Then, suddenly a loud crack as the bone gives. It's more due to the pressure than the knife.

Thomas drops the knife and tumbles to the floor. Dan lets go of the towel and steps back. Thomas looks up, expecting to see a bloody stump where the arm used to be. But the arm is still there, still attached. Now it's just dangling helplessly from the hole in the hatch. The fingers don't seem able to open or close anymore. Dark red fluid is gushing from the cut and dripping to the floor.

"Right, that's enough," Thomas hears himself say, as he swallows several times in an effort to keep down the nausea. "Now she can't scratch us."

Thomas picks up the pipe, feeling more like a sleepwalker than a wakeful person, and starts banging away at the hatch once more. The zombie child is still growling and trying to grab him, but the broken arm is as useful as a garden hose with a rubber glove at the end.

Dan suddenly turns away and throws up on the floor.

Thomas darts a look at Jennie. He has almost—amazingly—forgotten about her while focusing on the zombie child. The last screw of the radiator is still holding. If they're lucky, it will hold just long enough for them to get out.

Just as he turns his attention back to the hatch, the bloody arm disappears back up through the hole.

"No!" he shouts. "No, don't you fucking do it! Don't put your other arm down here! I fucking dare you!"

The thought of having to break the zombie child's other arm is too much to bear.

But the arm doesn't appear. Nothing appears. Instead, he can hear the zombie child getting to her feet. She walks away from the hatch.

Dan has finished puking and is wiping his mouth with his sleeve. "Where did she go?" he croaks.

"No idea."

A new sound comes down through the hole now: it's a whiny scratching noise. Like fingernails on glass. It takes Thomas a few seconds to figure out what the zombie child is doing.

"She went to the window," he mumbles. "Maybe ... maybe she saw something." He turns and points. "Check the windows in the other room, Dan."

Dan slips around Jennie, who reaches for him, and steps through the hole in the wall. Thomas holds his breath waiting. A few seconds pass. Then Dan shouts: "A car! Thomas, I can see a car! Someone's coming!"

Thomas feels his heart leap.

At that exact moment, something happens which turns the situation upside down completely inside the steamy basement: The last screw gives way and the radiator comes loose.

NINE

The atmosphere in the car is a whole lot cooler than the air outside. And it's not just the air conditioner.

"Could you at least put on a smile for when we see her?" Janjak asks, glancing over at Linda.

Linda pretends like she doesn't hear him, keeping her gaze firmly on the gravel road and the house coming up ahead.

"I mean, there's no reason for her to know we've been arguing."

"It's not arguing," Linda mutters. "Not when you're shouting at each other. That's called fighting."

Janjak sighs, running a hand across his forehead. His usual cocoa brown complexion has turned almost black thanks to the scorching summer sun. Linda hates how easily he tans; it just makes her look even paler.

"Okay, whatever," he says. "I just don't want her to worry."

"I know you don't."

"What's that supposed to mean?"

Linda shakes her head.

"Huh?" he persists, looking from the road to her and back again, a note of annoyance coming back into his voice. "Don't just clam up like that. Tell me what—"

"Fine!" Linda explodes. "You want to hear what I think? I think you're way too protective of her."

"Oh, that old song again …"

"Yes, that old song! You haven't heard from her in what, a couple of hours? And you blow off our weekend together to come running for her."

"It's been more than a couple of hours," he says. "And you didn't have to come."

"So I should just have stayed in the cabin all alone?"

"Look, she promised to call me yesterday but didn't, and this morning I couldn't reach her."

"The signal is terrible out here, you know that."

"But why didn't my mother call, then?"

"She probably forgot. It's not the point. The point is, you always put her first."

Janjak throws out a hand. "Of course I do! She's my daughter!"

"And I'm your wife. Once in a while, it'd be nice to be the one getting …" Linda cuts herself off as she realizes how pitiful she was about to sound.

She hates being in competition with the girl, hates having to fight for Janjak's affection. And she hates herself for actually despising the girl sometimes.

"All right, look," he says. "Let's just put this off until later, okay? All I'm saying is, I don't see the point in arguing when she's around. It would be … huh."

Linda looks over at him. "What?"

He nods ahead. "Someone's here."

Linda looks out the front window as they pull into the courtyard. Another car is parked on the gravel, and Janjak pulls up next to it.

"Who's that?" Linda asks.

"I have no idea, never seen that car before."

He turns off the engine, and Linda unbuckles.

"Hold on," he says, putting a hand on her arm. He's looking over at the house, frowning. "It might be better if you wait out here."

"Why?" Linda asks.

"Just because. We don't know who that car belongs to."

Linda looks from the strange car to the house, noticing the front door is standing wide open. "You don't … you don't think it could be … like, a home robbery?"

"I don't know. It's probably nothing. Let me just check it out first, okay?"

Linda nods, noticing absently how completely her mood has turned in a matter of seconds. The way he's suddenly acting protective of her has reminded her why she fell in love with him.

"Don't you … don't you think we should maybe … call someone?" she suggests.

"It's probably nothing," he repeats, offering her a brief smile. "Wouldn't want to call the cops without a good reason. Let me just take a peek, okay? I'm sure it's just friendly guests."

Linda nods, even though she doesn't feel like nodding.

Janjak opens the door, and suddenly she's gripped by a strong sense of dread. It makes her reach out and grab him by the shirt.

"Janjak!"

He looks back in at her. "Yeah?"

She wants to say "be careful," but that's such a cliché movie line, so instead she resolves herself with saying: "I'm sorry."

He smiles back at her, showing part of his big, white teeth. "Don't be. I'll be right back, okay?"

"Okay."

He exits the car and closes the door behind him. He walks towards the house, taking his time, casually surveying the surroundings.

Then he disappears inside.

Linda stares after him.

The sense of dread returns, fills up her chest.

She can't shake it.

Can't shake the feeling that she's just seen her husband alive for the last time.

TEN

"Hello?"

His voice quickly dies out in the silence of the house. He looks briefly around the scullery, finding nothing out of the ordinary. Nadia's shoes are there, which means she's probably in the house. Which should make him less worried.

"Nadia?" he calls out, stepping into the kitchen. "Sweetheart? You there?"

Still, no answer.

He walks through the kitchen and into the living room. "Mom?" he calls out. "You home?"

Weirdly, there's still no answer.

Besides the bedroom, there's only the upstairs. If his mom and Nadia are up there, they probably can't hear him calling.

He's about to head for the stairs, when he stops and looks across the living room. He didn't notice it right away, because the room is already full of his mother's weird stuff. But a lot of things have been tipped over, and furniture pushed around.

Janjak feels his stomach tighten.

It looks an awful lot like a fight or scuffle went down in here.

Oh, no ... please don't let anything have happened to my little girl ...

Then he hears it. A sound from below.

Janjak looks down to the floor, as though trying to look through the carpet and the boards underneath.

There's an old basement down there; he remembers playing down there as a young boy. But as far as Janjak knows, the basement has never been used for anything other than storing old stuff, and his mother scolded him badly for sneaking around down there.

There's another sound from the basement; someone saying something in a strained voice. Janjak can't make out the words, and he can't recognize the voice, either.

What the hell is going on here?

He heads across the living room for the door to the stairs. Just as he's about to open it, he notices the sound from another door a little farther away: the door to the bedroom.

Sounds like someone is scraping at the other side.

Janjak frowns. "Who's in there?" he calls out.

No answer, but the scraping grows more eager.

He steps closer, stops, listens.

A low, guttural growl mixes in with the scraping of nails. The noises are coming from the lower part of the door. Whoever is on the other side isn't very tall.

"Nadia?" he breathes. "I'm coming, honey."

Janjak turns the handle.

And begins screaming.

ELEVEN

The person in front of him is his daughter. And at the same time, it isn't. Or maybe it's more accurate to say that the person used to be his daughter.

One look into her eyes is enough to convince Janjak with absolute certainty that Nadia is no longer inhabiting the short, skinny body he knows so well.

She's wearing her nightclothes and is barefoot. Her light brown skin has turned ashy grey, her beautiful, dark hair is hanging in ragged threads.

The lower part of her face is smeared with something dark which Janjak instinctively recognizes as blood. Like she's been drinking a gallon of it and spilling most of it down herself.

But the most harrowing thing about her is the arm, which is both obviously broken and has also been torn almost clean off. A large, ragged gash above the elbow reveals the white bone underneath.

Nadia doesn't seem too bothered by the injury, though, as she simply staggers right out into Janjak's arms.

Part of him wants to recoil, wants to push her away, to run and get the hell out of here. But a deeper part, a part not concerned about his own survival, wants to hug her closely, to comfort her and call someone to help save her life.

She's already dead! a thought screams to him as his daughter reaches out her still working arm, grabs his shirt and pulls herself into him.

For a moment, Janjak takes the gesture as a plea for comfort, and he instinctively puts his arms around her. Then he feels the sharp pain as she bites down hard on the skin right below his solar plexus, her tiny teeth cutting right through the shirt.

"Ouch!" he yelps and tries to push her back a little, which only serves to make her clamp down harder, tearing off a big piece of skin and T-shirt.

"Stop that, sweetheart!" he hears himself say, even as Nadia lunges forward, snarling and snapping her teeth like an angry dog.

He manages to hold her at arm's length, but she pushes eagerly forward, forcing him to step backward. He steps on something round and his foot slips. He falls on his ass with a yelp of surprise. Nadia follows suit, stumbling down into his arms once more. This time, she's even quicker to bite him, and she takes a bigger piece of skin off.

Janjak screams in pain and shoves her back again, but she squirms and he can't get her off of him and she manages another bite, this time from his forearm.

"Stop, Nadia! Stop it!" his voice keeps repeating, even as his thoughts tell him that this is not Nadia, that this thing has got nothing to do with his beloved daughter, but somehow his brain can't connect the fact fully.

He manages to push her off enough for him to turn around and crawl towards the kitchen. He looks back and sees her coming after him, groaning and snarling, fresh blood dripping from her lower lip, his blood.

He crawls right into the kitchen island, banging his head against it hard enough for his vision to go blurry; or maybe it's from the blood loss, as the bite wounds on his arm and stomach are bleeding heavily now. As he looks down hazily, he sees the dark-red liquid pouring from him and coloring the tile floor.

He turns around and sits down on his butt, moving slowly like a sleepwalker, his thoughts turning sluggish as something akin to sleep is closing in. And as he sees the thing that once was his daughter come crawling at him on one arm like a crooked spider, he can only think: Why is this happening? What did I do to deserve it?

Then, gliding off into a freeing darkness, Janjak manages to actually reach out his arms, not to push her away, but to welcome her.

"It's okay, sweetheart," he croaks, not aware that the words are coming from himself. "Daddy's here now."

The last thing he sees as she crawls into his arms and pushes him down onto his back is the kitchen ceiling. And the last thing he hears is the sound of her eating away at him.

TWELVE

Once again, everything speeds up. Like fast-forwarding a movie.

Jennie staggers towards Thomas, dragging the heater noisily behind her.

Thomas is still standing on the second rung of the ladder. He turns just in time to see her, gives a yelp and jumps aside. Jennie's outstretched hands only catch the ladder. Thomas runs behind the nearest stool, lifting it up and holding it out like a shield. A gutted rabbit still dangles from the seat.

Jennie comes at him, not paying the slightest notice to the stool, even as Thomas thrusts it at her, knocking her backwards. She just regains balance and tries again, snarling hungrily.

Thomas backs away, bumping into the table, turning in another direction. He doesn't dare take his eyes off of Jennie, as they perform a bizarre dance: him backing up, her still dragging the heater on the cord. Thomas throws the stool at her face. She falls over backwards, but immediately tries to get back up. Thomas grabs the next stool, just as he notices Dan's head peeking in through the hole in the wall.

"Watch out!" Thomas roars. "She's free!"

His warning is redundant; Dan has eyes. In fact, he has very large eyes right now. They're staring at the reanimated corpse of his older sister, now sensing his presence and turning around to come at him, her thin fingers reaching for him, her mouth gargling eagerly.

"For fuck's sake, Dan! Get out of the way!"

This time, the warning is not redundant, as it snaps Dan out of his temporary trance. He disappears through the hole a second before Jennie bends over clumsily and tries to follow him.

Oh, shit! He'll be trapped in there! There's no room to move around her ...

Thomas's gaze falls on the heater still tied to Jennie's leg. He jumps forward, grabs it and tugs hard.

Her leg jerks backwards, causing her to slide into a painful split. With a grunt she tries to crawl on, but Thomas pulls the heater again, dragging her a few feet away from the wall. Jennie flails her arms, clawing at the concrete floor, as though to pull herself forward.

Thomas tugs again, and the cord breaks, sending him tumbling backwards into a stool. Jennie, finally free of her anchor, crawls eagerly forward and slips through the hole in the wall.

"Oh, fuck ... Dan! She's coming for you!"

"I'm safe!" Dan's voice calls back. "At least I think so ..."

Thomas steps carefully to the hole and looks into the other room. Jennie has come to her feet and is making her way through the maze of old furniture and junk. She bumps into things, knocking stuff to the floor, but keeps steering determined towards the far corner, where a large dresser is standing. For a moment, Thomas figures Dan must have locked himself inside the dresser, but then he sees him on top of it. There's little more than two feet between the dresser and the ceiling, but Dan has managed to squeeze himself into the tight space.

Jennie reaches the dresser and reaches up. The tips of her fingers are ten inches short of the top of the dresser.

"She ... she can't get to me ..." Dan says, looking like he might laugh or cry any minute.

Then, there's a loud, terrified scream from up above.

Thomas looks to the ceiling, then over at Dan. "I think our guests have met the zombie kid."

THIRTEEN

"I need to go on," Thomas tells Dan. "Are you gonna be okay?"

Jennie is still standing by the dresser, stretching her arms in the air, like a groupie trying to touch her idol on stage. She moans and steps a few inches from side to side, but makes no other effort to find a way to get to Dan.

"Do I have a choice?" Dan asks grimly. "It's okay, just go. I'll make it till you find help."

"Right. If anything happens, just call out as loud as you can."

"I will."

Thomas darts one last look at Jennie. She's completely absorbed with Dan and doesn't seem like she'll get tired of him anytime soon. Thomas is just about to turn around, when something comes to him. "Dan?" he says. "She's not your sister anymore."

Dan looks blankly at him from across the room. "I know."

"It's just ... don't get tempted to ... you know ... touch her or anything. Okay?"

Dan sends him a pale smile. "Don't worry."

"Right. I'll be back soon. Hang tight."

He runs to the ladder, steps up and stops for a moment to listen. Somewhere up there, he can hear footsteps running and a man's voice shouting, but it seems to come from farther away, probably in another room. Now that the zombie child is no longer right above him, he doesn't need to break down the hatch—he can simply reach his arm up through the hole and grope his way to the lock. He finds it, pulls it, and there's a loud click. Finally, he can push open the hatch.

Thomas sticks his head up into a room which appears very bright to Thomas's eyes, although there is only one window, and it's covered by red drapes. It's a bedroom with a single bed. More family photos on the walls. The door to the living room is open. He can't see or hear anything from in there. In fact, the house has suddenly fallen completely silent.

He climbs up and closes the hatch behind him. As he strides to the door, something sharp jabs at his heel.

"Ouch, goddamnit!"

He lifts his foot and sees a piece of broken glass protruding from the sole of his sneaker. He carefully wrenches it free and throws it aside. He pulls off his shoe and checks the damage. Only a small cut in his heel. It's bleeding a little, but nothing severe. As he pulls his shoe back on, he finally notices the broken glass strewn all over the wooden floor. There's also something which might once have been flowers, but now have been trampled to a mush. Almost all of the pieces of glass are sticky with something dark, and he can make out small, dark footprints all over the room. He reconstructs to himself how there must have been a glass vase with flowers standing on the night table. The zombie child then knocked the glass vase to the floor, breaking it, and then proceeded to wander around in her restless search for something to eat, for what looks like several hours, maybe even days, stepping on the shards, ripping her feet to bloody shreds.

Good thing for her she can't feel anything.

Thomas goes to the door and peers into the living room. It's a chaotic mess like he remembers it, with tipped-over chairs and stuff knocked to the floor. He also smells something sweet and metallic.

Whoever came went and opened the door to the bedroom, letting the zombie kid out right into his own arms.

Thomas makes his way through the room, noticing the bloody footprints on the carpet. A sound reaches him, makes him stop dead in his tracks. It's a wet smacking noise. Like a child eating Bolognese for the first time and making a mess of it.

It's coming from the kitchen.

Thomas looks around for a weapon. He didn't think to bring the pipe. Instead, he grabs a big, pink crystal rock from a shelf. It feels satisfyingly heavy in his hand, giving him the courage to go on towards the opening to the kitchen. A dreadful sight meets him.

In the middle of the kitchen, sprawled out on the vinyl floor, is a grown man. His skin is dark and he's wearing shorts and a T-shirt. The colors of his clothes are hard to discern, as they're completely soaked with blood.

His stomach is open. It reminds Thomas of something he saw in a medical documentary about open heart surgery. Something is hanging out of the side of the crater. It looks like a piece of raw sausage with the filling sucked out of it. The rest of the content of the poor man's stomach is mercifully hidden from view by the girl who's sitting on her knees, feasting away. With one hand, she digs eagerly into the man's intestines, transporting them to her mouth and chewing loudly. The other arm, which is broken, hangs limply by her side.

Apparently, this one-armed system isn't working fast enough to satisfy the girl's appetite, because suddenly she bends over and simply buries her face in the guy's stomach.

Thomas breathes firmly through his nose—which immediately proves a mistake, as it only intensifies the smell of blood and meat. He knows he needs to move on. That he's still in a hurry. That the guy on the floor might only be minutes from waking up, and then he'll have two zombies to deal with.

So, he slips through the kitchen as close to the wall as possible. His eyes are fixed on the girl, and that's why he doesn't notice the bottle of olive oil lying on the floor. He accidentally kicks it, and it rolls across the floor, hitting the table leg with a loud Clank!

Thomas freezes, raising the stone, ready to throw it at the zombie girl.

But she doesn't react at all to the noise; not even a flinch. She just keeps eating.

Thomas breathes a sigh of relief. He hurries on. Makes it out of the kitchen and into a hallway. There are a couple of closed doors. At the end is the scullery. He reminds himself about the fact that he can't know for sure if anyone else is in the house—living or dead. So, he keeps the crystal stone held high, ready to strike at anyone trying to surprise him.

He makes it through the hallway with no one doing so, and he finds the front door open wide. Before leaving the house, he throws himself at the scullery sink, turning on the faucet and drinking greedily in big, loud gulps until his belly feels like it's ready to burst. Immediately, he feels better.

Then, he steps out of the house into the bright daylight. The sun is still up, but it has lost some of its power. He hasn't got a watch, but he figures it's got to be around dinnertime.

His own car is parked where he left it. The door to the driver's side is open. Another car is parked next to it. It's empty.

Thomas takes out his phone and tries to activate the screen, but nothing happens.

"Come on, you piece of shit." He tries a few more times, before realizing the phone is dead. He must have spent all the juice trying to call 911 a hundred times down in the basement.

Dan left his phone at home by accident, and Jennie's is probably still in her pocket.

Which means his only option is to drive for help. He runs to the car, gets in, slams the door and turns the key, which is still in the ignition.

Nothing but a dry Click!

The car is as dead as his phone. He notices the gas is on EMPTY.

You gotta be fucking kidding me. I forgot to turn off the engine when I heard Dan screaming.

Frustrated, he gets back out of the car and goes to the other one. He grabs the driver's door, but finds it locked. He goes to check the back door and jumps backwards as a face appears inside the car.

FOURTEEN

"Holy shit!"

Thomas manages only by sheer effort of will not to turn around and bolt.

A woman is crouching on the floor of the backseat, obviously trying to make herself invisible and obviously not a zombie, as her face is full of emotions; terror, most of all, mixed with a healthy dose of shock. She points what looks like a nail file up at him.

"Stay away!" she yells, her voice trembling. "I've already called the police! They're on their way!"

"Thank God," Thomas sighs, holding up his hands. "I won't hurt you. I'm just—"

"Get away from the car!" the woman demands, stabbing the air with her improvised weapon. "It was you! You killed him!"

"I had nothing to do with what happened here. I was just delivering the paper."

The woman flicks her eyes, as though she doesn't really understand what he's saying. Her hair is red, her skin is pale and freckled. She's older than him, perhaps in her mid-twenties, and somehow, she seems vaguely familiar.

Thomas suddenly remembers about the three—soon to be four—zombies in the house, and that he left the front door open wide. He hurries to close it. As he returns to the car, the woman is now sitting on the backseat. Her blue eyes follow him intently.

Then Thomas remembers where he has seen her before. In the photo album in the basement.

"You're her daughter-in-law," he says.

The woman rolls down the window an inch or so and squints out at him. "What's that?"

"The woman who lived here. You're her daughter-in-law, right?"

Her eyes are still suspicious. "Why do you say 'lived'?"

"Because she's dead. Like the man and the little girl, who—" Thomas interrupts himself abruptly, as he realizes what he's saying.

But it's too late. The woman's face crumbles into tears.

You moron. That was her husband and her daughter.

"Uhm ... I'm sorry," he mutters stupidly.

The woman just sobs into her hands.

Thomas rubs his forehead and closes his eyes for a moment. It's finally over. Almost, at least. Before long, the police will arrive, and they will be able to pacify the zombies. If only Dan can hold out a few more minutes ...

"What is this?" the woman whispers in between her sobs. "What ... what happened to them?"

"They've become zombies," Thomas murmurs. "Like on TV."

The woman looks up at him with wet eyes and an expression like she had forgotten about him being here. "What?"

"Your mother-in-law made some fucked up ritual in the basement. I think that's how it started. Was she into witchcraft or some crazy shit like that?"

"Voodoo," the woman whispers. "But that's not ... that can't be ..." She starts crying again. "Oh, Janjak ..."

Thomas says nothing, and the woman cries for a minute. A honey bee buzzes by lazily. He listens for sirens but can't hear anything in the quiet summer air.

"Did the police say when they'd be here?" he asks. "My friend is trapped still inside."

The woman wipes her eyes and shakes her head. "I ... I didn't call the police."

Thomas gapes at her. "What? Why the hell not?"

"I left my phone at home to recharge."

"Goddamnit! Then why did you say ...?" He moans. "Forget it. We need to go get help. My car is out of gas, so we'll go in yours."

He's about to go to the driver's side, when the woman says: "My husband took the key with him."

Thomas stops and smacks himself on the forehead. "Of course he did. This just keeps getting better. How about your mother-in-law? She must have a car ..." He looks around, but sees neither car nor garage.

"Esther doesn't have a car."

Thomas flails his arm. "Come on! You can't live all the way out here without a fucking car! Christ! Right, you need to run to the highway. At least a couple of cars must come by every hour or so. You can stop one of them and ask them to call for help."

The woman shakes her head firmly. "No!"

Thomas steps closer to the window, and she pulls back like a scared animal.

"Listen, I've cut my foot, so I can't make it. My friend in there hasn't had a sip of water since we came here several hours ago. I'm afraid he might faint or go into shock or something. And then my girlfriend will probably get him. She's also—"

Something catches the woman's gaze behind Thomas as he is speaking, and she turns her head and screams.

Thomas spins around, ready to fight, but he's still alone in the courtyard, and the front door is still closed. But right next to it is a tall, narrow window. On the other side, the Black guy is pressing his face against the glass, his eyes flickering empty in their sockets.

So, he's woken up, too, Thomas thinks. That means Dan is now alone in the house with four zombies.

As though his thoughts have caused it, Dan's voice suddenly screams: "Thomas! Thomaaaas! Heeeelp!"

FIFTEEN

There is terror in Dan's voice, but to Thomas's surprise, the scream isn't coming from inside the house; it's coming from behind it.

Thomas starts running, ignoring the pain from his wounded foot. He rounds the corner of the house, passes by a terrace, jumps across a flower bed. As he runs, he wonders how Dan has managed to exit the house. He stops on the lawn of the back garden and looks around.

"Dan?" he calls out. "Where are you?"

"Here!"

Thomas turns. The basement window is halfway hidden behind a couple of giant dandelions. Dan's arm is waving frantically.

Thomas runs over and falls to his knees. As soon as he looks into the basement, he can tell that Jennie has either grown two feet taller or found something to stand on, because she's suddenly able to look over the top of the closet, and her arms are grabbing greedily for Dan, who is squeezing himself up against the window. Jennie's fingers grope at his shoes.

"She can almost reach me!" Dan cries. "Get me out of here, Thomas! Help me! Make her go away!"

"All right. Don't worry, Dan, I'll—"

"Help me! Get me out!"

Thomas studies the window. It's about four inches too narrow for Dan to squeeze through. The wall around it is brick. Even if he was able to find a hammer and a chisel, it would take him forever to make the hole wider.

Instead, he looks around for something else to use. The woman had a large vegetable garden, and a few garden tools are lying around. Thomas jumps to his feet and goes to grab a rake.

"Help me, Thomas!" Dan cries and grabs him as he returns. "She's got my foot!"

"Move aside," Thomas says, forcing the rake past Dan. "And let go of my arm."

Dan lets go and moves sideways slightly.

Jennie has got a hold of the laces of Dan's left shoe and is tugging at them. Thomas places the head of the rake against her throat and pushes her backwards. She is forced to let go of Dan's shoe. She growls, makes no attempt to remove the rake, only groping for Dan's legs, but now they're out of reach.

"She ... she tipped over a box," Dan says, breathing fast. "That's what she's standing on. I don't ... I don't think she did it on purpose, it was just luck. Please get me out of here, Thomas."

"I'm trying," Thomas says, concentrating on the rake, as Jennie moves from side to side, trying to find a way to reach Dan. "But you'll have to go the same way as I did: up through the hatch."

Dan stares out at him. "What about the other zombie? The kid?"

"She's somewhere in the house, and there are two more. But I don't think any of them will be in the room with the hatch."

Jennie jerks sideways, and the rake slips off her neck.

Dan screams as she tips forward, almost grabbing his foot by surprise.

Thomas pulls back the rake, plants it in Jennie's chest this time, and pushes her back once more. "You need to go for it," he hisses. "I can't hold her forever."

"O ... okay."

"On the count of three, I'll shove her back so she falls down. You'll have to jump down and get past her before she can get back up. You ready?"

Dan looks terrified, but Thomas can tell how he mans up. "I'm ready," he whispers.

"One ... two ... three!" Thomas thrusts the rake as hard as he can.

Jennie is shoved backwards and falls over. She drags a box of old junk down with her.

"Now, Dan!"

Dan has already crawled to the edge of the closet. He jumps down, and Thomas hears him land on the concrete floor. He gives off a loud, short shriek of pain. Thomas feels his own heart turn to ice.

She got him ...

A few seconds of commotion. Jennie snarls. Then Dan appears, making his way through the room towards the hole in the wall. He's limping on one leg.

"Did she bite you?" Thomas yells.

Dan doesn't hear him. He's obviously focused on one thing only: getting out of the room.

Behind him, Jennie appears, as she gets to her feet.

"Hey!" Thomas shouts, banging the top of the closet with the rake. "Hey, Jennie! I'm right here! Look at me!"

Jennie doesn't even seem to register his voice. She just staggers after Dan, who slips through the wall.

Thomas leaves the rake and gets to his feet. He runs along the outer wall, reaching the window with the red drapes. He knocks on the glass.

A moment later, the drapes are flung aside. Dan fumbles with the hasp. Behind him, the hatch is closed.

"Did she get you?" Thomas yells.

Dan shakes his head, not looking up, sweat pouring down his face. "No, it's my ankle. I hurt it when I landed."

Thomas feels a surge of deep relief. For a moment, he sees everything. How they'll make it. Dan opens the window and climbs out. They shut the window and trap all four zombies in the house. Then they go to the woman in the car and bring her along as they walk up to the highway. They flag down the first passerby and hitch a ride to the police station. That's how this nightmare will end.

Dan shouts from the other side of the glass: "How do I get this stupid thing open!?"

From the courtyard on the other side of the house comes a shrill scream. Thomas turns his head for a moment, thinking: That was her. I hope she didn't open the front door.

At that moment, he sees a movement through the window. Behind Dan, the door to the room is pushed open. The small girl with the broken arm, now all covered in blood, comes staggering into the room.

Dan hasn't noticed her. He's struggling with the window hasp.

Thomas looks down. "It's the old-fashioned kind. You have to hold it out and then push."

Dan seems to sense something behind him. He turns around and screams. The girl is slowly making her way around the bed. Her pale, fishlike eyes are fixed on Dan.

"Come on!" Thomas shouts and slaps a hand on the glass. "Concentrate!"

Dan wrenches his eyes off the girl and turns his attention towards the window. This time, he does it right, and the window opens. Thomas pulls it and lifts it up all the way. "Get out! Quick!"

Dan throws himself out the window. The girl is only a few steps away when he lands on the grass. Thomas lets go of the window, and it slams shut. The girl presses her face up against the glass, instantly covering it in sticky red blood.

Thomas steps back. He can't lock the window from this side, but the window is quite heavy, and the girl isn't strong enough to push it open.

He gives off a sigh of relief. "I think we're good. She can't get out this way."

He turns to look at Dan, who has crawled to a safe distance from the window. Now he's sitting on the grass, looking around in disbelief. "I'm out ... I'm out!"

"You all right?" Thomas asks. "Sure Jennie didn't scratch you?"

Dan checks both his legs. Then he shakes his head. "I'm good. But my ankle—"

He is interrupted by a second scream from the courtyard.

SIXTEEN

Dan looks up at him in alarm. "Who's that?"

Thomas wastes no time explaining. "Stay here. Keep an eye on the window." He spins around and runs back around the house. As he gets to the courtyard, he stops. It takes him a moment to understand what's going on and how it happened.

The dark man must have gotten the front door open somehow, because he's making his way across the courtyard. The redheaded woman has left the car—probably in order to try and talk to her husband. If that was her reason, though, she seems to have gotten second thoughts, because she's backing away from him, an expression of pure terror painted on her face, her eyes wide and her lips moving. The whispering words reach Thomas's ears.

"It's me, Janjak ... It's me, babe ..."

Her late husband is staggering towards her, arms outstretched, eager at the sight of its first, easy meal almost within reach. The woman bumps into the hood of the car. Instead of stepping sideways, she just stops and stares.

"It's me, Janjak ... Don't you recognize me?"

"He doesn't understand you!" Thomas roars. "Get out of the fucking way!"

The woman only reacts by blinking fast twice. She doesn't move and she doesn't take her eyes off the zombie, which is only a few paces away now.

Thomas has no other choice. He runs straight at the zombie and hits it with a perfect shoulder tackle. The dark man tumbles over and rolls around in the gravel.

The woman is finally able to take her eyes off her husband and instead looks at Thomas like a sleepwalker who just woke up. "He was ... he was ..."

"That's right, he was going to fucking eat you! Glad you finally caught on!" Thomas grabs her by the arm and pulls her to the passenger side. "Get in! Hurry! And lock the damn door."

She follows his order with dreamy movements. Just as she manages to hit the lock, the zombie gets back on its feet. Most of its guts seem to have spilled out of the hole in its stomach as it went sprawling, and are now dragging behind it like a bunch of bloody ropes, the gravel sticking to them.

Thomas feels the nausea rising to his throat, but he manages to force it back down. He backs away from the car. The zombie reaches out its arms, moans, then steps in its own intestines, trips and falls onto the hood of the car.

Inside, the woman screams.

The zombie gracefully slides off the car and dives back down into the gravel.

That gives Thomas a few seconds to think.

Gotta get him back into the house somehow. Can't risk him getting away.

He goes around the car and positions himself between the front door and the zombie struggling to get back up for the second time. As soon as it succeeds, it sees him and comes at him with a hungry growl.

Thomas backs up towards the house. The zombie follows along.

"That's right," he mutters. "Come on."

His plan is simple. As soon as he's back inside the house with the zombie, he'll lure it out into the kitchen. There he can run around the table and get back out to the front door, closing it behind himself and trapping the zombie in the house.

They're almost at the door now. "Come with me," Thomas whispers. "There's a good boy."

From the car, the woman screams again. She also bangs the windows and waves frantically.

"What?" Thomas yells.

Then he picks up the sound of gravel crunching right behind him. He whirls around and is face to face with the old woman just as she lunges at him. Thomas catches her arms clumsily, stumbles backwards, slips in the gravel and almost falls down. Her nails are clawing the air right above his face. He narrowly avoids her mouth as she snaps at his chin. He regains his balance and shoves her backwards, causing her to fall over, just as another hand grabs his shoulder and someone hisses right into his ear. Thomas turns his head just in time to see the open mouth. Less than a split second before the dark man bites his neck open, Thomas throws himself to the side. But the zombie has a firm grip on his shirt, so it follows along, trips him and lands on top of him. Thomas kicks wildly to get it off, feeling the dark hands groping eagerly all over his shirt, trying to rip through the fabric, searching for the skin.

Thomas goes into blind panic. He kicks, punches and writhes uncontrollably. In a stroke of luck, he manages to throw off the Black guy. He crawls backwards, panting, the zombie immediately crawling after, reaching for him.

A movement next to him. The woman is back on her feet. She's bending down to grab him, mouth open wide, her frame blocking out the sun.

Thomas screams.

Then, the zombie lady is abruptly jerked backwards.

Thomas catches a glimpse of Dan tugging at the woman's ponytail. He gives her another hard yank which sends her sprawling to the gravel.

Dan yells something, but all Thomas can hear is his own throbbing pulse. He gets up. Both zombies are also getting to their feet. Out from the doorway Thomas sees another figure coming. It's the girl who finally found her way out of the house.

It's too late, he thinks, his thoughts sounding oddly distant. There are too many. We can't get them back in the house.

Dan is still shouting. Thomas looks at him, dazed. A word makes it through.

"... car! ..."

Thomas staggers towards the car, Dan on his tail, jumping on one leg. The boys open the doors on either side and crawl in. Thomas hits the central locking.

The sound of the lock snapping somehow brings back Thomas's hearing. His own wheezing breath, Dan's gasping sobs, the growling of the zombies outside.

"Holy fuck," Thomas mutters. "I really thought I was done."

Dan looks at him. "Are you unharmed?"

Thomas lifts up his T-shirt. "You tell me."

"I don't see any scratches."

"I guess I'll live then."

A thud, as the black man bumps against the window next to Thomas. The girl staggers to Dan's side. The zombies start making futile attempts to push through the windows.

"Shouldn't we get out of here?" Dan asks.

"We can't. Car's out of gas. And she doesn't have a key." He looks to the car with the redheaded woman, where the zombie lady is standing.

Dan gives off an exhausted noise. "You're kidding me! So we're still trapped?"

Thomas nods grimly. "Looks like it."

SEVENTEEN

The clock in the car tells them it's almost nine. Thomas can't believe they've been here for nine whole hours.

The zombies are waiting patiently right outside. Snarling, snapping their teeth and groping the windows. Thomas tries not to look at them, but it's hard, considering how their empty eyes seem to devour him alive.

At least the sun has disappeared behind the house, leaving the courtyard in a pleasantly cool shade. Yet the inside of the car is still warm, and Thomas is sweating.

Dan has pulled off his sock, revealing a swollen ankle.

"How's it doing?" Thomas says, pointing.

"It's sprained," Dan mutters. "I did it once before, when I was skiing."

"So you can't walk?"

Dan shakes his head.

Thomas glances out at the nearest zombie. "I guess I'm the lucky one who gets to go for help, then."

"You think that's a good idea? Wouldn't it be better to wait for someone to come along?"

"It could be days."

Dan shrugs. "Someone's got to be wondering where we are!"

"Who would that be? I haven't spoken to my dad for months. And your parents are on holiday."

"Yeah, but Mom will probably call me or Jennie tonight; she usually does."

"And what then? I mean, when you don't pick up? You figure she'll go straight to the police?"

Dan hesitates. "Probably not. She'll probably try to call us again tomorrow."

"And when she does, and she still can't reach you, then she just might call the police, and that's great. Except the police have no idea where we are. If they come looking for us, they might find my car missing. And even if someone tells them about the paper route, this house was one of the last stops, which means they'll have to make a lot of house calls before reaching this place." Thomas shakes his head. "By that time we'll be long dead from thirst. I've given it a lot of thought, and I don't see any other way; I need to make a run for it."

"I guess you're right." Dan squints his eyes. "I'm so thirsty. I feel dizzy. You sure you don't have anything to drink?"

"Nah, I already told you—" Thomas suddenly lights up. "Holy shit, wait a minute ... I just might ..." He turns around and crawls to the backseat, checking the trunk. His heart leaps at the sight of the canned sodas. Out of the entire box, only three of them are missing. He grabs one and hands it to Dan. "Here you go. Sorry it's not cold."

Dan takes the can as though it is life itself. He opens it and drinks greedily.

Thomas grabs another three cans and crawls back over behind the wheel.

Dan burps and drops the empty can to the floor. "Another one," he groans.

"I think you'd better pace yourself," Thomas says, handing him another can nonetheless. "I don't think it's a good idea to drink too much too fast when you've been thirsting for ..."

But Dan has already opened the can and is pouring the Coke down his throat. And Thomas can't blame him. His own hands are shaking as he opens the can. He closes his eyes and lets the sweet, warm liquid flow down his throat. It prickles wonderfully. He sighs deeply. "That's got to be the best Coke I've ever had."

Dan burps wetly and laughs. Thomas can't tell if the tears in Dan's eyes are caused by relief or carbon dioxide.

"How many you got back there?"

"Almost an entire box."

"That means we can survive for days. You don't need to go out there anyway!"

Thomas becomes conscious of the zombies once again. Not that he ever forgot about them. But their moaning, hungry noises suddenly seize his attention. He looks out, past the Black guy, over at the other car. There are about ten feet between the cars. He can't see the woman inside, which means she's probably lying down. The zombie woman is faithfully standing guard by the rear door.

"She's probably thirsty," Dan says, guessing what Thomas is thinking.

"I'll try and call her." He puts his hands to the window and shouts: "Hey!"

The red hair of the woman appears. She looks over at them.

Thomas holds up a can.

The woman shows him a large bottle of water.

He sends her a thumbs-up. "She'll be all right. Good thing, 'cause I don't really see how we would get a soda over there anyway."

"Who is she?"

"She didn't tell me her name, but she was married to that guy." Thomas taps the window, and the Black guy attempts to bite his finger, but manages only to drench the glass in saliva. "The old hack was her mother-in-law. Oh, and she's not a witch, by the way. The old woman, I mean."

"No?"

"Nope, she was into voodoo."

Dan gazes out the front window, looking thoughtful. "Well, that makes sense."

"What?"

"Voodoo originated in Haiti. We learned about it in school. That's where the zombie myth came from. Did you know that?"

"I had no idea."

"There have been several accounts of voodoo priests waking up dead people."

"Seriously?"

"Yeah, I mean, it's only rumors, of course. But the voodoo people believe something about the human soul being split in two. One part keeps the body alive, and the other one is our personality and thoughts and stuff like that. So, in theory, the body can live on, even if the other part of the soul dies. You're just ..." Dan searches for the right word.

"Braindead?" Thomas suggests.

"No, not quite. You're a body completely without a brain. Without anything of that which made you a human." Dan sips his Coke. "It can't happen naturally; it requires someone to mess with the forces of nature."

"Then why would they eat other people? And why do they contaminate others?"

Dan shrugs. "The teacher didn't say anything about that."

A moment of silence passes by. The boys are both looking out at the zombies.

"So, you think the ritual in the basement …?" Thomas mumbles. "And all that nonsense we found in the book …?"

Dan breathes deeply. "Well, I think the girl died. Perhaps she fell down the stairs or whatever. And then the woman tried to bring her back to life. In a way I guess you could say she succeeded."

Thomas raises an eyebrow. "I don't think this was quite what she was hoping for."

EIGHTEEN

The night grows steadily dimmer. The time wears on at a painfully slow rate. Thomas slips in and out of a light doze.

"What do we do if they suddenly give up?"

Thomas opens his eyes and looks at Dan. He's on his fifth Coke. He already had to pee once, and managed to fill one of the empty cans. It's now in the trunk.

"What do you mean?"

"If they just decide to walk off? To find someone else to eat?"

Thomas looks out at the zombies. The man and the girl are still right outside, and the old woman is still by the other car. It's difficult to see clearly, due to the drool and dirt and blood smeared all over the windows, turning the zombies into vague figures in the twilight.

"I don't think they'll quit anytime soon. Not as long as we're here."

"No, but what if?" Dan persists. "I mean, we don't know for sure they won't get tired of trying to get in here. And if they walk away, won't we have to ...?"

Thomas nods. "You're right, we can't let them get away. It could mean the end of the world if they—" He grinds his teeth as a sharp pain suddenly jabs the sole of his foot. "Goddamnit!"

"What is it?"

"My foot," Thomas groans, pulling off his shoe. "I stepped on a shard of glass in the bedroom. It went right through the bottom of my shoe."

He hasn't really thought about it, but the puncture wound on his heel has been throbbing for at least the past hour. He pulls up his leg, looks under the foot, and finds a bloody stain on the sock the size of a big coin. He carefully pries off the sock to reveal a tiny, V-shaped wound.

"I think you need to clean it," Dan remarks.

"There's a first aid kit in the trunk. Grab it for me, will you?"

Dan climbs to the back of the car—Thomas notices how the zombie girl follows along on the outside of the car—and comes back with the kit. He opens it and goes through the content.

"I can only find these," he says, handing Thomas a packet of wet wipes. "It says they're disinfectant."

Thomas bites open the packet and pulls out the wipe. He carefully pats the wound, grinding his teeth as it starts to burn. "Goddamnit …"

"Does it hurt badly?" Dan asks. "Maybe the piece of glass is still in there?"

Thomas hadn't considered that possibility. He reaches up and turns on the small light in the ceiling. He gently opens the wound using two fingers, causing it to begin bleeding once more. "I don't see anything in there. I don't think there's any glass."

"Right. You want a Band-Aid? There's also gauze."

"A Band-Aid's fine."

Thomas covers the wound with the Band-Aid and puts his sock back on. His heel is throbbing warmly. He tries to ignore it and turns off the light again.

They sit for a little while in silence. Of course, the zombies make sure there isn't any real silence. Thomas leans back his head and closes his eyes.

"You still want to go get help?" Dan asks quietly.

"Yeah."

"Sure you can run with that foot?"

"I'll be all right. It's not that far."

"The town is miles away."

"I only need to get to the nearest neighbor. Or perhaps I'll meet a late-night car."

Dan looks out at the zombie girl who's snarling back at him. "They'll probably follow you."

"I'm counting on it. But they don't move very fast. I just need to keep ahead of them."

"And what then, when you find someone who can help? What about the zombies?"

Thomas shrugs. "I'll call the police. They'll have to deal with them."

"You think they'll get what's going on?"

"I have no idea. That's a problem I'll have to deal with if it comes to that." He runs his palm across his forehead. "Damn, I'm still sweating."

"That's weird," Dan says. "I'm actually freezing."

Thomas notices he has put on his sweater. "Grab me another Coke, will you?"

Dan has fetched the whole box which is now standing between his feet. He reaches down and grabs a can which he gives to Thomas. Thomas opens it and drinks three big gulps.

Dan looks to the other car. "What did you say happened to the keys for her car?"

Thomas burps. "She said he's got them." He nods towards the Black guy.

Dan bites his lip. "Maybe we can get it."

"How would we do that? You feel like reaching out and going through his pockets?" He drinks again and notices Dan staring at him. "What?"

"You're really sweating. Are you feeling all right?"

"Sure, I'm just a little hot." A bead of sweat drips from his nose.

Dan reaches over and touches his cheek. "You're burning up."

Thomas realizes Dan is right. His skin feels like it's on fire. His whole body is soaked with sweat. "My system is probably just a little hyped after all the stress I've been through," he mumbles. "I don't think that's any wonder."

Dan doesn't look convinced. "Thomas?" he asks quietly. "Could it be a fever?"

"Why would I have a fever?"

"You sure you didn't get a scratch?"

"You checked my back."

"Yeah, but ... we didn't check you everywhere. Are there any other places on your body that's hurting?"

Thomas scans his body. "Nope. Just my foot, but that's from the glass, and that can't be ... that can't be ..."

The words die out as an image appears in his mind.

The floor of the bedroom. Broken glass strewn all over. Glittering in the afternoon sunlight. Red from the blood of the girl, who has been walking around on them for hours.

The blood of the girl ... the blood ... Oh, no ...

The truth finally sinks in.

NINETEEN

"Fuck, fuck, fuck, fuck!"

Thomas screams and bangs his fists onto the steering wheel, harder and harder, more and more uncontrollably, until his hands are starting to hurt.

Finally, he sinks back into the seat, panting. "Why didn't I ... think of it before? Goddamnit ..."

"What ... what is it?" Dan croaks, staring wide-eyed at Thomas.

"The shards of glass were covered in the blood of the girl. I've been infected."

Several long seconds of silence pass by inside the car. Thomas closes his eyes. His foot is suddenly throbbing a lot worse than a minute ago. The pain is radiating all the way up to his knee. Perhaps it's only his imagination, but all of a sudden, he can almost feel how the infection is making its way up his bloodstream. Headed for his organs. Headed for his brain.

"Can't we ... can't we stop it?" Dan asks. "Maybe if we make a really tight bandage?"

Thomas shakes his head. "It's too late. I can feel it. Even if we cut off my whole damn leg ..." He sighs. "Why the fuck couldn't I just have watched where I was going?"

More silence.

Thomas feels like he's somehow full of emotions and completely empty at the same time. Random memories seem to pop up. His first bike. His parents' divorce. The day he met Jennie.

Is this what it feels like when your life passes in front of you?

He can't really grasp it. That his life is over. Only yesterday his greatest concern was breaking up with Jennie. Now she's dead, and soon he'll be too.

"It's not fair," he whispers. "I'm only eighteen, for fuck's sake."

He feels something on his arm, looks down and sees Dan's hand resting there. Dan's eyes are wet. "I'm really sorry, Thomas."

Thomas starts to cry himself. The tears just burst out. He sobs over the wheel, letting out a scream now and then, cursing the world, but mostly he simply cries, as the long life he had imagined for himself crumbles and falls away.

As the sobbing subsides, Thomas begins to feel an unexpected calmness. He wipes his eyes and mutters: "Could you please tell my dad I'm sorry for what I said the last time I saw him?"

"I ... I will," Dan whispers. "Anyone else you want me to ...?"

Thomas thinks. "My mom lives in Copenhagen. I haven't talked with her for years. And I don't really have any close friends." He glances at Dan. "I guess you're the closest one."

Dan tries to muster a smile. Then, his expression turns somber again. "What now?"

Thomas straightens up. "I can't run for help, that's for sure. Judging from how fast it went with Jennie, I'm lucky if I have half an hour left. So I guess we got to figure something out quick."

"Thomas," Dan says, pointing. "Look ..."

Thomas looks out his window. The Black guy, who has been patiently standing right outside his door the whole time, is now making his way around the hood of the car with wobbling steps. He unwittingly shoves the girl aside as he joins her in trying to get through Dan's window.

"Guess that's our solution," Thomas says. "They're no longer interested in me."

TWENTY

"Hold on," Dan says. "You sure that's a good idea?"

Thomas shrugs. "What have I got to lose?" He unlocks his door, opens it and steps out into the cool evening air. "Lock it again," he says, slamming it shut.

Dan immediately reaches over and locks it.

Thomas just stands there for a moment, looking at the zombies. They, on the other hand, won't even deign a glance at him. He turns to see the faint figure of the redheaded woman on the backseat of the other car. She has lain down with a jacket pulled over herself.

Thomas takes a step, and a lightning bolt shoots up his leg. He grunts in pain, stumbles and almost falls down. For a moment, he feels lightheaded, as the pain rolls through his leg in slow, intense waves.

Fuck me. Now I get why Jennie complained so much. Need to be careful. If I faint, it's over.

Out here in the fresh air, he can really feel the fever. His skin is burning and freezing all at once. He's standing on one leg waiting for the dizziness to subside.

Then, when it finally does, he jumps across the gravel to the woman's car and knocks on the window.

She jumps up and stares out at him. "What are you doing? Have you lost your freaking mind?"

"They won't hurt me," Thomas says. "Listen, if I get you the key, can you drive the car?"

The woman seems too surprised to answer right away. The zombie woman comes staggering around the car. For one terrible second, Thomas is sure she's coming for him. That he was wrong, that he's not immune after all. He jumps back a few steps. But the zombie woman only pays attention to the woman inside the car.

The redheaded woman stares from the zombie to Thomas. "Why ... why isn't she attacking you?"

"That doesn't matter right now. Can you drive the car?"

The woman looks down at his feet. "Why are you standing on one leg? What happened to your foot?"

Thomas sighs. "I've been contaminated, all right? That's why they won't eat me. I guess they can smell I'm already ..." He doesn't know how to finish the sentence.

The woman's eyes are even bigger now. "But ... but you ..."

"I don't have long, so could you please just answer my question? Do you ... know how to ... drive the car?"

The woman nods.

"Great. And do you happen to know where your husband keeps the key?"

The woman looks over at her husband. She says something inaudible.

"What's that?"

"In his pants pocket, I think."

Thomas turns around and jumps back to his own car. He supports himself on the hood as he jumps around to Dan's side where the zombies are standing. Both of them are completely absorbed by Dan, who's staring out with a frightened expression.

Thomas reaches out and nudges the Black guy. He sways gently, but doesn't react. Thomas sticks his hand in the guy's pocket. Nothing. To reach the other pocket, he has to position himself behind the guy. He grabs the guy's shirt for support. Still, the zombie doesn't seem to notice him at all. Thomas plunges his hand into the pocket and feels metal. He draws out a key ring.

"Bingo!" He jumps back to the woman's car and pushes the button to the central lock; nothing happens. "Why doesn't it work?"

"I control it from in here," she says.

"Well, then unlock it."

The woman peers out at him, worried. "Are you contagious?"

The zombie woman bumps into the side of him in order to get closer to the window where the redhead is sitting. Thomas shoves her back hard with both hands, causing her to topple over in the gravel like an overgrown toddler.

"No," he says, looking in at the woman. "It only infects via blood."

The woman doesn't look particularly appeased. "How do I know I won't get contaminated if I touch the key? How did you get it?"

Thomas briefly explains about the broken glass in the bedroom. "Now, please open the door. I guarantee you won't get infected."

The woman considers for a few more seconds. The zombie woman has climbed back to her feet and approaches once more. Thomas pushes her over once more.

The redhead finally decides to trust him and unlocks the door. She opens it a few inches. Thomas hands her the key. She immediately slams the door again.

"Good," Thomas says, grinding his teeth as a new avalanche of pain floats through his leg. "Now we just need to get Dan into your car."

The woman has already climbed to the driver's seat. She sticks the key in the ignition, turns on the engine and puts it in drive.

"Wow, wow!" Thomas bangs hard on the windshield. "What do you think you're doing?"

The woman glares out at him. "I'm going to get help, of course."

"No, damnit! If you drive off, we risk the zombies following you. We can't let them leave this place. Don't you get it? We put the whole world at risk if they get to leave."

The redhead looks like she's churning over an internal conflict. After several seconds of thinking, she finally shuts off the engine. "What do we do then?"

"We need to get Dan ..." Thomas sways, as a sudden fog clouds his vision, and he struggles to keep his balance.

"You okay?" The woman's voice seems far away.

Thomas rubs his temple. "Yeah, I'm all right," he manages to croak. "But we'd better hurry." He takes a few deep breaths, forcing his head to clear up. "I'll get Dan over here. Just be ready to open the door for him, okay?"

"He's not infected, is he?"

No, he's not infected, you stupid fucking bitch, Thomas thinks, feeling a raging fury. So don't worry, I'm sure you'll get out of this with your freckly ass in one piece!

He knows the rage is really because he's afraid, and he understands the woman's worries, so he says calmly: "No, he's not infected."

"All right," the redhead nods. "I'll be ready."

Thomas skips back to his own car once again, now starting to feel surprisingly weak and tired. He feels like lying down, but he knows he probably won't get up again if he does.

"Listen, Dan," he says through the window. "You need to get into her car. I'll help you. If you get out over here on my side, I'll make sure none of them touch you."

Dan doesn't look like he approves very much of the plan, but makes no objections.

"You ready?" Thomas asks, spitting into the gravel, his saliva sour from fever.

Dan nods.

"Right, go!"

Dan climbs over the gearshift, hits the button, and the central lock snaps open.

The Black guy and the girl have already begun to make their way around the car, as Dan opens the door and steps out onto the gravel. He stands on his good foot, and Thomas grabs him by the arm. Together, they jump awkwardly towards the woman's car. Behind them, father and daughter lumber after.

The zombie woman apparently senses more accessible meat behind her, because she turns around and comes towards them. Dan instinctively draws back, but Thomas drags him along, reaching out his other arm and pushing the zombie hard backwards, feeling for a brief moment like a quarterback making his way through the defense.

Then, he accidentally puts weight on his wounded foot, and a flood of acid instantly eats its way from his heel all the way to his hip. He falls down with a hoarse cry.

"Thomas!" Dan screams.

"Around the car," Thomas groans. "Get to the other side!" He's only partially aware exactly what's going on around him, as everything takes place behind a red veil of excruciating pain.

Dan skips around the car as fast as he can. The two zombies still on their feet stagger right past Thomas, and Thomas, without time to think, stretches out his leg and kicks the Black guy's ankle hard, causing him to stumble and fall over. But the girl continues, reaching the woman's car just as Thomas hears the sound of a car door opening and then slamming shut again.

He made it, Thomas thinks, laying back his head, resting it on the cool gravel. Dan made it, and now I faint.

He drifts off to a pleasant darkness.

TWENTY-ONE

A voice from very far away calls to him.

Slowly, reluctantly, Thomas is drawn out of his daze. It feels like awaking from the deepest sleep. He opens his eyes, blinks, and into focus drifts a clear, dark sky full of stars.

"... Thomas ..."

He wakes up a little further. Begins to remember. The pain is what brings him back completely.

He moans and sits up with an effort. His leg is one big blaze of fire. The foot has swollen to twice its size, and the sock seems about to burst. The skin on his ankle is deep blue.

Am I dead? Am I a zombie?

"Thomas! Over here!"

He turns his head. His sight flickers for a moment, then comes back into focus. The Black guy is standing in front the car. From the side window, Dan's pale face is staring out.

Thomas rubs his forehead. The skin is hot as lava. He feels the side of his neck. There is a weak pulse.

Guess I'm still alive.

He comes to his feet, using all of the strength left in his body, willing it to obey. He hobbles to the car, shoving aside the Black guy and leaning heavily against the car door, rasping for breath, croaking: "Why ... are you ... still here?"

"We need to kill them, Thomas," Dan says from the other side of the glass. "We can't go before they're dead."

Thomas moans. "Just fucking run them over."

"I already suggested that. But she says she can't do it. And I don't know how to drive."

Says she can't do it, Thomas thinks, bending down and darting the woman a burning look.

He skips to his own car. Every step is sending waves of pain up and down his leg. His head is swimming, his temples are throbbing. He opens the trunk and takes out the tire iron.

This is turning out to be a real zombie flick, he thinks, almost smiling to himself. In a real zombie flick they always use a tire iron or an axe.

He skips back to the other car. The zombie woman is closest to him, which means she'll be the first to go. That's only fair. After all, she started it all.

Thomas positions himself behind her, using a few seconds to secure his unsteady balance. The woman doesn't even register him. From inside the car, Thomas notices Dan telling the redhead to look away.

That's right, don't look at me doing your dirty work. Wouldn't want to cause you any distress, you stupid cunt.

Thomas pulls back the tire iron and bites down hard. He releases the swing with all his might. It connects perfect, the impact sending a jolt all the way up to his shoulder. The woman goes down sprawling, her skull visibly cracked open.

"Next, please," Thomas mutters, a string of saliva dripping from his lower lip. "Please step up to the counter, sir."

He hobbles round the car and repeats the procedure on the Black guy. But this one doesn't go down instantly like the old woman. He requires nothing short of four powerful blows. Even as he finally collapses, Thomas has to administer two more to keep him from getting back up. At last, the skull gives way at the temple, causing the tire iron to get stuck. Thomas twists it sideways, producing a sound both wet and crisp. As he pulls his weapon free, there are greyish lumps of brain matter stuck to the metal.

From inside the car, the redhead starts bawling loudly like a toddler. The sound brings Thomas a highly inappropriate feeling of joy.

Hope she's watching. Hope she's enjoying the show.

His breath is very shallow now, like his lungs almost can't manage the effort anymore. "You're the only one left," he wheezes at the girl. "Last zombie standing."

On the inside he feels something akin to excitement. Even though he's dying, he'll get to save the world first.

How many people in history can say that? How many can say they actually—

Thomas skips forward, and a new, flaming stab of pain rolls up through his leg. And this time, it doesn't stop at the hip, but flows out to his entire body. The pain is too intense. It short-circuits him.

Thomas doesn't scream. He merely gives off a sigh. And collapses.

TWENTY-TWO

Dan sees Thomas go down for the second time. This time he doesn't think he'll be able to call him back. It looked like a minor miracle when he woke up again the first time around.

The woman is sitting with her face in her palms, sobbing. Of course, she looked away as Thomas put down the zombie who just a few hours ago had been her husband. But the sound of the blows could be heard even inside the car.

"He didn't get the girl," Dan mutters.

The woman lifts her head and stares at him, her eyes wet and swollen. "What?"

"Thomas is out again. He didn't manage to …" Dan points out the window at the girl who is still snarling at them hungrily.

The woman looks from the girl to Dan. "What … what do we do then?"

Dan breathes deeply through his nose. "I think we have to do it. With the car."

The woman immediately shakes her head violently. "No, I can't. I won't. You can't make me!"

"I know it's tough, but we might be talking about the fate of the world. If we don't—"

"I just lost my husband! And now you want me to run over Siva? Forget it!" She turns the key and starts the engine. Suddenly, she seems very adamant. "I'm going to the police now. They'll have to handle it."

"I lost my sister too," Dan says quietly. "If we drive off now, we might lose more of our friends and family members. We might lose everything."

The woman has put the car in gear, but now she hesitates, staring stiffly out the front window.

Dan can tell how she's fighting an internal battle. "Was she your daughter?" he asks.

The woman shakes her head. "She was my husband's. I ... I guess I cared for her, but we didn't get to build a very close relationship. Janjak was very protective of her, since her mother died a few years back."

"What's your name?"

The woman looks at him. There's the hint of a smile at the corner of her mouth. "Linda."

"She's already dead, Linda," Dan says softly. "It's just some crazy disease keeping her body moving. You would only be giving her peace."

Linda nods in resignation. "I'll try. I can't promise anything. But I'll try." She places her hands on the wheel, but makes no attempt to drive anywhere.

"You can back it up," Dan says quietly. "If you do, I think she'll walk in front of us."

He's not sure Linda has heard him, and he's just about to repeat, when she suddenly slams the car in reverse and backs up several yards. The zombie girl, as Dan predicted, staggers out right in front of the car and follows them. She's a pretty terrifying sight to behold in the sharp gleam of the headlights.

Linda turns them off.

"Good idea," Dan mutters and fastens his seat belt.

Linda whispers something under her breath, too low for Dan to pick it up. Then she puts the car in first and steps on the gas. The tires spin violently, gravel is banging against the underside of the car as it lunges forward.

Dan senses the figure of the girl right before the front end of the car collides with her. He even feels the jolt all the way up his seat. The zombie girl is flung forwards and tumbles across the courtyard, rolling over several times. Linda—to Dan's great surprise—doesn't slow down, but keeps on the gas and hits the girl again. This time, the tiny body goes underneath the car. It feels to Dan like driving over a curbstone. He is jerked back and forth in his seat.

Then Linda hits the brakes. As the car comes to a halt, she's still clutching the wheel and staring out the windshield. Her voice is stiff as she asks: "Is she dead?"

Dan turns to look back. He can make out the girl in the red gleam of the rear lights. She's not moving.

"I think she is."

Linda gives off a sound somewhere between a sigh and a sob. "Let's get out of here ..." She's about to drive off.

"Wait," Dan says. "There's still Thomas."

TWENTY-THREE

Linda really steps on the gas. The headlights follow the curvy country road. The car races through the summer night headed towards the town. Neither of them speak.

Dan can't quite relax. Even though it's actually over, it's not really. He's constantly listening for sounds from the trunk.

Was it a mistake?

His thoughts are oddly dissolute. Like he can't really collect them. Perhaps it's due to exhaustion. Perhaps hunger. Or shock. A single question keeps presenting itself, though.

Was it a mistake to bring him along?

He's not sure. But what else could they have done? Run him over like they did the girl? He was still alive, for God's sake. Dan heard the faint, rattling breath as he, with the help of Linda, lifted Thomas up into the trunk.

Linda breaks the silence. "Do you think they can save him?"

"I don't know. It never works in the movies. There's nothing the doctors can do, because there's no vaccine."

Linda throws a look into the rearview mirror. "What do we do if he … wakes up?"

Dan runs a hand through his hair. "I have no idea."

They speed past the town limit and the first houses appear on each side of the road. Linda slows down as they reach the somewhat comforting light of the streetlamps. The streets seem only sparsely trafficked. At the first traffic light, Linda runs a red light.

"You'll have to tell me the way," she says. "I'm not from around here."

Dan guides her through town. They reach the hospital.

"Pull over here," he says, pointing. "This is the A&E."

Linda parks, pulls the handbrake, but keeps the engine running. She looks at Dan. "I think it's best if you explain it to them."

Dan unbuckles and steps out of the car, avoiding stepping on his injured foot.

The glass doors of the building glide open, and a young man in scrubs comes out. "You can't park here. It's only for ambulances."

"We have a seriously ill person," Dan says, hobbling to the trunk.

The man looks down at his leg. "It just looks like a sprained ankle to me. You'll have to get her to remove the car, so we—"

"It's not me," Dan interrupts and opens the trunk.

Thomas is lying there, in fetal position. His eyes are closed, his mouth open. A string of drool has run from his lower lip, and the skin is completely white. Thomas is obviously dead. And at the sight of him, Dan is struck be deep terror. Suddenly, he realizes how stupid it was to bring Thomas to the hospital, and just how dangerous the situation is.

What was I thinking?

The nurse shoves him aside. "Geez, what happened?" He reaches down to feel Thomas's neck. "I can't find a pulse. Don't move him, I'll get help." He runs back in through the glass doors.

Dan just stands for a moment, paralyzed, thoughts darting back and forth inside his head. Thomas will wake up any moment. The doctors have no idea of the danger. If they bring him inside the hospital to try and resuscitate him—

His train of thought is abruptly interrupted when Thomas opens his eyes. But as the empty, milk-white balls turn to look at him, Dan can tell at once it's no longer Thomas peering out of them. He utters a hiss and reaches up to grab him.

Dan acts out of instinct: he grabs the lid and slams it down. Thomas immediately starts scratching on the inside.

Dan skips round the car to Linda's side, and she rolls down the window.

"What happened?" she asks.

Dan shakes his head. "It's too late. He's—"

The nurse comes running back out, bringing two colleagues and a gurney.

Dan steps out in front of them, his heart pounding, holding up his hands. "He's dead! There's nothing you can do!"

The nurse doesn't pay any attention to him, he simply pushes him aside and grabs the handle to the trunk. "How do you get this open?"

"Listen to me!" Dan yells, his voice pleading now. "We can't ... it's dangerous ... he's no longer human!"

One of the other nurses—a young Indian-looking woman—exclaims: "I can hear him in there! He's regained consciousness." She turns to seize Dan by the arm. "Open that trunk lid, right now!"

The male nurse is still struggling to open the lid, tugging at it hard. Dan is close to panic. He only sees one way out of the situation, so he screams: "Go, Linda! Drive!"

The engine roars and the car skids forward.

"No!" the nurse yells, letting go of Dan. "What the hell are you guys doing? Stop the car!"

Linda pulls out onto the road and guns it. Dan runs after the car as fast as he can with his aching ankle screaming to him for every step.

"Call the police!" one of the nurses calls from behind him.

Luckily, none of them take up the pursuit. Dan waves at the car, and the brake lights shine as Linda stops and backs it up.

Dan opens his door and throws himself inside. "Go," he gasps.

Linda has already floored the pedal, and a moment later they once again speed through town. From the trunk Dan can hear fumbling, scratching and growling.

"Oh, no," he whispers, rubbing his head with trembling hands. "Oh, no, oh, no ..." He turns and looks back. "Can he get to us?"

"I don't think so," Linda says. "Unless he scratches his way through the seats." She darts him a quick glance. "What now? And don't tell me I have to run him over. I'm not doing that again."

Dan tries to collect his thoughts. The shock of the nearly averted disaster slowly settles, and an idea comes to mind. "I think ... I think I might know what to do. Do you smoke?"

"What? No."

"Then pull over at the gas station coming up on the left."

Linda glares at him. "Are you going in to get fucking cigarettes? Right now?"

"Just pull over, please," Dan says, trying to shut out the sounds of Thomas from the trunk.

Linda pulls over and stops in front of the gas station.

"Wait here, it'll only be a moment," Dan says, getting out. His ankle is worse now, all swollen and throbbing. He can't put his weight on it, so he skips into the store on one leg. He's met by the smell of coffee and chocolate, but the store is empty.

The cashier comes out from a backroom. It's a young, pimply teenager, around Thomas's age. "Hey there," he says absentmindedly, not even looking at Dan. "You paying for gas?"

"No, I just need a lighter." Dan skips to the counter.

"Sure thing. We got 'em here." The cashier points to a rack next to the counter.

Dan grabs one and also takes a packet of Kleenexes, putting both items on the counter.

"Forty-five kroner," the cashier says.

Dan goes to his pockets and finds a fifty-kroner bill all crinkled up and damp from sweat. He was going to spend it on a cold soda on their way home from the paper route.

The cashier gives him the change. Dan grabs the lighter and the paper tissues, turns and skips towards the door.

"Hey, what happened to your foot?"

"Soccer practice," Dan mutters over his shoulder right before hobbling out into the cool night air once again. He opens the door and jumps in.

Linda stares at the lighter. "You ... you're not thinking about ...?"

"Drive out of the town," Dan says tonelessly.

TWENTY-FOUR

They pull over at the first rest area they see.

Linda turns off the engine and looks at Dan. "For the record, I still think we should call the police."

"They won't believe us," Dan tells her for the fourth time.

"We just need to explain to them what happened. If we tell them not to touch him—"

"It's still too risky."

"But we can—"

"No!" Dan interrupts, amazed at how stern he sounds. He goes on more softly: "We need to end this. It was too close a call before at the hospital."

In the trunk, Thomas is rummaging around, growling and snarling.

"Sure there's no better way of doing it?" Linda asks hoarsely.

"I can't think of any. Can you?"

She bites her lip then shakes her head. "And you're sure he won't …?"

"I'm sure. He doesn't feel pain anymore."

"All right."

"Do you have anything in here you want to keep? Better bring them, then." Dan opens his door and steps out onto the asphalt. He takes a deep breath, filling his lungs with the cool, crisp air, smells the surrounding fields and listens to the silence.

Linda comes out of the car, carrying her jacket, purse and a pair of sunglasses. "Okay," she mutters. "All clear."

"Right. Step back then." Dan opens the back door. He pulls open the packet of Kleenex and shoves them down between the seats one at a time. Thomas scratches and moans more eagerly from the trunk, as though he can sense Dan is close by.

"I'm so sorry," Dan whispers as he tears up. "But I have to do it. I think you'd understand. And thank you for saving us, by the way."

He flicks the lighter, looks at the flame for a moment, then he lights the tissues and shuts the door.

Linda has gone several yards away, and Dan skips over to her.

From inside the car comes a faint, flickering orange light. It quickly grows brighter. Soon the flames become visible. They eat the seat greedily, licking at the ceiling.

In a matter of minutes, the whole car is ablaze. Dark smoke begins to seep out of cracks in the doors. Dan can feel the heat even this far away.

He sits down heavily on the asphalt, resting his forehead on his knees. He's never felt this tired before. The fatigue is coming from inside his bones. He has lived through the worst possible nightmare, and now all he wants is to—

"Dan!" Linda exclaims. "The trunk is open!"

Dan lifts his head. She's right; the lid of the trunk has opened a few inches. A burning hand suddenly appears, followed by the rest of Thomas.

Dan stares in utter horror at the rear end of the burning car. Thomas's hair and clothes are gone. Same goes with most of his skin. And yet, he stubbornly fights his way out of the trunk and slumps down to the ground. His movements are oddly stiff. The legs don't seem to function properly. Instead of getting to his feet, he begins dragging his way towards them.

"Do something!" Linda yells and backs away. "Do something!"

Dan gets to his feet, unsure what to do or where to go.

Then, Thomas seems to lose his strength. He drags himself a few feet farther, but then he slows down. His groans and moans grow fainter, and with a final sigh, Thomas lies his head down on the asphalt and dies for the second time, the naked flesh still seething all over his body. He has left a broad trail of sticky blood all the way from the car. Dan can smell the burning flesh. He forces himself to look away, and instead he sees Linda.

She's standing with her hand over her mouth, staring from Thomas's burning corpse to Dan, her eyes wet from fear and tears. "It's over now, right? Tell me it's over."

"It is," Dan mutters. "It's finally over."

But just as he utters the words, a realization hits him like a lightning bolt.

Jennie! Oh, shit! How could I forget about her?

Linda says something, but Dan doesn't even register it. He can only think of one thing.

The hatch. The hatch to the basement. I locked it. I know I did ... didn't I?

TWENTY-FIVE

Dennis looks up at the dark house looming under the starry night sky, and everything within him screams for him to turn his bike around and get out of here as fast as possible.

But he can't.

Not until he finds the gris-gris.

He can't remember having been this scared in his entire life.

At least not since last night.

All the gruesome things that went down right here, in Esther's house, Dennis will never forget. And he'll probably suffer from nightmares for the rest of his life. The bloody images are already haunting him, the dying screams echoing inside his skull.

And now he needs to go back inside.

Because he lost his most important possession, the one thing he can never lose no matter what; that's what Mom instructed him, anyway.

To Dennis, the amulet is really not much else than what any person would see looking at it: a small leather pouch. Inside are a few tiny items which don't hold any particular significance either: a feather, a piece of bone, a rock and a white marble.

To Mom, however, the gris-gris is a magical amulet protecting Dennis from harm as long as he wears it. When she made it for him several years back, she demanded he wore it on a string around his neck at all times.

When Dennis started going to school, she agreed—after he pleaded with her repeatedly—to let him keep it in his pocket so the other kids wouldn't see it and make fun of him. There are already plenty of things about Dennis for his classmates to make fun of—like the fact that he's slow-witted—and he certainly didn't need another one.

Dennis has always been careful about not losing the gris-gris. He would take great pains in removing it from his pocket before his pants went to the laundry basket, and it would sit right beside his bed every night, so he was sure to see it first thing in the morning and remember to bring it.

He's never lost it.

Not until yesterday.

On the worst day of his life.

He didn't even notice until right after dinner.

Suddenly he felt something missing from his pocket, the tiny bulge always resting against his thigh. When he stuck his hand down there, he found nothing but a hole at the bottom.

The gris-gris must have slipped out without him even noticing. Not surprising that he didn't notice, though, as he had plenty of other things on his mind at the moment.

Of course, he couldn't tell Mom. Not on a regular day, and especially not after what they'd been through yesterday. He could feel she was also affected by it, even though she tried not to show it. In fact, she acted like it never happened, and she told Dennis to do the same, and to never mention anything to anybody about it. They would both go to jail if he did, she said, and Dennis believed her; he would never breathe a word to anybody.

So, he just waited anxiously in his room for night to come. And as soon as Mom had stuck her head in and said good night, he climbed out the window, got his bike from the garage and rode the couple of miles down road to Esther's place.

He was careful when he approached the driveway, looking for flashing lights or any other signs of police. But both the house and the driveway are completely dark.

And now he's standing here, next to his bike, trying to convince himself to go inside the house. Something awful obviously went down here. The front door is standing wide open, inviting him.

The dark piles lying around the gravel are not so inviting, though. Dennis doesn't want to look at them, but he can't help it. And he can't pretend like he doesn't know what the piles are, either.

They're dead people.

Real dead people.

The ones who stay dead.

Come to think of it, Dennis actually prefer this kind of dead people, even though they scare the life out of him. But at least they don't get up and come for you.

Or do they? Maybe they will once I get closer ...

The thought nails him even firmer to the spot, his legs refusing to move. He glances at the bike, considering calling the whole thing off.

But he can't.

He knows that.

As much as he's scared of the dead people and the house and what happened here, none of it can hurt him.

But Mom can.

And she will if she finds out he lost the gris-gris.

So, Dennis breathes deeply and forces himself to walk towards the front door. He doesn't look at the dead people—but he can't help but glance at them out the corner of his eye.

One of them is a man with dark skin, lying with his face turned towards the sky, his eyes closed and his mouth open.

The other is Esther; Dennis recognizes her all too well. After all, it's only been around twenty-four hours since he last saw her. She's still wearing the white dress, and her face is turned away from him, which Dennis is grateful for.

The last dead person, the one closest to the front door, is much smaller, and Dennis recognizes her too, without having to look closer.

It's the girl.

Nadia.

Dennis feels like crying, and he manages to up the speed as he passes by the dead girl.

He reaches the front door and stops there, peering into the darkness of Esther's scullery.

"He ... hello?" he whispers, causing himself to jump.

There's no answer.

The house is completely silent.

Which is good.

But also very scary.

Dennis steps inside, reaching for a light switch, but changing his mind at the last second. It's not a good idea to turn on any lights. Someone passing by might see it from the road. Best to get by with the light of his cell phone.

He takes it out and activates the screen. It's almost midnight. Dennis is usually sleeping tight by now.

He lights his way into the hallway, searching the floor for the gris-gris, stepping carefully so as to not bump into anything or make any kind of noise.

Once he reaches the living room, he finds it even more messed up than he remembers. Someone else has obviously been here since yesterday, and it looks like they've been fighting.

Dennis checks the floor all over. As the light falls on the dark spot from where Old Niels died, he feels a wrench in his gut and he hurries on.

The gris-gris isn't in the living room, either. Dennis begins to suspect he might have dropped it outside the house.

But there's one more room he needs the check.

The one he fears the most.

He turns slowly towards the door to the bedroom. It's ajar. A pale gleam of moonlight shines out from inside, luring him closer.

Dennis slips across the floor, pushes the door open very gently and peeks inside the bedroom.

It's empty except for the bed; just like he recalls it. The only thing different is the broken glass strewn all over the floor, and the dried-up blood prints glistening in the moonlight. The hatch to the basement is open.

He can't see the gris-gris anywhere.

Maybe it's under the bed?

He steps inside the room, careful about avoiding the shards of broken glass, as he makes his way towards the bed.

Just as he kneels down, lifts up the side of the sheet and looks under the bed, there's a sound from below. It's a bump. Dennis freezes. And then he sees a movement from the other side of the bed.

A hand comes up from the open hatch, groping at the air for a second, then clamping on to the floor as another hand appears.

Dennis stares at the hands as they turn into arms and then a golden-haired head with shoulders.

A girl a few years older than Dennis comes up from the basement, halfway climbing, halfway dragging herself, her movements slow and clumsy.

Even before she's all the way up, she turns and stares directly at Dennis. The sight of her face makes him gasp for breath. The girl has obviously been very pretty very recently, but now she looks like something out of a nightmare. Her eyes are white and fishlike, bulging from their sockets, her mouth is open and drool is dripping from her bottom lip. And her skull seems to have been almost caved-in on one side, making her face crooked and reminding Dennis of that awful picture of a man screaming on a bridge he once saw in a museum.

The girl isn't screaming, but she's making a sound from deep down in her throat, a sound of hunger, as she begins to make her way towards Dennis, climbing like a crab on land.

Dennis is finally able to move. He pushes himself back and jumps to his feet, stumbling backwards, feeling the walls behind him as he squeezes into the corner.

The dead girl gets to her feet, too, looking like a toddler walking for the first time, unsteady and wobbly.

In a flash of sheer panic, Dennis realizes he's literally cornered, the only thing between him and the girl being the bed. Then he notices the dead girl deciding to walk around the bed instead of simply crossing it, which would have left Dennis nowhere to run.

Now, he has the chance, and he grabs it.

He leaps onto the bed and down on the other side, then heads for the door. He forgets completely to look where he's going, and his foot bangs into the open floor hatch, sending a flash of pain through his toes. He falls forward and rolls around on the floor, missing by sheer luck any of the broken glass.

There's no time to whine about the pain, so he immediately jumps back up to see the girl coming right at him.

Dennis screams and jumps back, hitting the doorframe. The girl reaches out her hands, missing his face by mere inches as Dennis manages to back out into the living room.

He grabs the door out of pure instinct and slams it in the dead girl's face. It only connects with a bang, sending her backwards, but not closing all the way.

Dennis jumps forward to push at it, but the girl manages to get one arm through the crack a split second before Dennis can close the door.

She flails her arm wildly, clawing blindly at him, missing his bare arm by less than an inch. Dennis yelps and backs away from the door. He turns around to run, only to stumble directly into the coffee table. He wheels sideways and trips over a tipped-over chair, landing between the table and the couch.

As he looks up, he sees the open door and the girl who comes staggering out from the bedroom. She's lit up from behind by the sickening yellowish moonlight, and the scene is so terrifying it causes every muscle in Dennis's body to cease working; he can only lie there and see her approach.

"Please don't," he whimpers as the girl maneuvers around the chair that tripped him. "Please get away from me ..."

The girl pays no attention whatsoever to his pleading, but simply moves in closer, towering over him.

"No! No, please don't!" Dennis begs, beginning to sob and scramble backwards, pushing into the couch, but there's nowhere for him to go. "I'm sorry! I'm sorry!"

He doesn't even know what he's sorry about—but, miraculously, it seems to work.

The girl suddenly stops.

She's bent down halfway, her arms reached out to grab Dennis's leg, when she simply ceases moving, like a robot who had its battery cut.

Dennis sobs and looks up at her, her empty dead eyes staring right past him as she sniffs the air once, almost like a bloodhound.

Then she gives off a groan, stands up straight, turns around and simply walks out of the living room, making her way through the furniture like a drunk person.

Dennis lies there and stares after her, completely nonplussed. He can hear her through the entire house as she heads for the front door.

Then, only silence.

Dennis listens to his pounding heart and his baited breath.

"What ... what just happened?" he whispers, as though the empty room can give him an answer.

When none comes, he decides to get up and get away in case the girl changes her mind and comes back for him.

And as he makes to get to his feet, he suddenly feels it; the thing he was lying on.

It's the gris-gris.

Dennis picks it up like it was made of crystal glass, holding it with both hands as he studies the leather pouch like for the first time.

Dennis puts the gris-gris in his pocket and leaves the house.

Outside, in the courtyard, there's no sign of the girl. The other three dead people are still lying around exactly where they were when Dennis came.

He can't help but take out the gris-gris and look at it once more.

Perhaps Mom was right after all. Perhaps it really does work as a protective amulet.

Then there's a pair of headlights cutting through the night as Dennis sees a car coming up the driveway. His first thought is that it's Mom who has found out he's missing and has come looking for him.

But as the car comes closer, he can tell it's not Mom's car. He runs to his bike and pulls it across the gravel to the garage where he crouches down and peeks out.

The car comes into the courtyard, and Dennis sees to his utter horror the word written on the side of it. Even though Dennis is terrible at reading, he knows that word.

Police.

The car stops without turning off its engine or headlights, and two men step out.

"Holy hell," one of them exclaims as he sees the dead people. "Call for backup!"

The other one runs back to the car as the first officer crouches down and begins examining Nadia—perhaps hoping she's still alive.

Dennis uses the chance as the officers are both busy to drag his bike back out of the garage and out to the driveway. As soon as he's a fair distance away, he jumps in the seat and begins pumping the pedals.

He doesn't slow down even once on the entire way home. He does pause briefly every thirty seconds, though, to check that the gris-gris is still in his pocket.

DAY 2

The following takes place on
Sunday, July 27

ONE

Selina is awakened by a scream.

She sits bolt upright and looks around. She's in her room. The sun is streaming in through the window, and the room is already too hot. It's got to be at least 10:00 AM. For a moment, she feels utterly confused.

Did I sleep in?

Slowly, some of her memory returns. She's not going to school today; it's Sunday. She was out partying with her friends last night. They got pretty drunk. As though to confirm this, a throbbing headache takes root in her temples.

Was someone screaming just now? Or did I dream it?

Another scream answers her question. It comes from the garden. This time, she can tell it's not a real scream, just a kid playing.

Selina lies back down with a heavy sigh.

Now it's all coming back to her. It's Louisa's birthday. She's having all the girls from her class over.

Perfect, Selina thinks, pulling the blanket over her face. Just what my hangover needed.

It soon gets too hot under the blanket. In fact, she's already sweating. So, she gets up, squinting against the sunlight as she opens the window and lets the fresh, lukewarm air in. She leans against the windowpane and peers down into the garden. On the terrace are tables laid out with flags and balloons. Three girls are chasing each other around the lawn. They are the ones screaming.

Selina gazes out over the open fields. They stretch out endlessly under the blue dome of the summer sky. She's still not really used to living out here. Just like she's not used to Louisa or Ulla, either. Or rather, "Little Sister" and "Mom," as Dad insists on her calling them. Like that's ever going to happen.

Something catches her eye. It looks like a person is walking across one of the fields. It's hard to tell for sure, though, with the sun blinding her, and the fact that she surprisingly remembered to take out her contact lenses before going to bed last night; it could simply be the wheat moving in the breeze.

A new wave of headache.

How did I even get home? That's right, Jonas drove us. Oh, shit, did I kiss him? I think I did ...

Selina lets out a moan and rubs her forehead. If she really did kiss Jonas goodbye, she might as well lie down and die right here and now. Krista is never going to stop teasing her as long as she lives, even if it was only a tiny peck on the lips as they said goodnight in the car.

Selina looks around for her cell. She can't see her purse anywhere, so the phone is probably somewhere in her clothes, which are strewn about the floor. She starts going through it, careful as she bends down, so as to not provoke any further headache. She doesn't find anything. She calls off the search for now and instead goes to the bathroom. She gulps down a couple of mouthfuls of water and removes the worst of the makeup. Then she sits down to pee, closing her eyes for a moment.

The window is open, and she can hear a car come rolling into the courtyard.

Probably more rug rats here for the party.

Two car doors opening and slamming. Steps in the gravel. The front door opening.

Her father's voice: "Morning, Officers. What can I do for you?"

Selina freezes. Officers? What the fuck? The police are here!? She immediately feels guilty. Had Jonas been drinking when he drove them home last night? Were there any drugs in the car?

"Morning, sir," a man's voice says. "We're from the local police."

"I figured as much," her dad says. "Is something wrong?"

Selina quickly finishes up and goes to the window. From up here, she can see her father and two uniformed police officers. One of them is older and has a grey beard. The other one is pretty young, maybe mid-twenties, and pretty handsome. The younger officer appears to be rather nervous, as he keeps darting glances around the courtyard.

"My name is Soren, and this is Allan," the older officer says.

"Torben," Selina's dad says, shaking hands with the older officer. He also offers his hand to the younger officer, but he doesn't notice it.

"Allan?" the older officer asks.

Allan turns his head, smiles apologetically and briefly shakes Dad's hand, before going back to searching the surroundings with his eyes.

Why is he so paranoid?

"We're looking for a young girl who went missing last night," Soren explains, taking out a phone. "Her name is Jennie Nygaard. If I could ask you to take a look at her photo …"

Dad studies the screen for a moment, before shaking his head. "Sorry, I haven't seen her. Is she from around here? My daughter and I just moved here last month, you see, so we don't really know—"

He's interrupted by a scream from the backyard. Soren raises his grey eyebrows, and Allan's hand goes instinctively to his belt, even though Selina can't see any gun there.

"We're having a kid's birthday party," Dad explains. "That's just the girls playing."

"Could we have a word with you inside?" Soren asks.

"Sure, come on in. My wife is out shopping, but she'll be back in ten minutes or so. Maybe she knows the girl."

The officers follow Dad inside the house. Just before they disappear out of sight, Selina notices Allan throwing one last look over his shoulder. Then the front door closes.

Selina is so curious she has completely forgotten about her headache. She runs to her room, gets dressed and puts in new contacts. Just as she's about to leave her room, she notices something outside the window.

It's the figure in the field again. This time, she's sure it really is a person, because they're a lot closer. She can tell it's a girl around Selina's own age. She's heading straight for the garden, where the kids are playing. Only a row of rosehips separates the lawn from the surrounding fields.

But something seems odd about the girl, Selina notices. She's staggering along in a precarious fashion, almost like a sleepwalker. Her arms are outstretched in front of her, like she's grabbing for something. Her hair is messy and covers most of her face.

Could that be the girl the police are looking for? I'd better tell the officers …

Selina runs downstairs.

TWO

On her way down the staircase, she's met by a pack of girls laughing loudly.

"Heey!" one of them shouts. "Are you Louisa's big sister?"

Selina doesn't bother to answer, but rushes past them. She finds her dad with the officers in the kitchen.

Allan turns immediately as she steps into the room. His eyes are surprisingly dark and handsome, but also nervous, almost scared.

"Do you suspect something happened to the girl?" Dad asks. He's pouring coffee and hasn't noticed her.

"We can't discuss the case," Soren says, taking the mug with a grateful nod. "But you'll hear about it in the media before the day is over, I can pretty much guarantee it."

Selina suddenly feels awkward. Allan is still the only one to have noticed her presence, and he's doing nothing but silently staring at her, which is making her uncomfortable. She clears her throat.

Dad turns around. "Good morning, missy. How's the head?"

"It's fine," Selina mutters.

"This is my daughter, Selina."

"Morning," Soren mumbles through a sip of coffee as he eyes her thoughtfully. "How old are you, Selina?"

"Uhm ... sixteen."

"Do you happen to know Jennie Nygaard? She's a year older than you."

"I don't know her, but I think—"

She's interrupted as three girls come barging into the kitchen. Louisa is one of them. "Torben! Can I open my presents now? Hey, who're these guys?"

"These are officers from the police," Dad explains.

"Wow!" Louisa gasps, eyeing the men. "Are you like real policemen?"

"We sure are," Soren says, smiling. "And how old are you, my girl?"

"Seven!" Louisa exclaims proudly, holding up the same number of fingers.

"Louisa!" One of the other girls pulls her sleeve. "Where's your dog?"

"Yeah, you said we could see it," the third girl chimes in.

Louisa's expression turns sad. "It's gone."

"Louisa's dog unfortunately ran away a few days ago," Dad explains. "But we put up posters, and I'm sure someone will find it. Go show your friends your room, Louisa."

The girls leave the kitchen and run upstairs.

"Please, sit down," Dad says to the officers. "My wife will be here any minute."

Soren sits down, but Allan walks past the table and instead stands in front of the window to the back garden, where the kids are still running around playing.

Selina takes a breath. "I think I might have seen the girl you're looking for."

Everyone's attention turns to her at once. Even Allan turns away from the window to stare at her.

"I see," Soren says evenly. "And when was that?"

"Right now. Just a minute ago. I saw—" At that moment, Selina sees something through the window.

The girl from the field comes crashing through the rosehips. The thorns are tugging at her clothes and leaving bloody scratches on her arms, yet the girl doesn't seem to pay notice. She just stumbles out onto the lawn with stiff, staggering steps.

The face of the girl leaves Selina speechless. Her messy hair can't hide the greenish hue dominating the skin nor the milky white eyes which belong to a dead fish rather than a teenage girl. The gaze is fixed on one of the girls who is standing with her back to the rosehips only a few yards away.

"Selina?" Dad asks, pulling her back. "What's wrong?"

Selina lifts her arm and points.

Allan has already turned his head to look. "Shit!" he exclaims, spinning on his heel and running to the hallway.

"Allan!" Soren exclaims, getting up from the table. "What are you doing?"

But Allan doesn't answer, and a second later the front door slams.

Selina is still pointing and staring at the window, unable to move or speak, trapped as though in a nightmare, everything suddenly moving painfully slow. She sees the girl who's got to be Jennie Nygaard descend upon the girl; it looks most of all like a clumsy embrace, causing both of them to fall to the grass. For a few seconds, they scramble around.

Then the girl screams. This time, it's a genuine scream. A scream of pain and fear.

"What the heck?" Dad says. "What's she doing? Is that the girl you guys are—"

"Stay in here," Soren commands, running through the living room and opening the terrace door.

Dad follows him.

Selina still can't move. Events seem to speed up again, reaching an unnatural pace. She sees and hears everything from the window, which is ajar.

Jennie Nygaard is sitting astride the girl who is still screaming, now in very shrill, batlike tones. Jennie Nygaard throws back her head, and Selina sees the bloody chunk between her teeth. It disappears quickly out of sight, as the teenager gulps it down and promptly bends down for another bite.

What the fuck? She's ... she's ... biting her!

"Hey, you!" Soren calls as he comes running across the lawn. "Stop that right now!"

Jennie Nygaard doesn't react the slightest to his call, but keeps doing what's she doing.

"Hey!" Soren yells, grabbing her by the shoulder. "I told you to—"

Selina sees the officer freeze in place, his expression turning to utter horror. "What the hell are you doing? Stop! ... Stop that!"

He shoves Jennie Nygaard aside, giving Selina a clear view of the girl on the grass. The sight makes her gasp. There's a giant bloody crater in the neck of the girl. She's no longer screaming.

"Allan!" Soren roars, kneeling down by the girl. "Allan, goddamnit! Where are you?"

Jennie Nygaard is laboriously making her way back to her feet, and the officer seems for a second to have forgotten about her completely. The lower part of her face is covered in blood. She makes a sound halfway between a gurgle and a growl, then turns towards Soren.

Suddenly, miraculously, Selina's voice returns. "Watch out! Watch out behind you!"

THREE

The policeman reacts to Selina's warning, but too late. Jennie Nygaard bends down and sinks her teeth into the back of his neck.

Soren roars with pain and throws her off. He touches the back of his neck, then stares with disbelief at his bloody fingers. Jennie Nygaard has fallen down once more, but that doesn't stop her reaching for his leg and trying to bite his ankle.

The officer pulls back his leg. "Stay down! Stay down, I say!"

Jennie Nygaard isn't listening; she's crawling stubbornly forward, her nails digging into the grass, her mouth snapping. Soren makes a move which looks rehearsed: he quickly steps to the side, plants a knee in her back, twists both her arms back and slaps a pair of handcuffs on them.

At that moment, Allan comes running around the house. He has a gun in his hand.

"Tend to the girl!" Soren shouts. "I don't think she has a pulse!"

Allan hesitates for a moment at the sight of Jennie Nygaard. Then, he drops down by the girl. "Holy shit! Her windpipe is totally gone ... she's already ... oh, fuck me!" His free hand goes to his head.

Selina is once more unable to move, and that nasty feeling of being trapped in a dream has again taken hold of her. A single thought keeps repeating.

This can't be happening. It just can't.

"Jesus Christ, she's completely out of it," Soren snarls, trying to hold down Jennie Nygaard. She twists violently from side to side, bending her back in obtuse angles, making it look like her spine might snap any moment. She doesn't seem to be in pain, though, as her main concern is still trying to bite Soren.

"Stop resisting!" he shouts at her. "Do you understand what I'm saying? Lie still!" He darts a look around and fixes on Allan. "What are you waiting for? Get them to send an ambulance!"

Allan takes out a walkie-talkie, his movements slow and hesitant.

"What's going on?" it's Dad's voice, as he suddenly appears on the terrace.

Soren points at him. "Get the kids out of here. Take them inside."

The remaining kids—whom Selina hasn't even noticed till now—run to her dad crying, and he disappears inside with them.

"Central," Allan says into the walkie. "We have an injured …" He stops. He's staring at something outside of Selina's view. Not until he takes a stumbling step sideways does she see it. The dead girl is now sitting up.

Selina's first thought is that the girl wasn't really dead after all. But then she sees her eyes, as the girl turns her head and glares hungrily at the officers.

This is a bad dream. It has to be. I'll wake up any moment now …

But a part of her knows she's not dreaming. A part of her understands that all of this is terribly real. A word is ringing somewhere at the back of her mind. That word is zombie. And that knowing part of her understands that zombies aren't just something on television anymore.

The girl exclaims something which might have been a growl, had it not been for the torn-up throat, which only produces a gurgling rattle. She gets to her feet. Her white summer dress is completely covered in blood still oozing from the open hole in her neck. She reaches out her arms and staggers eagerly towards Allan, looking grotesquely like a little girl who wants her daddy.

Allan hesitates, shakes his head, staggers backwards.

"Allan!" Soren shouts, still struggling against the cuffed zombie. "What the hell are you doing? Help her, for Christ's sake!"

Allan keeps stepping backwards. He drops the walkie on the grass. Instead, he raises the gun.

"Allan, goddamnit!" Soren roars. "What the hell are—"

The shot rings out over the garden, surprisingly loud. It stings in Selina's ears, and the glass in front of her vibrates for a second. The girl's head is thrown back, revealing a gaping hole right above her eye. She manages to take another step, then she collapses on the grass.

A few seconds of terrible silence.

The only thing Selina can hear is a shrill ringing in her ears, and Jennie Nygaard still growling and trying to get free. Selina notices absently how her dad comes rushing past behind her, herding a flock of kids.

Outside on the lawn, Allan is staring down at the dead girl. His mouth opens and closes a few times.

Soren stares at his partner. "You ... you shot her ..."

Allan turns around to face Soren. He looks very ill. He mutters something Selina doesn't catch. It sounds like: "... had to do it ..."

Maybe because Soren is distracted, Jennie Nygaard finally manages to twist around just enough to plant her teeth in his thigh.

"Auv, goddamnit! Let go! Let go of me!" He sends a fist directly into her face, once, twice, three times. Jennie Nygaard ignores the punches and keeps gnawing away fiercely, ripping the pants and causing blood to spurt. Soren gets up and steps back. The zombie clamps down and is dragged a few steps before it finally loses its grip.

Soren limps backwards, clutching at his leg. "Bloody hell, she got me good ..." He's still bleeding from the wound on the back of his neck, the blood running down both sides of his neck like strings of red hair.

Jennie Nygaard still has her hands caught behind her back, which means she can't get up. Instead, she wriggles after Soren like a giant worm. A piece of his pants leg is still lodged between her teeth.

Allan steps between them. He aims the gun at Jennie Nygaards's head.

"No, Allan," Soren begins.

He's interrupted once more, as Allan pulls the trigger the second time. The shot is just as deafening as the first time.

Jennie Nygaard immediately ceases to move.

FOUR

The silence that follows is even louder than the two gunshots.

The first noise Selina registers is kids crying somewhere nearby. Then she hears something much closer: a gurgling sound coming from her own throat. She doubles over and throws up onto the floor. The sweet taste of Malibu brings her fleeting memories of last night.

Her stomach is quickly empty. It cramps up a few more times, and Selina spits into the puddle. Outside in the garden she can hear the officers shouting at each other.

"Have you gone completely insane?"

"They were zombies, goddamnit!"

"Give me the gun! Let go of it!"

Selina looks out to see them fighting over the gun.

Then her dad is by her side, pale-faced. Without a word, he grips her arm and pulls her towards the stairs.

"Dad, wait ..."

But Dad doesn't seem to hear her. He hauls her upstairs and into Louisa's room, where a flock of scared girls—including Louisa—are standing or sitting around the floor, sobbing or staring in wide-eyed silence.

"We stay in here," Dad says to no one in particular. "All of us. We're safe in here."

"What about Josefine?" one of the girls immediately asks.

Selina figures Josefine must be the girl splayed out on the grass down in the back garden with a bullet in her brain.

"She's fine, Josefine is fine," Dad lies and finally looks at Selina. "Stay in here with the girls. Comfort them if they get scared." He strides back towards the door.

"Dad!" Selina says, following him. "You can't go down there ..."

"You'll do as I say!" Dad shouts and spins around to point a finger in her face.

Selina steps back, amazed. Dad has never yelled at her before. She looks at him and realizes he's trembling, his eyes flickering.

"I have no idea what's going on down there," he murmurs. "But it's obvious they don't have the situation under control, so I'm calling the police, and I'm also calling Ulla to tell her not to come home." He pats his pockets. "My phone is downstairs. I'll be back up as soon as I've made the calls."

He leaves the room without further explanation, slamming the door and turning a key on the other side.

Selina turns to look at the scared girls, most of them staring back at her, unsure what to do or say. At that moment there's a shout from the garden. Selina runs to the window. Looking down, she sees the policemen rolling around the grass, still struggling for the gun.

Soren wins the fight and gets to his feet, panting, holding the weapon. He points it at Allan as he limps backwards a few paces. "You're ... under ... arrest ..." he wheezes.

"You've been infected, Soren," Allan says, sitting up, his shirt and hair all ruffled. "You'll become—"

"Shut up!" Soren shouts. "And stay down!"

Allan holds up his hands. "Listen to me, goddamnit. We might still have a chance of stopping it!"

Soren doesn't answer, but picks up the walkie. "Central," he says.

"No!" Allan shouts. "Don't call for backup! We can't risk any more people getting infected!"

Soren steps a little farther away. "Yeah, we need an ambulance ... one officer is wounded, two civilians are dead ... We found what we assume to be the missing person ... she's dead."

Someone pulls at Selina's sleeve. She turns to see Louisa. Her lips are trembling. "Selina? Why is this happening on my birthday?"

"I don't know," Selina mutters, realizing how all of the girls are staring at her. She forces a smile. "There's no need to be scared, we're safe up here."

"What about Josefine?" one of them asks.

Selina glances down onto the lawn and feels a cold shiver down her spine despite the heat. "I'm ... I'm not sure about Josefine."

Louisa leans forward to look, but Selina pushes her gently back. "Just take a seat, okay? It'll be over soon."

"I want Mommy," Louisa says and starts crying.

"Your mom will be here in a minute," Selina promises her.

But Louisa keeps crying, and it sets off a chain reaction. Soon all the girls are sobbing. Selina looks out the window again.

Allan is still sitting on the grass, his head in his palms, looking like he's brooding over a serious problem. Soren has sat down on one of the lawn chairs. The gun is on the table next to him. He's tending to the bite wound on his leg. The other wound, the one on his neck, is still trickling blood.

"Soren," Allan says, suddenly lifting his head. "You need to listen to me. I'm not crazy."

Soren sends him a brief look, but doesn't say anything.

"You saw her yourself," Allan goes on, gesturing towards the body of Josefine. "She was dead. I know you saw it. How do you think she could just get up again?"

"Apparently, she wasn't dead after all," Soren growls. "Not until you shot her."

"Yes, she was! She was dead as a doornail. I checked her pulse."

No answer from Soren this time.

The girls' sobbing is starting to get on Selina's nerves. It's making it hard to hear what the officers are saying. She turns and shushes the girls, but they hardly notice her.

"Hey," she says. "Be quiet, all right? You need to stay quiet."

The girls sniffle, and a few of them actually stop the waterworks.

Selina turns her attention to the open window once more.

"How about her, then?" Allan asks, pointing to Jennie Nygaard. "Did she look alive to you when she charged at you? She has been dead for at least twelve hours, and you know it!"

Soren glances at the corpse of Jennie Nygaard, but still doesn't reply.

Allan goes on pleadingly: "This is a form of disease. It's killing people fast and then bringing them back so they can attack other people and spread the infection. I knew it as soon as I saw the three bodies. I should have told you, but I knew you wouldn't believe me until you saw it." Allan hesitates for a moment. Selina can tell how he weighs his next words. "You're already infected, Soren. I'm really sorry, but ... there's nothing we can do. And if you don't call off that ambulance, you'll spread the infection to a whole lot of other people."

Soren scoffs. "This isn't a movie, Allan."

"No, it's real. Do you really want the end of the world on your shoulders?"

Soren gingerly touches the wound on his neck and mutters something Selina almost can't pick up. It sounds like: "... hurts like hell ..."

Even from up here, Selina can tell how the skin around the wound is already starting to take on a greenish color; the same color Josefine's skin had when she woke up again.

Selina's stomach is doing somersaults. What Allan is saying is completely ludicrous—but for some reason, it also makes sense. If it works like in the movies, then Allan is right: It's game over as soon as you get a scratch or get bitten. It's only a matter of time before you'll be walking around like a flesh-eating monster yourself.

Selina bites her lip. Tries hard to think. Is there anything she can do? She assumes it's too late to help Soren. But can she in anyway prevent the ambulance from getting here? Or that Soren gets in it?

Not as long as he has the gun ...

She looks down at the gun on the table. Soren is leaning back in the garden chair, moaning and closing his eyes for a moment, his forehead gleaming with sweat.

This is insane, Selina thinks. But I have to try ...

FIVE

Selina closes the window and turns to the girls. "Listen up, girls. I need to leave the room for a minute. But you guys just stay here, all right? Nothing will happen."

"You can't leave," Louisa remarks, wiping her nose on her sleeve. "Your dad locked the door."

"I'll climb out the window."

The girls look at each other, then back at her.

"Isn't that dangerous?" Louisa asks.

"Where are you going?" another one asks.

"When will you be back?" a third one asks.

Selina puts a finger to her lips. "You need to be quiet, remember? It's very important you don't say anything once I open the window. I'll be back in less than five minutes. But I don't want you to look out the window while I'm gone. You need to stay seated, okay? Do you understand?"

A few of the girls nod.

From the other side of the door, Selina can hear Dad's voice talking on the phone. "Yes, two officers, and one of them has gone insane ... no, Louisa is fine, just don't come home right now, okay? ... Listen, I keep telling you: I don't know!"

Selina opens the window again. It opens all the way like a door. Dad has been wanting to put a child safety-thing on it, but luckily, he hasn't gotten around to it.

By sitting on the windowsill, she can reach the drain pipe running down the wall. She swings out her legs, and for a moment feels dizzy. It's probably due to the hangover, because she's never been afraid of heights—in fact, she used to do quite a lot of tree-climbing when she was little.

"Selina," Louisa whispers behind her.

Selina turns her head and shushes her.

"I just wanted to say be careful," Louisa whispers. "I don't want you to fall down and hurt yourself."

Selina sends her a quick smile and whispers: "Don't worry." Then, she leans out and grabs a hold of the drain pipe. The metal is already hot from the sun. The pipe seems to be securely fastened to the wall and can easily carry her weight.

She looks down at the terrace one more time. Soren is still sitting with his eyes closed. Allan, who's sitting on the grass, looks up at that exact moment and meets Selina's eyes. He looks like he's about to say something, but then thinks better of it. He then simply glances at his partner and back up at Selina. He nods discretely, once.

Selina slips out and begins climbing down the drain pipe. The metal gives off tiny sounds under her weight, but luckily, Soren is complaining about the pain, so he doesn't notice.

"Bloody hell," he moans, leaning forward on the chair. "I'm burning up here ... when's that ambulance coming?"

Selina keeps descending. She's only about six feet above ground, when her sweaty palm slips on the pipe, producing a high screeching sound. Selina freezes.

Soren lifts his head. His eyes are hazy. "What was that?" he mutters and looks around.

"Soren!" Allan says loudly, drawing his attention. "Why won't you listen? You need to call and cancel that ambulance ..."

"You shut up, now. You're under arrest, remember? You have the right to remain silent, so use that right."

Selina slides down and lands on the terrace without another sound. Her heart is beating wildly as she sneaks towards Soren and the table where the gun is. She's only five steps away.

"The future of the world might depend on it," Allan goes on, keeping Soren's focus away from Selina's direction.

"I don't want to hear anymore from you," Soren says, blinking and wiping sweat off his brow. "Until help is here, you don't open your mouth—you got that?"

Selina glances at Allan, and he glances back. Unfortunately, Soren looks at Allan at that moment, and he sees his partner's eyes flicker.

"What are you looking at?" he mumbles and turns in his chair. He stares directly at Selina, and his eyes grow wide. "Hey! Will you get back in that house!" He reaches for the gun, but the movement seems uncoordinated, and his hand misses the table, almost causing him to tip off the chair.

Before he can go for it again, Selina jumps over and snatches the weapon.

"Stop that!" Soren shouts, grabbing her by the arm.

Selina almost drops the gun, as it's a lot heavier than she anticipated, and she pulls to get free. "Let go of me!"

But Soren's grip is firm. He gets to his feet and grabs her with his other hand, too. She can feel the heat radiating off him as he fumbles to take the gun away from her. She fights to keep him off, and suddenly, Allan is there, pulling the weapon out of her hand and turning it on Soren. "Let her go, man. And sit back down."

Soren lets go of Selina, takes a wobbling step backwards and holds up his hands, blinking dully. "All right now. Take it easy, Allan."

Selina steps away from the officers. She can tell Soren is in a really bad state now. In fact, he's struggling to even keep upright. His eyes are watering, his voice is drooly. He's a terrible sight with the dried-up blood all over his neck, and his skin appears ash grey in the sunlight.

"Put down that gun, Allan," he mutters dreamily. "You don't know what you're ... what you're doing ..."

"Sit down, Soren," Allan says without lowering the gun. "You've got a bad fever."

"Do I?" Soren asks in a wondering voice, running his hand across his forehead. He looks at it and finds it dripping with sweat. "Well, what do you know? I do have a fever ..." Then his eyes turn to the sky and he faints.

SIX

Selina stares from the unconscious policeman on the terrace tiles to the armed policeman standing a few feet away. Allan is looking at his partner while breathing heavily through his nose.

"Are you ... are you going to ...?" Selina asks meekly.

Allan looks at her like he has for a moment forgotten all about her, then nods briefly. "Thank you for helping me. You'd better go inside now."

"Are you ... sure there's absolutely no other way? Like, completely sure? The ambulance will probably be here in a minute, and if they can help him in some way ..."

"They can't," the young officer says, shaking his head grimly, a drop of sweat falling from his chin. "There is nothing anyone can do. Once you're bitten ..." He nods towards the house. "Go inside, please."

Soren gives off a noise. It's halfway between a gasp and a cough. He twitches for a moment, but doesn't open his eyes.

"He's already slipping into a coma," Allan mutters, gripping the gun with both hands and spreading his feet slightly. "Go now."

Selina goes towards the terrace door.

Suddenly, her dad's voice calls from upstairs: "Selina! What the hell are you doing?" She looks up to see him hanging out the window, disbelief and horror on his face. "Didn't I tell you to stay up here?"

"But I had to—"

"Close that window!" Allan shouts. "I don't want the children to see this ..."

Dad looks at Soren and then at Allan. "Christ, I hope you're not thinking about shooting him?"

"He's already dead."

"No, he's not, I can hear him breathing all the way from up here! He's only wounded. He needs medical attention. I've already called the police, they're coming."

"Dad, you don't understand," Selina begins.

"Selina, get inside the house!" Dad shouts.

"But he's been—"

"Shut the fuck up, both of you!" Allan roars. He points a finger at Selina's dad. "You, shut that window. And you ..." He points at Selina. "Go inside—now!"

Dad obeys and closes the window, but only after sending Selina one last, meaningful look. Selina goes through the terrace door and closes it behind her. She doesn't feel like looking out, but she can't help it.

Allan is still poised above Soren with the gun. He looks up at the window on the first floor, as though to check no one is looking down. It's only a second. But it's enough. It happens very fast. Soren sits up abruptly and opens his eyes. His pupils are white, empty, dead, alive, hungry.

Selina screams.

Soren leans in and bites Allan's ankle.

Allan gives a yell of pain. He aims the gun and shoots Soren through the head.

The shot rings through the house for the third time.

Soren dies for the second time.

Everything stops moving for several seconds.

Selina is staring out at the young officer through the glass of the terrace door. He bends down slowly to lift up his pant leg, revealing his ankle and a bloody bitemark. Then, he straightens up again, his expression completely blank. His eyes fall on Selina, but it's more like he's looking right through her.

Selina holds her breath as Allan raises the gun and places it under his chin.

No, Selina thinks, but she can't move, can't talk, can't even take away her eyes.

Allan's face has become a mixture of emotions. Selina prepares mentally for another loud bang.

But—it doesn't come.

Allan lowers the gun again.

Selina blinks and finally starts breathing again. He can't do it ...

Then Allan does something else. Something completely unexpected. He spins on his heel and runs limpingly around the house.

What's he doing? Where's he going?

Selina runs through the living room and out into the kitchen.

Her dad comes running down the stairs, yelling: "Selina? Where are you? You come to me!"

Selina doesn't answer. She goes to the kitchen window and peers out, just as Allan comes running into view. He jumps into the police car.

Dad comes into the kitchen behind her. "There you are! What were you thinking? Come here!" He grabs her shoulder.

Selina pulls free with a strong tug. "Let go, Dad! I need to see what he'll do …" She stares out at Allan who starts the engine, revs it up, twists the wheel around and races out of the courtyard, leaving a cloud of dust.

"He … he ran away," Selina whispers.

"Good thing," Dad says. "Go and lock the front door, Selina. In case he comes back. I'll call the police again, ask them what the hell is taking them so long!"

Selina goes to the front door, suddenly feeling very unreal, like she's in a movie. She just stands there for a moment, staring at the knob. She sees everything unfold in her mind's eye. Allan, driving on the highway. Allan, becoming more and more ill behind the wheel. Allan, arriving at the hospital. Allan, dying in the hall. Allan, receiving CPR from a doctor. And finally Allan, reawakening in a building full of people …

Right now, Selina is the only one aware of this danger. She's the only one who can prevent this scenario from becoming real.

I have to stop him.

She doesn't know what else to do, so she rips open the door and runs out across the courtyard. Down by the end of the gravel road she just sees the police car as it turns left onto the highway—headed for town.

SEVEN

Dan's eyes are stinging, making it hard to see the road in front of him clearly. He forgot to change his contact lenses when he was at the house to get the scooter. Now his retinas have dried up.

Luckily, there isn't really any traffic on the roads out here. The road slopes lazily through the open fields. On his left is a forest, and underneath the scooter's tires, the asphalt is seething from heat. Dan is sweating.

In his backpack are a large bottle of water and two sandwiches. He made three of them back at the house, but he already gulped down one as he walked out to the garage. It's all he had to eat for … for how long? He's not sure what the time is, and there's no clock on Jennie's scooter, but judging from the position of the sun, it's got to be around noon. Which means it's been more than twenty-four hours since this whole thing started.

Dan blinks and tries to moisten his eyes. He feels like rubbing them, but he's not comfortable with taking one hand off the handlebars, and there's no time to make a rest stop—he already lost too much time. First by trying to talk Linda into going with him. He needed someone to drive him, but she didn't budge, no matter what he said.

"Listen to me, Linda …"

"No, you listen. I'm done. You get that? I've lost my husband, for God's sake!"

"But we need to find my sister. She might be—"

"I don't care! I already did enough! I agreed to burn the car, didn't I? I'm going to the police, and I'm telling them about everything that happened."

"No, you can't do that! They'll just—"

"I don't care! If your sister is still a … zombie, or whatever, then the police need to deal with it. That's their job, not mine!"

At that moment, a car had pulled over onto the rest stop where they were standing next to the rubble of the still burning car. A man had jumped out and asked them if they were okay. Linda went to him and began explaining everything.

Dan made a quick decision and ran for it—as much as he could with his busted ankle. He was headed back towards town when a firetruck came screaming by, closely followed by a police car. Dan jumped into the ditch and hid until both had passed. Then he continued onwards.

He still can't really believe he made the half mile back to town, but he did. Maybe it was the thought of Jennie keeping him going. If she got out of that basement, it would be his fault, since he was the one who forgot to lock the hatch. In that stuffy basement, Dan had fought for his own life. Now he was fighting for the future of the world.

He had limped through town as a new, hot day had broken, and the few cars on the roads this early didn't even notice him. As he fought on, he considered his options. His parents were out of town, so they couldn't help him. And it was also pointless to contact the police, as he was sure he couldn't convince them about what was really going on. Besides, Linda had probably already told them the whole thing by now. They were most likely already headed out to the house where everything had started. And where Jennie might be waiting for them …

When Dan finally reached his home, he knew he had to go out there himself. So, he took Jennie's scooter, and he—

A sound pulls Dan out of this train of thoughts. He looks to the side and sees a police car coming at him fast from an adjacent gravel road.

Dan yells out and squeezes the brake hard, causing the scooter to slide sideways and almost throw him off.

The police car veers to the side at the last second and narrowly avoids hitting him. But the driver doesn't seem to pay any notice, because the car doesn't slow down; it simply makes a sharp turn, the tires screaming against the hot asphalt, and then it races off in the direction towards town where Dan has just come from. Less than two hundred yards down the road, it slams on its brakes, turns sharply again, disappearing into the forest.

Holy shit, Dan thinks, feeling his heart under his chin. Wonder if that had anything to do with …

He doesn't need to finish the thought, because he already knows the answer. He had a brief glimpse of the driver of the car—a young man in a police uniform—and the pale face with the wide eyes told Dan everything he needed to know about what the guy had seen.

He looks around and notices the mailbox by the side of the gravel road from which the police car came. Number 214. The house where it all began was number 216. This is the neighbor, then. And that means Jennie probably—

Dan sees the girl running up the gravel road. For one terrible second he takes it to be Jennie. The girl does look a little like his late sister; around same age, same height and build. The hair is a little shorter and darker, but that's not readily apparent from this far away, and the only thing keeping Dan from twisting the gas handle and getting the heck out of Dodge is the way the girl moves. She's way too fast and steady on her legs to be a zombie. And now she raises one arm and waves at him.

Dan pulls off the helmet.

The girl reaches him and slows down, panting. "Did you ... did you see ... where he went?"

"That way," Dan says, pointing in the direction without taking his eyes off of the girl. "He drove into the forest."

The girl places her hands on her knees, heaving for breath, sweat beading on her forehead. Dan scans her quickly for any signs of blood or wounds, but doesn't see anything.

"What happened?" he asks.

"I need to borrow your scooter. I don't have time to explain, but I need to follow that guy."

"Why? Who was he?"

"I said, I don't have time." The girl grabs the handlebars.

"No!" Dan objects. "You can't have it. I need it."

"It's very important!" the girl says earnestly. "You'd never believe me, but the future of the world might depend on it."

Dan stares at her for a moment, as something falls into place. "I believe you," he says. "I've seen them."

The girl's eyes grow big. "Oh, no ... does that mean they already ...?"

"No, I don't think they've spread very far. As far as I know, it all began in the next house down the road from here. Only one of them escaped. It was—"

"Jennie Nygaard?" the girl interrupts.

Hearing his sister's names forms a lump in Dan's throat. He nods.

"She came to our house," the girl says, talking fast. "She killed one of the kids, and the officer shot her, then … then he got bitten, and then he ran. That's why I need to find him. I think I can talk him into his senses before he dies and infects anyone else."

"So … Jennie is dead?" Dan asks hoarsely.

"Yes. The officer is the last one, at least from what I've seen. That's why you need to lend me your scooter!"

Dan pulls his helmet back on. "Get on. I'll drive."

The girl looks at him with surprise for a second. Then, she jumps on and grabs him around the waist. Dan turns the scooter around and takes off down the road.

"Did Jennie bite anyone else?" he asks over his shoulder.

"Yes, another officer and a small girl. She was …" She doesn't seem to want to finish the sentence.

"They both dead?" Dan asks.

"Yes."

"How?"

"Allan shot them."

"Is Allan the guy we're after?"

"Yes."

"Did he shoot them through their heads?"

"Yes."

"How about Jennie?"

"Same."

Dan feels his stomach tighten up thinking about Jennie being really dead. But at the same time, strangely, he also feels a fair amount of relief.

He slows down as they reach the place the police car turned into the forest. There's a narrow forest road, and as they turn and head in between the trees, the air becomes slightly cooler and more pleasant. The girl tightens her grip around Dan. The feeling of her arms around him combined with the faint smell of her perfume gives Dan a brief flutter of butterflies in his stomach. Odd how his brain is even capable of registering something like that given the situation. Dan has always been shy around girls, and even though he's almost fifteen, he still has never kissed a girl.

"Do you know where this road leads?" she asks him.

"No idea," Dan replies. "I don't live out here, I was just doing a paper route."

"I just moved here, so I don't know the area either. I'm Selina, by the way."

"My name's Dan."

The road makes a sudden left turn and reveals the police car on the side of the road, its front up against a tree. Dan's first impression is that the driver has intentionally parked the car in a weird, crooked way—but then he notices the crunched hood of the car and the white smoke rising up from it.

"He has crashed it," Selina says, jumping off the scooter before it comes to a complete stop. "He might be dead."

Dan wants to tell her to be careful as she approaches the police car, but there seems to be no need: Selina walks over to it gingerly, ready to run at any moment. Dan keeps his hand ready on the gas.

Selina peeks in through the open driver's door, then shakes her head. "The airbag has blown, and it's stained with blood, but he's gone."

Dan steps off the scooter, puts it on the jack and takes off the helmet. He throws a look around but sees no one in sight.

"Shut off the engine for a moment," Selina says.

Dan turns the key, and silence descends over the forest. A couple of birds are singing carefreely and a bumblebee comes buzzing by. Besides that, nothing.

"You think he went on down the road?" Dan asks.

"That would make the most sense, I guess," Selina says, looking around. "I don't know how to track people—do you? Do you happen to be a Boy Scout or something?"

"Nah," Dan says. "But I think it's something about looking for broken twigs and stuff. That's how they do it in the movies."

Selina runs a hand through her hair. "I just don't get why he would drive in here in the first place. I thought he was going to the hospital."

"Maybe he's not aware what he's doing. If he lost a lot of blood, he might already be—"

A shrill scream interrupts Dan. It lasts for some seconds and echoes throughout the forest.

"Fuck," Selina whispers, her eyes wide. "I don't think that was him."

Dan shakes his head. "No. It sounded like a woman."

EIGHT

"Wake up, Dennis!"

Mom's voice—urgent, almost agitated—pulls him from deep sleep with a violent jerk. He opens his eyes, then shuts them promptly again as Mom rips aside the curtains, causing the sunlight to stream in.

"What ... what's the matter, Mom?" Dennis croaks, rubbing his eyes.

"Did you see it?"

Dennis squints up at Mom towering in front of his bed, a blurry silhouette against the bright daylight.

Dennis is completely nonplussed. He was sound asleep just a second ago. He thought it was still nighttime, but apparently, it's past noon. He normally never sleeps that long.

Then he remembers with a gasp what he did last night. It all comes back to him with a rush of panic. To make it all worse, Mom has somehow found out. She knows he lost the gris-gris and that he had to sneak back over to Esther's place to get it. She knows all about what—

"Did you see it?" Mom demands again—obviously interpreting his reaction as an answer to her question. "Where is it?"

"I ... I had it right ... right here ..." Dennis mutters, feeling immensely guilty as he looks around the bed for the gris-gris. Then he remembers it's hanging around his neck, and he grabs it and holds it up for Mom to see. "Here! It's right here! See? I didn't lose it!"

His eyes are getting used to the light by now, and he can make out Mom's expression. It's one of annoyed confusion.

"No, not your amulet. The dagger! Have you seen the dagger?"

Dennis blinks and stares at Mom for several seconds as it dawns on him he has completely misunderstood the situation. He shakes his head slowly. "No, I haven't. Not since ... you know."

"Damnit," Mom spits, then looks around the room. "You sure? Could it be in here somewhere?"

Before Dennis has time to answer, Mom begins rummaging through the dirty clothes and his toys lying around the floor.

"Why would your dagger be in here, Mom?"

She doesn't hear him. Seeing his mom like this—nearly frantic—is even more frightening to Dennis than the thought of her finding out about his nighttime venture. She's usually calm and collected no matter what happens.

"Did you … did you lose your dagger?" Dennis asks.

Mom stops abruptly, straightens up and stares into empty space. For a terrible second, Dennis is sure he has insulted Mom with his question and that she's about to punish him.

Then she whispers: "Of course. The car." And she rushes out of the room.

"Mom?" Dennis calls after her, but she doesn't answer.

He gets up and follows her through the house—not even worrying about getting dressed. She exits the house through the front door, leaving it open for Dennis to peer out into the bright sunlight.

He sees Mom march to the car parked in the courtyard. She opens all the doors and begins to search the car like the police do on the TV shows Dennis watches now and again when they are looking for weapons or drugs. Mom checks between the seats, under the mats and even in the glove compartment.

Dennis steps outside, the gravel is warm under his bare feet.

Finally, Mom pulls back out of the car and slams the door. "It's not here," she mutters through gritted teeth, her eyes searching the gravel around the car absentmindedly. "I've looked everywhere. It's not here."

Dennis builds up the courage to ask: "Did you lose the dagger, Mom?"

She snaps her head around to look at him, and Dennis pulls back reflexively. Mom looks like a bird of prey and Dennis feels like a mouse.

Then, her expression softens somewhat. "I did. I should have never put it in the pocket of my gown. It was sharp enough that it cut right through the thin fabric. It must have fallen out somewhere." She looks toward the house. "I've looked everywhere. It's not here."

Dennis knows the dagger is very precious to Mom. She values it almost as much as her amulets and her books. It's made purely from bronze and it's very expensive. But that's not the reason Mom holds it so dear. It was a gift she got from a man in a country far away, the man who taught Mom the things she can do.

Still, Mom reacting this way over losing the dagger seems excessive to Dennis. It was just a knife, after all. It held no magical powers.

He clears his throat. "Can't you … can't you just … get a new one, Mom?"

She sighs. "You don't get it, Dennis. We need to find that dagger. It's very, very important that we do."

"Why?"

Mom looks at him for a long moment, like she's trying to answer his question with her gaze alone. Dennis shrugs to show her that he still doesn't get it.

Mom says in a low voice: "Because it's evidence, Dennis. And if the police find it, they'll know we were there."

The gravity of the situation opens up to Dennis like the ground opening beneath him. "Oh, no," he breathes.

Mom nods. "Exactly. We need to find that dagger, Dennis. Which means we need to go back to Esther's place."

Dennis shakes his head without even knowing it. The mere thought of going back over there after what happened last night is enough for his bladder to give way, and he accidentally lets out a few drops into his boxers before he manages to regain control and squeeze shut.

Luckily, Mom doesn't notice. She's staring at the car, thoughtfully. "We can't just drive over there. It'll be way too conspicuous." She looks over at Dennis, biting her lip. "It needs to be you. You take your bike and ride over there. You—"

"What? No, Mom!"

"Yes. You need to—"

"I-I-I can't! I can't go over there again, Mom! Please don't make me! Please don't—"

"Listen to me, Dennis. It'll be fine. You don't need to go inside the house. I just want you to go and check if anybody is still there. If you see cars parked over there or anything else that suggests the house isn't empty, you just come right back home again. Okay?"

NINE

They listen for a moment, in case there's another scream. But there is not. The forest is once again dead silent.

"Which way did it come from?" Dan asks.

"This way, I think." Selina begins running farther down the road, waving for Dan to follow her. "Leave the scooter, we can't hear anything with the engine going."

Dan leaves the scooter rather reluctantly. His ankle is still throbbing, but once he starts walking, he realizes to his amazement it actually feels a little better. Perhaps it's not sprained after all; perhaps it just got twisted.

Still, he needs to hurry to keep up with Selina. She suddenly stops outside a driveway Dan almost didn't notice. A small house is halfway hidden among the trees.

"It must have been here the scream came from," Selina says, walking towards the house without a second thought.

Dan is for a moment struck by how determined and brave she is. In fact, she reminds him of Thomas. Had he been here, he would also have been the brave one, the one walking in front whenever there was danger.

Is the world full of brave people? Or am I just a coward?

Perhaps he's simply the type to let someone else take charge, he reflects. And perhaps that's why Thomas is dead and Dan is still alive. The brave die, and the cowardly live on.

He shakes off the thought and hurries on to catch up with Selina.

There's a small gravel courtyard in front of the house. In the carport a tiny white car is parked.

Dan is just about to say something, when the front door of the house suddenly opens and a woman steps out holding a hunting rifle. "Who are you?" she shrieks. "What are you doing here? I already called the police!" As if to prove this statement, she shows them a cell phone.

Dan holds up his hands stupidly. "Uhm … we didn't … eh …"

"We don't want to cause you any harm," Selina says. "We're just looking for a young man who might have been here. Did you see him?"

The woman looks at them, assessing the situation. She's around retirement age and wears a bandana around her head. Dan can't see any hair, and combined with how thin the woman is, he guesses she might have recently undergone chemotherapy.

"It's really important we find him," Selina goes on. "He's wounded and he needs help."

The woman seems to decide to trust them, because she points the rifle into the ground and steps a little closer. She glances towards the carport and lowers her voice. "He ran into the workshop, so I locked the door behind him."

Dan notices a small shack adjacent to the carport. The door is still closed, and there are no windows.

"Did he hurt you?" Dan asks, discretely scanning the woman's bare arms for any visible scratch marks.

She shakes her head. She's close enough now that Dan can smell peppermint on her breath. "He just ran right past me, like he didn't even see me. He came out of nowhere, I thought I was going to have a heart attack when I saw him, his nose was all bloody and … and he was limping." She shakes her head in disbelief and looks at them. "Goodness, what happened to him? I thought it looked like he was wearing a police uniform, so I thought he might have been … I don't know, attacked by some criminals … that's why I locked the door behind him."

"He is a policeman," Selina explains. "But he hasn't been … uhm …" She glances at Dan for help.

"He crashed his car," Dan says. "We came by the crash site and followed him here."

"Yeah, and if we don't help him, he'll bleed to death," Selina adds.

"I already called an ambulance," the woman assures them, once again holding up the cell phone absentmindedly.

"They won't make it all the way out here in time," Selina says. "We need to get to him right now. Where's the key?"

The woman hesitates, glancing from the shack to Selina. "I don't know if it's a good idea ... I mean, he seemed very out of it ... perhaps it's better to leave him be until help arrives."

"No, we have to help him!" Selina insists. "Please give us the key. I know him. His name is Allan. I'll never forgive myself if he doesn't make it ..."

Dan is surprised at how convincing Selina sounds.

The woman still looks doubtful. Her hand goes to her pocket, but then stops. "If only Paul was here ... he'd know what to do ..."

A loud bang from the shack makes all three of them jump in unison. The woman raises the weapon and backs away.

"That was him," Selina says. "He needs help. Give me the key ..." This time, it's not a question, and she doesn't wait for an answer; instead, she steps to the woman and plunges her hand into the pocket.

"No, wait!" the woman says, but Selina already pulled the key out and is now headed for the shack.

"It's probably best if you go inside the house," Dan tells the woman.

She doesn't seem to hear him, she's still staring at Selina, who unlocks the door to the shack.

Dan steps a little closer, whispering: "Careful, Selina. Be ready to jump aside."

Selina sends him a quick glance, nods, then pulls open the door. She lets out a gasp, but doesn't move, simply stares into the shack.

"What is it?" the woman calls out. "Is he okay in there?"

Selina doesn't answer.

Dan goes to her side, peering nervously inside. He thinks he's mentally prepared for what awaits him, but the sight still shocks him.

Allan is no longer in the shack. Not all of him, anyway.

Dan swallows forcibly to keep down the nausea as the sweet, warm stench of blood rolls out at him. The shack is arranged like a small workshop, a bench and some tools. Dan hardly notices, though; he's staring down. The concrete floor is more red than gray. Allan has lost what appears to be a gallon of blood. Way more than what could have been caused by the bitemark on his ankle or the nosebleed he had gotten from the airbag. In the middle of the pool, Dan sees the explanation. The lower part of Allan's leg is still wearing the shoe. The saw is lying next to it.

"Oh, fuck," Selina whispers, putting her hands in front of her mouth and nose. "He sawed it off ..."

"Where is he?" the woman asks, joining them. But as soon as she gets a glimpse of the blood, she backs away, uttering a scream loud enough to pull Dan out of his trance.

He sees the bloody trail leading from the pool to the far end of the shack. A back door is standing wide open.

"He left that way," he says, pointing.

"You think he's still ...?" Selina doesn't need to finish the question.

Dan looks down at the blood once more, then shakes his head. "You don't survive losing that much blood. And you don't just walk away after cutting off your own ..."

Behind them, the woman screams again. Dan looks back to see her sitting in the gravel, the weapon lying next to her. She's clutching her head, screaming and crying.

She's going into shock, he thinks faintly. And he can't blame her. If he hadn't been hardened by what he'd seen during the past twenty-four hours, he would probably sit down next to her and begin screaming himself.

"But perhaps he died for real," Selina says. "Like, naturally, I mean. Perhaps the infection or whatever didn't reach his vital organs. That's why he did it: he tried to stop it." She stares at Dan with an almost painful look of hope in her eyes. As though he's the one to decide the fate of the policeman. "I mean, couldn't that be? Couldn't he have left the shack while he was still alive, and now he's dead somewhere nearby? That would also explain why he hasn't come back to attack us, right? Right?"

Dan shakes his head slowly. "I don't know. Maybe. We need to find him to make sure. But we have to be very careful, in case he didn't stop the infection in time."

A movement behind the leg of Selina catches Dan's eye, and he almost yells out in surprise. Then he realizes it's only a cat, black as the night. It's strolls over and rubs itself against Selina's leg before it slips into the shack.

"No, Whiskers!" the woman exclaims, as she finally stops screaming. She gets to her feet and staggers towards the shack. "Don't go in there! Come back here ..."

The cat completely ignores her call and sniffs the blood pool curiously, before it licks at it. Dan feels the nausea returning.

The woman squeezes past them, enters the shack and bends down to scoop up the cat. "No, Whiskers, stop that!"

Whiskers is in no mood to get told off, so he gives off a hiss and strikes at the woman with his front paw, causing her to let go immediately. The cat lands on its feet, darts past them and disappears behind the house.

The woman steps back out of the shack, looks at her arm where Whiskers's claws have left three thin scratches, and starts sobbing uncontrollably, sinking to the ground once more.

Selina looks at Dan. "Are you staying with her? I don't think she should be alone. I'll go look for Allan."

Dan doesn't like the thought of him staying here, and he likes even less the thought of Selina walking around the forest alone, looking for a person who might have turned into a zombie. Luckily, at that moment, he hears the sound of sirens.

"That's the ambulance," Dan says. "They'll care for her."

"All right, come with me, then."

"Wait," Dan says, pointing to the gun. "Do you know how to use that?"

"Not at all. But maybe we won't need it."

Dan hesitates for a moment longer. His gut tells him they just might need the gun. He doesn't think the chances of finding Allan as a regular corpse are very good. And he really doesn't care to enter the forest unarmed.

"Are you coming?" Selina asks, walking towards the trees.

Dan makes a decision. He goes into the shack, careful not to step in the blood, and looks at the tool rack. There are screwdrivers, a hammer, a crowbar, even a small axe.

Everything you need to kill zombies, Dan thinks, suppressing nervous laughter.

He reaches up and grabs the hammer. Then he goes back out.

Selina looks at the hammer in his hand. "Are you seriously going to use that?"

"If I have to," Dan says, trying to sounds more confident than he feels.

TEN

For the second time in less than fourteen hours, Dennis is approaching the house which used to belong to Esther.

His legs are shaking a little as he pedals the bike up the long gravel driveway. The house appears up ahead, and Dennis immediately hears Mom's voice: "As soon as you see the house, get off your bike and walk the rest of the way. That way you'll be harder to see from the house, if anybody is still up there."

Dennis stops and gets off the bike. He takes it to the side of the driveway and lays it down in the tall grass, taking a mental note of the place.

Then he walks on up the driveway. The courtyard comes into view more and more, and Dennis can't see any cars. No police cars and no regular cars. Which is very surprising to him; he had expected the place would be buzzing with policemen, like a crime scene on television.

Maybe they already did all their investigations and left again?

The thought brings a glimmer of hope.

And as he gets closer still, he realizes the bodies are also gone—all of them. Which brings him even greater relief. The thought of seeing the dead people in bright daylight was quite horrible.

Luckily, though, he'll be spared that. The police must have cleaned up everything.

Even the house looks empty. Of course, it's hard to tell from a distance, but all the windows are shut and so is the front door.

The relief in Dennis grows with every step.

He reaches the courtyard and stops to look around. There're marks and traces in the gravel from where the bodies were lying. He can also make out some dark stains, which is probably dried blood. It makes him shiver despite the baking heat. But a little blood is nothing compared to what he was expecting.

He recalls the next part of Mom's instructions: "If there are no cars parked in the courtyard, make sure no one's in the house. Don't go inside, just check the windows."

Dennis goes to look inside the scullery. It's empty. He moves on to the kitchen. Empty as well. His courage rises still further. He then rounds the corner and goes to look into the living room—but just as he's about to do so, something catches his eye.

Dennis turns his head and glares at the three police cars parked along the tree line flanking the side of Esther's house.

He just stands there for several seconds, unable to move.

Then, when he's finally able, he turns his head and looks into the living room.

Several people are walking around in there. Some in police uniforms, some in weird suits. They're talking to each other, and—miraculously—none of them has noticed Dennis, who's standing in clear sight.

He drops to his hands and knees; his heart feels like it explodes inside his chest. All he can think of is getting out of here, so he begins crawling frantically back towards the courtyard. Just as he rounds the corner and is about to jump up and run, the front door opens and two uniformed men come out.

Dennis throws himself back behind the corner of the house. He holds his breath and listens—the roaring of his pulse in his ears makes it difficult to hear, but he makes out one of the men saying: "... I'll get it from the car ..." And steps come this way.

Dennis freezes completely as he realizes the policeman will come around the corner any second.

There's nowhere to hide.

The policeman will see him.

Dennis prepares himself mentally for the shock of seeing the policeman step out in front of him, when he realizes he's staring right at an open window. It's just above ground and it's dark inside.

Before he has time to think, Dennis climbs through the window.

ELEVEN

From behind the shack a narrow path runs into the woods where it's quickly swallowed up by the greenness.

Dan looks down to see a trail of blood drops on the ground. "Looks like he followed the path," he mutters.

"You want me to lead?" Selina asks.

"No," Dan says quickly, surprising himself as he walks past her. "I'll lead. I'm the one with the weapon."

Perhaps I'm not a complete coward after all.

Selina sends him a faint smile, and Dan feels a jolt of excitement and pride. It's a short-lived pleasure, though, and is soon replaced by fear, as they venture deeper into the forest. He clutches the hammer tightly, listens intently for any sounds, looks around for any movement. He keeps blinking to keep his eyes from watering. The only sounds come from birds singing, the only movements are branches bobbing in the high-noon breeze.

Dan keeps anticipating a one-legged zombie jumping out in front of them. The hammer begins to seem like a silly idea. He might as well be walking around with a bouquet of flowers. He would never be able to successfully defend himself from an attacking zombie at close hand; it just doesn't work like in the movies. To take down a zombie with a hammer, you'd need several hard, precise hits to the head, and the zombie would still have plenty of time to attack you between blows, as it wouldn't be deterred by pain or fear.

Why didn't we take the rifle?

But he knows why. As long as none of them knows how to use the damn thing, it would probably be even less useful than the hammer; at least using the hammer doesn't take any particular skills.

"The blood gets less and less," Selina remarks, pulling Dan out of his head.

He looks down to see she's right. Only a few, scattered blood stains are visible on the forest floor.

"Perhaps he found some way to close the wound," Selina suggests with an unmistakable sound of hope in her voice.

"Yeah, perhaps," Dan mutters, feeling still more convinced the trail of blood won't lead them to anything living. He thinks it more likely the dwindling blood is a sign that the body from which it came is simply empty.

The only thing still giving him hope is the fact that the trail leads away from them. They have to be the closest humans around for at least a few miles, and that means the closest prey for a zombie. So why would it be walking away from them, if it really was a zombie?

Perhaps it picked up the scent of something better ...

It feels like they have been walking forever, but it's probably no more than ten minutes, when the forest suddenly ends. They step out into a ditch and find themselves right by the road again, a few hundred yards from where they turned into the forest road.

Dan looks in both directions, and his heart leaps when he sees the police officer walking by the side of the road a fair distance away in the shade from the trees. He's facing away from them, headed towards town, and his gait is completely crooked, since one leg is notably shorter than the other.

"Oh, shit," Selina gasps. "There he is!"

She's about to run after the policeman, but Dan grabs her by the arm. "Wait. He's no longer ..." He doesn't need to finish what he's saying, because at that moment, the officer stops and turns around in an awkward movement.

Even at this distance, and despite his itchy eyes, Dan can make out the milky white stare of the zombie. The blood has been gushing from the broken nose and drawn what looks oddly like a bib on the front of the shirt.

That's why it couldn't smell us, Dan thinks dimly. Its nose is completely busted up.

But even though the nose might have been put out of play, the mouth seems to work just fine, as the zombie opens it wide, snarls at them and starts staggering towards them.

"It's too late," Dan hears himself say, as he begins backing up, dragging Selina along. She doesn't need much persuasion, though she seems to have a hard time taking her eyes off of the dead policeman.

She finally manages to look briefly at Dan, her face pale now. "We need to ... how do we do it?"

Dan holds up the hammer hesitantly, feeling anything but eager to use it on the zombie. "I don't know if I can do it."

"But we have to," Selina pleads, looking from Dan to the zombie still coming towards them. "We can't just let him ... hey, look!" She points.

Dan looks past the zombie and sees the car coming. It's a black BMW and it's going way over the speed limit, the roar of the engine growing quickly louder.

The zombie seems to sense the potential meal coming quickly closer, because it turns around and wobbles out onto the road, headed straight for the car. In its eagerness, it slips on the amputated leg and falls down on its hands and knees.

What happens next takes place within a few seconds of time, yet Dan picks up every detail.

The police zombie struggles to get back up. The BMW is way too close to avoid it, and even though the driver locks the brakes, the car runs right over the zombie. The body is thrown around violently underneath the car like a wet sock in a tumble dryer, arms and legs flailing helplessly before it comes out behind the car, rolling round in a series of somersaults and finally coming to rest at the side of the road.

The car, which has made a long track of black rubber on the asphalt, comes to a stop not far from where Dan and Selina are standing. The engine is still going. Through the smoke from the burned tires Dan can make out the dumbstruck face of a young guy still clutching the steering wheel.

Dan is overwhelmed by a sense of exhilarated joy. It's dead! He crushed it completely ...

The zombie is lying dead, still where it landed.

The driver gets out of the car.

Selina lets out a gasp. "Jonas?"

The young guy doesn't appear to hear her. He walks back towards the zombie.

"No, wait!" Dan calls out. "Don't get too close!"

"Jonas!" Selina shouts, running after him. "Hey, Jonas!"

Jonas still doesn't hear. It must be because of the shock. Or perhaps the rumbling of the BMW's engine drowns out Selina's voice. He walks up to the zombie and kneels down.

It's okay, Dan tells himself, running after Selina as best he can on his hurting ankle. It's dead. It has to be. It can't hurt him.

But his thoughts are proven wrong in the very next second, as the zombie lifts its head—even from this far away, Dan can tell how the neck is twisted in a completely unnatural way—and grabs Jonas around the leg with a bloody hand.

Jonas, who is wearing shorts, lets out a yell of surprise and tries to pull back, dragging the zombie along. Most of the broken body seems to be put out of function as the bones are crushed. The free arm and both legs look like limp elastic bands, as Jonas jerks his leg back again and again in order to shake off the zombie. But the arm holding on to Jonas is still working fine, and the zombie isn't intent on giving up without a fight.

Jonas trips and lands on his buttocks, kicking wildly at the zombie. "Let go of my leg, goddamnit!"

Selina comes to the rescue and starts kicking the zombie in the ribs. It doesn't seem to have even the slightest effect, though, as the zombie just keeps on tugging at Jonas's leg in its desperate attempt to reach it with its mouth.

"What the fuck are you doing, dude?!" Jonas shouts. "Stop that! Let go of me!"

Finally, one of his kicks connects, hitting the zombie squarely between the eyes. Its head is flung backwards, producing a crunching sound loud enough for Dan to hear over the rumbling of the engine.

A couple of uncontrolled twitches go through the body of the zombie, as the last circuits in the already damaged spine are cut. Then it lies down limply, as Allan dies for the second time in his life.

TWELVE

He comes into a dark stairwell, crouches down on the steps and turns to look back out the window.

Half a second later, a pair of legs wearing black pants and boots comes walking by, causing Dennis to jump. He stretches his neck and looks after the policeman, who strides to the nearest of the cars, opens the door, reaches inside and takes out a folder. He then closes the door again and walks back past the window—Dennis pulls back, even though the policeman isn't looking down at him, but is focused on the folder in his hand.

As soon as the policeman is out of sight, Dennis lets out a long, trembling breath he didn't even realize he was holding. Beads of sweat are prickling his back and forehead, and his entire body is trembling.

He looks up the stairs and sees the dark rectangle of door with light streaming in through the cracks. He can hear voices coming from up there. It must be the living room.

Dennis looks down and sees another door. This one is open. It leads to the basement. He can hear nothing from down there, so Dennis begins descending the dusty stairs carefully.

He reaches a room lit up by a single, naked lightbulb. It's crammed full of old stuff and furniture. On two sides sit windows high up, leading out to the back garden—but they're too narrow for Dennis to squeeze through, he can tell just by looking at them.

Instead he looks around the room for another door. There aren't any. But there's a hole in the wall which, judging from the pieces still lying on the floor, was made recently.

Dennis maneuvers through the stuff and over to the hole. And as soon as he looks into the adjacent room, he recognizes it and pulls back instinctively.

It's where it all happened.

Dennis feels his heart pound away in his throat, which already feels dry from the warm, dusty air of the basement.

The room next to him is dark, but Dennis knows what's in there; he doesn't need the light to remember.

And even though he doesn't want to, he can't help but look in there. He has to.

And he sees it.

Lying right there, below the ladder leading up to the hatch in the ceiling.

Mom's dagger. The handle shining orange. The blade sticky with dried-up blood. It must have fallen out the last time Mom climbed the ladder.

Dennis needs to go in there and get it.

But he can't. His body won't do it.

Go on, he tells himself. Go get it. You have to!

Finally, he manages to force his arms and legs to get moving. He ducks down and steps into the room, slipping across the floor, bending down and picking up the knife. It's very cold and very heavy.

Then there's a sound, and light comes down from above. Dennis peers up to see the hatch in the ceiling open up.

"All right, John, you come with me, please," a voice says as a man steps into view. He's looking and pointing at someone else up there. "We'll get things ready for the forensics."

Dennis spins around and bolts back to the hole in the wall, jumping through it and almost knocking over an old chair. He looks frantically for a place to hide just as a pair of legs appears from the open hatch behind him and begins descending the ladder.

There's a tall cupboard beneath one of the windows, but Dennis knows from playing hide and seek that a cupboard is a way too obvious hiding place. Instead his gaze falls on a big, heavy chest squashed away in the corner. He quickly makes his way over there and opens the lid. The chest is empty except for dust.

"You guys take the next room," the voice says. "Go over it again, make sure we didn't miss anything important."

Dennis climbs into the chest—his legs are shaking so much he almost can't make them obey his will. He's just about to crouch down when notices the key sticking out of the lock. He wriggles it, pulls it out and puts it in his pocket. Then he sits down and lowers the lid.

Once it closes, a complete darkness enrobes him. Dennis can feel it pressing against him from all angles, like black tar. He concentrates on breathing through his mouth and making no sound while he listens.

Within what feels like a couple of minutes, the police begin searching through the room outside. Dennis can hear them rummage through things while they talk together in low voices.

"Pretty nasty stuff, huh?"

"Definitely the worst I've ever seen. Like straight out of a movie."

"The press will be all over this. You know they already got a hint of it? They called the chief this morning, begging him for an interview …"

The conversation goes on, but Dennis doesn't register the words. He listens instead to the sounds telling him where the men are exactly. He can tell they're making their way over here. His heart is already thumping away in his chest, but now it climbs up into his throat.

He realizes with a sinking feeling that they might open the chest to check inside it—and he'll be found right away, clutching the bloody dagger.

He lifts a hand and feels the inside of the lock. There's a tiny metal plate but no hole. Of course, the chest can't be locked from the inside—why would it?

Instead, Dennis grasps the metal plate and pulls it down, holding the lid tightly shut. Then he waits and listens.

Suddenly—so suddenly that Dennis jumps—there's a pull at the lid. Dennis holds it down as firmly as he can. The lid lifts a couple of millimeters, but that's it.

"Huh," a voice says right on the other side. "Was this thing locked before?"

"Nah, it should be open."

Another tug at the lid, harder this time. Dennis holds on with all his might.

"Funny, I can't get it open."

"Probably rusty hinges. Never mind, though, nothing's in there."

"You sure?"

"Uh-huh. Just dust."

Dennis can hear the man stand by the chest for another moment. Then he moves on and begins checking other things.

Dennis breathes out a long, quivering breath. But he doesn't let go of the plate; he keeps holding on firmly while the men search the rest of the room.

THIRTEEN

Jonas immediately jumps to his feet and backs away from what used to be a young police officer not many hours ago but now only bears a faint resemblance to a person.

Everything went by so fast, that Selina almost didn't have time to take it all in. She acted out of pure instinct when she started kicking Allan, and not until now, as the immediate danger has passed, does she realize how easily she could have been bitten. Had Allan let go of Jonas and instead turned to the side, she might not have been able to act quickly enough to get out of the way.

But that didn't happen. The zombie didn't let go of Jonas, and now she's staring at the bloody scratch marks on his ankle.

"What the fuck, man," Jonas wheezes, glaring from the dead officer to Selina. "I mean, what the fuck! What just happened?" He raises his hands halfway to his head, as though not sure where to put them. "He fucking attacked me ... You saw it, he fucking attacked me! I didn't mean to ... I wasn't trying to hurt him, I just ... I had to ... holy shit! What the fuck ..."

"It's okay," Selina says, trying her best to sound reassuring. "You didn't hurt him, I promise you. He was already ..." For some reason, she can't get that final word out.

Jonas stares at her, his eyes wild. "Was already what? What the fuck happened to him, Selina? His eyes, man, I tell you ... they were all fucked up ... and where is his fucking foot?" Jonas's voice is rising in pitch. It's clear to Selina he's about to have a panic attack or maybe even faint.

She wants to tell him it'll be all right, but she suddenly can't speak. Maybe because she knows it will be a lie. Jonas won't be all right. Not at all.

Dan steps closer. Selina notices he's still holding the hammer.

Like he was ever going to use it, she thinks, feeling a sudden violent anger towards Dan, like it's all his fault. What a great hero. Keeps out of harm's way until it's all over.

"Did you get ...?" Dan asks, but shuts up as his eyes fall on Jonas's leg.

Jonas doesn't hear the question. He doesn't even seem to register Dan's presence. He grabs his hair and repeats over and over again: "What the fuck ... what the fuck ..."

"Oh, no," Dan sighs, rubbing his forehead. "What now?"

Selina just shrugs. She can't take any more in. Can't deal with any more decisions. Can hardly think. Allan is dead, but he managed to scratch Jonas before he went. Now it all begins over again. Another innocent person will die. And this time, it's someone she's known for more than a few hours. Someone she was kissing only last night.

What is he even doing out here? Couldn't he just have stayed home?

Selina feels like crying and screaming at the same time. It's all she can do to keep herself together.

The sound of another car engine makes her turn and look down the road. A police car is coming this way very fast, no lights or sirens on.

"Shit," Dan says behind her. "We need to get out of here, Selina."

He goes to grab her by the arm, but she pulls free. "Let go of me," she hisses.

"But ... we need to hide," he says. "If we get arrested then no one will be able to ..." He glances at Jonas, who has sat down in the middle of the road, still mumbling to himself.

"Be able to what?" Selina snarls. "Kill Jonas?"

Dan swallows. "I just mean we're the only ones who get how serious this is."

The police car is getting closer, and now it actually does turn on the sirens.

Selina shakes her head, suddenly feeling very adamant. "I'm done running around playing soldiers. I'm going to tell them everything. They need to handle it."

"They won't believe you!" Dan pleads. "Not until it's too late."

"You don't know that. Allan was a policeman and he understood it."

"No, don't ..."

Selina turns away from him to wave at the police car.

Dan runs into the forest.

The police car stops and an officer jumps out. "Stop, police!" he shouts and runs after Dan.

Selina looks at the other officer, a woman, who steps out and comes over to her. She's not holding her hand on her gun, like Selina has seen so many times in American movies, but she still looks very vigilant as she approaches slowly and scans the scene with her eyes.

"What happened here?" she asks, her gaze stopping at Selina. "You guys had an accident?"

"I guess you could say that," Selina mutters and points to Allan.

The female officer hasn't seen Allan yet, as he has been blocked from her view by Jonas's car. But now, as she sees him, she runs to him and is just about to crouch down, then seemingly changes her mind. "Oh, God …" She points to Jonas and Selina. "You two, stay where you are!"

Selina nods. Jonas doesn't seem to hear the command, but he's obviously not going anywhere.

The officer pulls a radio from her belt and says with a voice slightly trembling: "I found the rest of Allan."

The other officer comes back out of the forest, dragging Dan along. Dan doesn't make any attempt to escape, he just stares resignedly at Selina. There's a twig in his hair.

An ambulance arrives, and the paramedics check on Allan and quickly pronounce him dead before covering him with a blanket. Then they talk to Selina and Dan, checking them for any physical injuries. They exchange a word with the male officer, who then takes Selina and Dan to the police car and puts them in the backseat.

Through the window, Selina sees the paramedics tend to Jonas, who is still sitting on the asphalt.

The female officer gets into the car and looks back through the metal grid at them. "I'm taking you two to the station, where they'll ask you further questions about what happened here."

Her voice is calm now, and Selina notices she avoids the word "arrested." Selina isn't really sure if you even can get arrested when you're only sixteen.

"How about Jonas?" she asks.

The officer looks at her. "The paramedics are taking a closer look at him. He seems to have gotten quite the scare."

Again there's a word the officer deftly avoids: "shock." The officer turns the car around, and Selina looks out at Jonas's face as they roll past. He's looking at the paramedics, his eyes dazed.

What had he even been doing out here? He lives in the town. The only thing she can think of is that he might have come to visit her. Strangely, that thought almost makes her tear up, and she thinks about the stupid goodnight kiss in the car last night.

"It won't be more than a couple of hours," Dan whispers.

Selina glowers at him. "Before what?"

"Before he dies, of course. We need to explain to them how dangerous he is."

Selina feels the anger contract in her chest. "Don't you start again."

The officer hears them and turns her head. "Please don't speak to each other."

Selina is more than happy to obey. She looks out at the fields gliding by. Out there everything is normal. The wheat is green and lush, the swallows are flying about playfully. No zombies in sight, no dying Jonas. All of that suddenly seems like a distant dream.

Dan pokes her thigh.

Selina sends him a burning look, which he apparently misses, because he hands her his phone. She takes it reluctantly and reads the message he has typed.

Promise me you'll tell them what's going to happen to him. We need to convince them. Or it all will have been for nothing. The future of the world is at stake.

Selina already knows it all. But for some strange reason, she doesn't want to hear it anymore, doesn't want the responsibility. She just gives Dan the phone back and looks away once more, feeling how he's looking at her in silent amazement and desperation, but she doesn't care, she just wants to look out at the fields.

Then he pokes her again, offering her the phone again. She shakes her head, but he keeps on trying to hand it to her. She folds her arms. He holds the phone in front of her face so she can't help but read the new message. It's very short.

Please ... Jennie was my sister.

The words hit her like a punch in the gut. She finally looks at Dan and realizes he has tears in his eyes. And when she sees how tired and scared he looks, she feels terrible about how she has talked to him. Of course, she knew he had been through some stuff before they met up, but she had no idea he had lost a sister. Maybe he even watched her die.

Selena deletes his message and writes a new one.

How did it happen?

Dan takes back the phone and types for several minutes. When he hands her the phone once more, she reads a short summary of the last twenty-four hours of his life—and they sure haven't been boring.

Selina feels the car slowing down. She looks up and sees they've reached town. The police station is just a few blocks away. She writes a short answer.

Sorry about your sister. Will tell them about Jonas. Here's my number. Call me afterwards.

Dan puts the phone away just as they pull over by the station.

FOURTEEN

It's not at all what she expected. None of it. The police station, the officers, the questions. Everything is very unlike what she's seen in movies. There are no cigarettes or lukewarm coffee cups or suspicious looks. No cramped rooms with one-way mirrors or grueling bright ceiling lights. The officers act like regular, friendly people. They believe what she says. There's even a female psychologist who smiles at her and listens to her talk.

It all passes by in an odd sort of haze in front of Selina. It feels like she doesn't really take part in it.

They offer her something to eat when she says she hasn't really eaten anything since last night. A sandwich and a Coke appear in front of her. She fights down a few bites, mostly to please the officers.

She tells them everything—but she never mentions the word "zombies." If she does, she knows they'll never take her seriously. She makes sure though to emphasize several times the fact that Jonas is incurably contaminated with some strange virus which he got from Allan. Even as the words leave her mouth, she can hear how crazy it sounds, and the more she insists, the less believable it becomes.

Then her dad is suddenly there, and the sight of him makes her burst into tears. The situation reminds her of that time in the first grade where she fell down and broke her wrist and her dad came to pick her up at the hospital. He wasn't angry with her back then, and he isn't angry now, only worried, and that makes her cry even harder.

"You go home with your dad and get some rest," one of the officers says. "We'll call you if we need to ask you anything else. And if you feel like talking to someone, you have the number for the psychologist."

Selina nods and wipes her eyes, feeling like a little girl. Dad puts an arm around her shoulders and leads her towards the door.

"Hold on," Selina says and turns around. "What about Jonas?"

The officer smiles reassuringly. "Don't worry about him."

"But ... what will happen to him?"

"We can't say for sure until after the preliminary hearing. I suspect he might get a fine for speeding and he might face charges for manslaughter, but—"

"That's not what I mean," Selina says. "Will he be ... cured?"

The officer comes to Selina and lowers his voice. "We talked about this, Selina. Jonas is fine. There is nothing wrong with him."

"No, but there will be. He's infected. If you don't do anything ..."

"Jonas is getting the medical attention he needs. The detention center has a doctor who tends to him."

"Does ... does the doctor take blood samples and stuff like that? So he can detect the virus in his blood?"

The officer smiles again. "I'm sure the doctor knows what he's doing. Don't think any more about Jonas. You can probably go and visit him tomorrow if you feel like it."

"I would like to visit him now. Can I?"

The officer's eyes flicker.

"Selina," Dad says.

"He's my friend," Selina exclaims. "I just want to see how he's doing."

"Maybe tonight," the officer says, his smile returning. "I'll look into it and get back to you. All right?"

Selina looks at the officer, and in her head, she suddenly hears Dan's voice: "They won't believe you! Not until it's too late ..."

"All right," Selina mutters.

"Come on, honey," Dad says, and they walk out of the building together.

FIFTEEN

Selina is lying on her bed about to drift off when the phone suddenly vibrates next to her.

When she and her dad returned home earlier, Ulla was there to greet them with worried hugs. The dead bodies of Jennie Nygaard, Josefine and the policeman had all been removed, and the terrace had been washed clean, no trace of blood left. Ulla told them how the police had taken pictures and tests of everything before cleaning up.

Selina headed straight up to her room. She had never felt more exhausted. And yet she couldn't sleep. Her thoughts kept creeping back to Jonas.

Now she sits bolt upright, groping for the phone, and almost drops it. It's a number she doesn't know. She answers.

"Hello?"

"Selina Peterson?"

"Yes?"

"This is David Mortensen from the police, we spoke earlier today."

"Yes."

"How are you holding up?"

"Fine."

"That's good to hear. I promised to contact you concerning Jonas Westholm, and ..." A short hesitation. "Unfortunately, it seems like he has taken a turn for the worse. He's been moved to the hospital."

Selina feels a cold shiver down her spine and closes her eyes.

"The good news is that he didn't have any traces of alcohol in his blood, so he's no longer being detained, and I'm sure you could go visit him if you still—"

"Where is he?"

A short pause. "Room eight, fourth floor. As far as I understood, his mother is with him, so of course you need to check with her if Jonas is all right with having a visitor."

"Right. Thank you."

The policeman once again encourages her to talk with the psychologist, but Selina is only halfway listening. She just says "yes" and ends the conversation as quickly as possible.

Then, she runs downstairs. In the living room Louisa is watching a cartoon. Ulla is in the kitchen cooking dinner. She sends Selina a smile. "So, did you get some rest?"

"Kind of," Selina mutters. "Where's Dad?"

"In the backyard, I think. Could you tell him dinner's ready in five?"

Selina steps into her shoes and leaves the house. Even though it's almost seven o'clock, the air is still hot. The heat wave is meant to last at least two more weeks, if you are to believe the weather experts.

She finds her dad on the terrace, where he is busy scrubbing one of the chairs with a sponge. He's working hectically, his T-shirt is all damp.

"Dad?"

He looks up in surprise, blinking. "Oh, hi, honey. I just noticed some ... well, blood." He wrings the sponge into a bucket of soapy water. "How are you feeling?"

"Fine," Selina repeats herself. "That officer just called to tell me Jonas has been hospitalized."

Dad wipes sweat from his forehead. "Really?"

"Yes, he's taken a turn for the worse." Exactly like I told you he would, she adds in her mind.

Dad stretches his back. "Look, honey, I know what you're thinking. But please don't believe everything you've seen in movies. This is not like that. The doctors will deal with whatever is wrong with Jonas, and I'm sure he'll be fine."

"I would still like to go see him."

"Sure thing. I'll take you there first thing tomorrow morning."

"I would like to go now."

"Right now? I think dinner is almost ready."

"I'm not hungry."

"Well, I am."

Selina crosses her arms.

Dad sighs. "Come on, Selina. You have to eat something." He drops the sponge into the bucket and dries off his hands on his shorts. "Besides, the visiting hours at the hospital are probably over for today. We'll go tomorrow right after breakfast, all right?" He puts a hand on her shoulder.

Selina looks up at him and thinks to herself: Tomorrow it's too late. She forces a smile and says: "All right, Dad. Ulla said to tell you dinner's ready in five."

"Thank you, honey. I'll be right there."

Selina goes back around the house, her steps firm, and her mind determined. She knows what she must do. She finds her phone and searches for a number online. Instead of going to the front door, she darts one quick look over her shoulder to make sure Ulla can't see her from the kitchen window, then she walks across the courtyard, putting the phone to her ear.

"You've reached Top-Taxi, and we're happy to help," a female voice says.

"Hello," Selina says, as she walks out of the driveway. "I need a taxi as soon as possible …"

SIXTEEN

Just as she gets into the taxi, she gets a text from Dan.

I'm still with the police. Can't go home until my parents come back. Of course they don't believe me about the zombies. What about you?

Selina writes back: I got to go home a few hours ago.

The answer comes almost immediately: And Jonas? Did you hear from him? They just keep telling me he's fine.

On my way into town to see him now. He's in the hospital.

A few minutes pass before Dan writes back this time. Selina imagines how he's considering his answer. He's probably thinking about writing something like: I told you, or: You know what to do, or the worst possible one, the one Selina really doesn't want to hear: You need to kill him.

But apparently Dan decides none of those are necessary, because when the text finally does come, it's very short: Be careful.

The taxi arrives at the hospital two minutes later. Selina pays the driver and gets out. She looks up at the tall glass building, the evening sun flashing in the windows. She takes a deep breath and walks up to the entrance. The automated glass doors let her into the air-conditioned entrance hall. And as she walks towards the elevators, she realizes she has no idea what her plan is—other than to find Jonas, of course. But after that, well, she simply didn't think about that until now.

If he really is infected, then he will die and come back just like Soren and Allan and Josefine did, and there will be no other choice than to kill him again. The thought alone makes her nauseous and makes her want to turn around.

And why not? She didn't ask for any of this. She just wants to go back to her life of being a teenage girl whose biggest problem is that her best friend saw her kissing a guy last night and is bound to tease her for it. In fact, Krista already texted her a bunch of times, but Selina hasn't replied. And they're going to Prague Monday morning! The whole class, as a summer school trip. She had almost completely forgotten about that. She needs to go home and pack. And she could do so. Just pretend like this whole thing is over and go to Prague with her friends.

But if she does that, she might have the end of the world on her conscience—although she can hardly fathom that thought. A thing like this simply doesn't happen in real life. The fate of the earth can't be resting upon one person's shoulders.

But the fact of the matter is that she and Dan right now are the only two people who know what's most likely going to happen to Jonas, and seeing as Dan is still being kept at the police station, she's the only one with the power to do something about it.

An old lady with a bouquet of flowers is waiting by the nearest elevator. As it opens, she steps inside, turns and sees Selina. "You going up too?" she asks, smiling.

Selina nods and steps inside.

"What floor?"

Selina looks at the old lady. "Sorry, what?"

"What floor are you going to, dear?"

"Uhm ... fourth."

The lady pushes the button and the doors close. With a feeling of absolute unreality, Selina feels the elevator start moving.

"My husband had an operation on his heart," the lady says. "He just woke up, and the procedure went fine."

"I'm ... happy to hear that," Selina says, managing a polite smile.

"Who are you here to visit?"

"A friend."

"What's wrong with him?"

"He ... was in an accident."

"I'm sorry," the old lady says, real regret in her voice. "Young people simply aren't careful enough behind the wheel."

Thankfully, Selina doesn't have to come up with an answer, because the elevator stops and the doors open.

"I hope your friend feels better," the lady smiles as Selina steps out.

"Thank you," she mutters back, right before the doors close again.

Then, she's alone in a long hallway. Room eight, she thinks and makes her legs start moving, even though they aren't exactly keen on it. The numbers on the doors glide by and she reaches number eight way too quickly. It's closed. She stares at the knob. The door feels like an unbreachable barrier. She has no idea what's waiting on the other side.

Selina closes her eyes. She's nauseous. Or maybe it's hunger.

She reaches for the knob and opens the door.

SEVENTEEN

The room is stuffy and dim, since the windows are closed and the blinds are pulled shut.

In the bed lies Jonas. He's on his back, eyes closed, mouth slightly open. His face is red and swollen, his forehead wet from sweat, and his breath comes in tiny, wet thrusts. One leg is protruding from under the blanket. A neat bandage is wrapped around Jonas's skin at the place where Allan scratched him. The skin surrounding the bandage is fiery red.

Selina just stands there for a moment, searching for the courage to step closer, when a totally unexpected voice says: "Hi?"

Selina jumps and spins around, staring at the woman sitting on a chair in the corner with a magazine. She's around Ulla's age with the first signs of grey in her bangs.

"Oh, I'm ... I'm so sorry," Selina mutters, swallowing in an effort to force her heart back down her throat. "I didn't see you."

"That's okay," the woman says, getting up and offering Selina her hand. "I'm not sure we've met. I'm Pennie, Jonas's mom. Are you Selina?"

"Ehm, yes, I am," Selina says with surprise, shaking the woman's hand. "How did you ...?"

Pennie nods towards the bed. "Jonas told me you were there when the accident happened. You were the one he was going to see, weren't you?"

"Uhm, I ... to be honest, I'm not sure."

"I think so. It was something about you forgetting your purse in his car."

"Oh, right!"

Pennie smiles. "He wanted to give it back to you. I still think it's in his car, actually. You can get it back tomorrow if you swing by."

Selina nods and rubs her arm. "Thank you. Listen, is it okay for me to be here?"

"Of course, dear! The doctor said nothing about no visitors. He just told me to let Jonas sleep off the fever."

Selina looks at Jonas and steps a little closer. She can feel the heat coming off him, it's almost like vapor rising from his skin. It's surprisingly painful to see him like this. She has naively been telling herself all the way out here that Jonas was just an acquaintance, someone she happened to give a casual kiss last night, and nothing more. But hearing Jonas's mom tell her that he had come to give her back her purse once he realized she had forgotten about it, somehow changed the way she now looks at him. She might have only known him for a couple of months, since that night Krista introduced them to each other, and although she had an inkling right from the beginning that Jonas had a crush on her, she didn't really find him to be her type, so she has been ignoring his attempts at getting closer.

Until last night.

"Are you his girlfriend?" Jonas's mom asks, as though she read Selina's mind.

"Uhm, no," she mutters. "We're just friends."

"Hmm," Pennie just says, a tiny, knowing smile at the corner of her mouth.

Selina clears her throat and quickly changes the subject. "Why does he have a fever? I mean, what caused it?"

"The doctor said it's probably just from the shock. But he might also have some mild infection, because of the wounds on his leg, so they're running some tests just to be sure, and they put him on antibiotics."

"Did they say anything about when they'll have the results of the tests?"

Pennie squeezes her arm. "Don't worry about him, dear. He'll soon be on his feet again. My Jonas is a strong boy. He's always been."

Selina struggles to smile back. "I'm just … scared for him."

"There's no need to be. The doctor said nothing serious is wrong with him."

"What about the scratch marks?"

"They've been disinfected, and …" Pennie frowns as she looks down at her son's leg. "Goodness, he's really turning red." She walks around the bed and puts her hand on Jonas's leg. "My God, he's burning up. I felt him just ten minutes ago and he was fine."

Jonas gives off a grunt. It sounds like his breathing is becoming more and more troubled. Selina feels her heart beat faster, as she looks at Pennie, who just stares at her son's face.

"Do you think we ought to call someone?" Selina asks finally.

Pennie nods without taking her eyes off her son. "Will you stay here with him?"

"Sure."

Jonas's mom leaves the room, leaving the door ajar.

Selina goes to the bed and carefully lifts up the bandage. The scratches are scarlet, oozing and swollen. The skin around them has taken on a sickly greenish hue. Selina lets out a whimper of despair. She has kept a small secret hope up until this point that Jonas perhaps was not infected after all. That hope dies in this moment.

Then Jonas suddenly begins twitching all over. It looks like tiny cramps going through his limbs. His neck is bent violently backwards, causing him almost to lift himself into a bridge, his clenched teeth are bared in a silent sneer and the veins pop out on both sides of his throat like thick cords. Still, he doesn't wake up, and Selina realizes he's way beyond waking.

She backs away, both hands in front of her mouth. No, no, no! Not now! Not already ...

EIGHTEEN

Do something!

Selina has been standing there, staring at the bed, for what feels like an eternity spanning a few seconds, when the thought comes through. Jonas's tremors have almost passed, and he has once again sunk back down onto his back.

"Jonas?" she croaks. "Can you hear me?"

No reaction whatsoever.

She tries shaking him gently. Not as much as a flicker of an eyelid. His breathing is a lot more shallow now. He looks like someone in a coma.

It's a matter of minutes …

Selina goes to the door to lock it but finds no lock. She looks around the room for something to bar the door with, but finds nothing heavy enough.

Need to get him out of here.

But how? She can't lift Jonas, and he's not able to walk on his own. Then, she sees it. Parked in the corner is a wheelchair. Selina grabs it and rolls it to the side of the bed. She pulls the blanket off Jonas and starts maneuvering his legs out of the side of the bed. It's not easy, and it requires all her strength, but she manages to get him into the wheelchair.

Suddenly, she hears voices from the hallway.

"… burning hot. I've never felt anything like it."

"I'll take a look at him."

Selina thinks fast. She pushes the wheelchair with Jonas out into the bathroom and closes the door behind her half a second before Pennie and a doctor enter the room.

"What the heck?" Jonas's mom exclaims. "Where is he?"

Selina stares at the bathroom door, her heart pounding. What was she thinking? She's trapped. Any moment one of them will open the door and find her. Then, out of nowhere, an idea occurs to her. Before she can think about it, she flushes the toilet and goes to open the door.

Pennie and an elderly male doctor are standing by the bed, both of them turning as they hear her. Selina makes sure to close the door quickly behind herself.

"There you are!" Pennie says, her eyes wide. "Where's Jonas?"

Selina looks at the empty bed, trying to conjure up a look of surprise, but feeling absolutely transparent. "I ... don't know. I was just in the bathroom for two minutes."

"He probably felt better and went for a stroll," the doctor suggests.

"Or he's wandered off in a delirious state!" Pennie exclaims, turning to Selina. "Why didn't you keep an eye on him like you promised?"

Selina shrinks. "Sorry ... I really needed to pee."

"I want him found—right now!" Pennie demands, looking at the doctor again. "He's definitely not well, and I can't bear to think what might happen if he's wandering about all confused ..."

The two of them leave the room. Selina stays behind unnoticed. She waits for a couple of seconds, then goes to the bathroom, pushes Jonas back out and checks the hallway to make sure the coast is clear. It is.

Selina rolls Jonas down to the elevator, trotting fast and looking in every direction. She can't believe she's really doing this. It's like her body is acting on its own. She almost feels dizzy.

An old man comes out from a room just as Selina passes it, and she almost gives off a scream. But the man is a patient and looks very fragile. He hardly looks up as he shuffles past her.

Selina rolls on, reaches the elevator and pounds the button. The doors open right away. It's empty. She rolls Jonas inside and stares at the row of buttons. Where will she take him? What is the plan? She hadn't really expected to come this far. If she brings him out of the hospital, they'll soon attract attention. And where would she go? No, she can't leave the building. She just needs to find somewhere without any people.

She pushes the lower most button. The doors close and the elevator takes them down through the building.

Selina wipes sweat from her eye and looks at Jonas. His chin is resting on his chest. He's still breathing, but very faintly so.

The elevator stops and the doors open.

The basement hallway is empty in both directions. Against the wall is standing a row of unused beds and wheelchairs. Selina pushes Jonas aimlessly down the hallway. She passes a door and stops to check it. It's a broom closet. She tries the next one. That one's locked. The third door is the lucky one: it's a tiny room with a lot of shelves filled up with all kinds of tools. And the door has an inside lock.

Selina pushes Jonas inside and checks one last time that no one is around to see her—there isn't—and then she closes the door and locks it. As her fingers turn the lock, she gets a moment of strange clarity.

She realizes without a shadow of a doubt that the next time her fingers will touch this lock, those fingers will have done something absolutely horrible, something she'll probably never forgive herself for.

And even if Selina lives to be a hundred, the next few minutes will be the worst minutes of her life.

NINETEEN

She spends ten minutes preparing herself. She knows it's exactly ten minutes, because she keeps checking her watch. As though that would somehow help her. Like she's hoping time will suddenly jump ahead an hour and all of this will be in the past.

It doesn't work like that, of course. She needs to go through with it. She needs to act.

Jonas's breathing has become less and less audible until the point where she's not sure whether it's still there. He hasn't moved at all. He's obviously far away, like in a coma maybe.

Still, she decides to pull out her shoelaces and use them to tie his wrists to the wheelchair. Just in case.

Her gaze has reluctantly started scanning the shelves. They're full of tools and equipment. Full of possibilities. Like fate decided to put her in exactly this room.

There are hammers, crowbars, screwdrivers, even a saw, not to mention a wide variety of electrical instruments. She can make this like something out of a movie. She can make it exactly as dramatic as she wants.

But Selina doesn't want it to be dramatic. She just wants to get it done as easy and painless as possible. She decides on a box cutter on the lowest shelf.

Her legs shake as she goes to take it. She fumbles a little with it before she manages to push out the blade. It's brand new and very sharp. She glances at Jonas's wrists. She might even be able to make it look like suicide. If she gets it done quickly and makes sure to be far away from the hospital once they find Jonas, they'll probably think that he—

Selina bursts abruptly into tears. What is she thinking? It's Jonas. She's going to kill him. And she's worried about what will happen to herself. How selfish can a person be?

"I'm so sorry," she whispers, sniffing, as she steps carefully closer. "I'm sorry, Jonas. But I have to do it."

She reaches out her hand—the one not holding the knife—and strokes his cheek. It's no longer warm. In fact, it's pretty cold.

"It was nice of you to bring the purse. I wish you hadn't, though."

She almost begins crying again, and she pulls back her hand. She doesn't know what else to say. A prayer? That doesn't seem right. She's not religious and she doubts Jonas is.

Do it then.

She gingerly turns Jonas's palm so it faces the ceiling, exposing the thin blue veins in his wrist—it's not easy because of the laces, but she manages.

He's already dead, she tells herself and closes her eyes. He's already dead. He's already dead.

The sentence becomes a monotone chant in her head. She focuses on it hard, shutting out all other thoughts. She needs to open her eyes in order to see what she's doing. Her hand shakes so much she can barely steer the point of the knife, and she has to grip it with both hands to get it to land on the soft skin of Jonas's wrist. The blade pushes the skin down a few millimeters.

All right, just a slight push and then pull down.

Selina stares at the knife, but it doesn't move. Her arms are trembling violently. Her body is fighting back. It won't obey.

Come on. He's already dead. He's already dead!

But the mantra doesn't work anymore. The thought of Jonas's blood about to burst out of his wrist is too much. She can't do it. She can't kill him. Not like this. Not with his sleeping face right in front of her.

She removes the knife, drops it on the floor and lets out a small scream of despair. She grabs her hair and looks up into the ceiling. She feels like vomiting. The temperature in the cramped room swings between frosty and stifling hot. Everything spins around. Selina realizes she's about to faint. In a few seconds she will—

Then a noise cuts through.

Selina stares at Jonas. He's still sitting in the same posture. But his neck is doing tiny twitches. His breath is audible again, although very faint and raspy.

It's happening!

Selina is gripped by panic. She turns to the shelves, goes through them frantically, searching for something, anything she can use, just not something that will make it bloody. She pushes stuff to the floor, it's all either for cutting, stabbing or bludgeoning, and she can't do any of those things to Jonas, she just can't, but she—

Then she sees it. The solution. It's been right in front of her the whole time. She just dismissed it. It's a plastic bag full of nuts and bolts.

She grabs it and empties it on the floor. Then she goes to Jonas, gets behind him and—before she has time to think—resolutely pulls the bag over his head and tightens it firmly.

Jonas's breathing quickly becomes even more strained. The bag is expanding and contracting in small, rapid thrusts, the inside soon fogged up and the plastic starts to cling to his hair. Strong tremors go through his body.

"Sorry!" Selina tells him and starts bawling loudly. "I'm sorry, Jonas, I'm sorry!"

She grips the bag as firmly as she can, pulling it shut around his neck with all her strength. She cries and apologizes and strangles. She doesn't know for how long. Maybe a minute. Maybe three. But suddenly, finally, Jonas is no longer twitching, and he's no longer breathing.

Selina sobs and keeps clutching the bag tightly. She needs to be absolutely sure, so she counts to a hundred. When she's positive that it's done, that Jonas is really dead, she lets go of the bag and staggers away until she hits the wall. Her legs give way and she slumps to the floor. She begins crying again, but this time she also cries from relief.

It's over. You did it. You saved the world.

The thought bears little comfort.

TWENTY

Dennis realizes he's drifted off and sits up abruptly, banging his head against a ceiling.

"Ouch!"

He looks around but sees nothing but darkness. For a couple of minutes, he has no idea where he is.

Then he remembers. The chest. In the basement. At Esther's place.

The fear immediately comes rushing back. The police were right outside! Dennis was listening to them for what felt like hours. Then, at some point, they must have left, because Dennis remembers listening to the silence and beginning to feel sleepy.

He listens intently, but he can't hear anything.

What time is it? He has no idea, no way of finding out. It could be nighttime.

Dennis decides to open the lid and check.

He lifts it very carefully—only an inch—and peers out. The basement looks like he remembers. The daylight coming in through the windows has turned orange. It must be late evening. Dennis can feel hunger gnawing in his stomach; he hasn't eaten anything all day. Mom must be very worried for him by now.

He opens the lid all the way and steps out. Then he sees the dagger and picks it up. He can't put it in his pocket—it's too big and also too sharp, he would risk cutting himself.

A noise makes him spin around. He stares at the hole in the wall. Right on the other side, his back turned toward Dennis, is a man in a white suit. He's bent over the table, busy doing something.

Dennis holds his breath as he begins backing away. He has to peel his eyes off the man to make sure he doesn't bump into anything.

He reaches the stairs and begins walking up them one step at a time, praying that none of them will make any noise.

The guy from the other room mutters something, and Dennis stops dead. But apparently, the man was just talking to himself, because nothing else happens.

Dennis reaches the window he came in through. It's still open. Dennis pushes it open farther and looks outside. There are no signs of the police cars. Only a single, white van is parked there now.

Dennis climbs out the window, very careful not to make any sounds. The grass is wet from dew and the air is pleasantly chill. Dennis gets up and looks around, making sure no one is there.

Then he slips over to the corner of the house and peers out into the courtyard. Also empty.

Okay. You just need to make it past the courtyard. Then you're out of here.

Walking across the courtyard would be very stupid—he would be plainly visible from all the windows at the front of the house. And he has no idea if anybody else is in there.

So, Dennis instead runs over to the carport and makes his way behind it, coming out at the far end of the courtyard. From here, once he runs out the driveway, he will be visible for a brief second from the house, but he will be a fair distance away, and besides there's no other way.

Dennis peers around the corner, looking up at the house. The front door is open, but no one's there.

He takes a deep breath, then steps out and begins running.

He's only taken three steps when someone shouts from behind: "Hey, you! Stop!"

Dennis is so surprised, he actually stops and looks back. A man in a white suit—Dennis can't tell if it's the same guy from the basement—is standing off to the side, holding a cup of coffee and a cigarette. He wasn't visible from Dennis's viewpoint until now, because he was standing behind Esther's drying rack, where a white sheet is hanging.

The man begins walking toward Dennis. "Who are you? What are you doing here?"

Dennis spins around and bolts out the driveway.

"No, stop! Come back here! This is a crime scene!"

Dennis runs as fast as he's ever run in his life. His legs are pumping up and down, his arms flailing at his sides, his lungs are heaving for breath and his vision is going blurry with exertion.

He reaches the place where he left the bike and jumps out into the ditch, almost landing atop the bike, pulling it up onto the driveway and flinging himself onto it.

He then pedals away like a madman. He keeps looking back, expecting to see the guy come running after him.

He doesn't.

Dennis keeps looking though, even after he reaches the highway. He rides his bike home as fast as he can, the dagger still clutched in his hand.

Ten minutes later, as he reaches the house, he can barely feel his legs anymore. The front door opens, and Mom comes running out.

Dennis stops the bike and gets off. His knees buckle, and if Mom hadn't caught him, he would have collapsed. She takes the dagger from him, then hugs him.

Mom never hugs him, and Dennis breathes in the scent of her as she whispers into his hair: "Thank heaven!"

Dennis wants to tell her everything. About the police and where he found the dagger and how he had to hide all day in the dusty old chest and the man in the white suit who saw him.

But Dennis can't say anything. Instead, he simply begins to cry. And for once, Mom doesn't scold him for it. She just holds him like she hasn't done since Dennis was very little.

TWENTY-ONE

Something vibrates somewhere close by.

Selina sniffs and takes a few deep breaths. It's probably her dad. But she can't talk with him right now. She can't talk with anyone. Yet she pulls out her phone.

It's Dan.

Selina answers and says hoarsely: "I did it."

A bated breath on the other end. Then: "How?"

"I strangled him with a plastic bag." Selina can't really understand the words coming out of her mouth. It has to be someone else speaking. Another Selina in another reality. A reality where that Selina just killed another Jonas.

"You sure he's dead?" Dan asks gingerly.

"I'm sure."

"So he didn't turn before you did it? I mean, he was still alive?"

"Yes."

"Okay." Dan lets out a long sigh of relief. "Good job."

Good job, Selina's mind echoes. Like she passed a test in school.

"Did you ... get any scratches? I mean, I imagine he must have struggled. I think he could have infected you even though he wasn't dead yet."

"I didn't get any scratches."

"Was anyone else near him? You think anyone could have touched him?"

"There are no others."

"We just need to make sure that—"

"Listen to me, Dan. Jonas didn't infect anyone else. He was already halfway in a coma when I came to the hospital." She looks at Jonas while she talks. His head, which is still in the bag, has slumped to the side. Luckily, she can't see his face from this angle.

Dan is quiet for some time. "Okay," he mutters. "I guess it's over then."

"It is."

Selina is about to disconnect, when Dan goes on: "I just got this ... I don't know, it keeps bothering me. I feel like we overlooked something."

Selina sighs. "Like what?"

"I don't know. Maybe I'm just paranoid, but ... I've been here before, you know. Where we thought everything was over. And then I remembered my sister ..." Dan interrupts himself.

"I think you're just paranoid."

"Maybe you're right. How about you? How are you feeling?"

"How do you think I'm feeling?"

"Terrible."

"Bingo."

"I'm sure the police will understand. I don't think you'll go to jail or anything."

"Dan, I don't want to talk about it."

"Sure, I understand."

More silence.

"Bye," Selina says.

"Bye," Dan says.

Selina puts the phone back in her pocket. She slowly gets to her feet. Makes sure not to look at Jonas as she passes by him. But as she stops by the door, she can't help but look back one last time.

Now she can see his face. His eyes are closed. The bag is full of moisture, and the droplets are clinging to his face like tears. His mouth is open.

Selina squeezes her lips together. She can't leave him like this, she just can't. Tied down and like an animal. She goes back and is just about to untie the laces, but then hesitates.

No. This is always how it happens in the movies. That final, stupid mistake.

She doesn't believe Jonas will reawaken. She's sure he really is dead. But she still can't bring herself to untie him. Her instincts tell her not to.

At least the bag, then. Just so he doesn't get found like this.

Selina carefully grips one corner of the bag with two fingers and lifts it up. It sticks a little to his head, so for a brief second his face is hidden from view. When the bag comes off and she can once again see his eyes, they are open.

Selina freezes in the middle of the movement. She's too shocked to react; she just stares dumbly into Jonas's irises, which are no longer blue, but milky white, as her exhausted brain struggles to understand what she sees.

She has no time to pull back when Jonas opens his mouth with a primal grunt, lunges forward and bites down over her fingers.

At first, Selina's scream is pure surprise. But as Jonas bites down even harder and she hears the bones in her fingers splinter, the scream changes to one of pain.

TWENTY-TWO

Dan puts down his phone and lies back down onto his bed.

It's over. It's finally over. This time, it's for real.

He sighs deeply. It's just past nine o'clock, and he has now officially been awake for thirty-seven hours. That's a whole workweek. And it feels like it, too. His eyes are stinging, his muscles aching with exhaustion.

He has been through more these past two days than most soldiers go through on an entire tour to Iraq. That's what the psychologist told him, anyway.

But now it's over.

But then why can't he believe that?

Something bothers him. A small thing he overlooked. He's been over the events again and again in his mind. Played the film back and forth. He just can't see what detail escapes him.

Perhaps there's nothing there. Perhaps his brain is still just running in overdrive. He'd probably better get some sleep. There's nothing more he can do now anyway.

He turns over and shuts his eyes.

From the living room he can hear the television. The sound can't quite drown out his mother's crying or his dad trying to console her. Dad has been in here every fifteen minutes or so since they got home. As though to make sure Dan doesn't suddenly disappear. Their only remaining child.

Dan feels a lump forming in his throat at the thought of Jennie. She was the hardest part telling their parents about. Seeing their faces crumble as they received the news just made everything worse—more real, somehow. The possibility of all this being a dream fell away when Dan saw his parents burst into tears. Nightmares don't affect other people.

He still can't grasp it. He can't imagine a world without Jennie. How could he? He has never seen a world without her. She's been here since before Dan was born. And now she's lying on a table somewhere.

He pushes that image out of his mind. It doesn't exactly help him to fall asleep.

Wonder what the doctors will say once they examine the many corpses? What will they even find? If the zombies were animated by some voodoo magic, will there even be a virus in the bodies? On the other hand, if there's no virus, then how were they able to contaminate others?

The answers will surely come within the next days. Once everything returns back to normal. Smart people will get on television and explain it all. How it could have happened, what went down and how it was all stopped in the last second.

Will people ever know how close the world came to ending? Will Dan be recognized as one of the people responsible for stopping it? Will some people even come to see him as a hero?

He sure doesn't feel like one. A hero would probably have saved the world and his sister.

His eyes tear up once again, but Dan is too tired to cry; he simply doesn't have the strength, and finally, his thoughts begin to drift further away as sleep comes sweeping like a freeing darkness, pulling him down deeper and deeper.

Dan sleeps as the evening grows dimmer outside his window. He doesn't notice how the door to his room is opened a few times, as his dad's face, eyes all red and puffy, peeks in and then disappears again.

Dan doesn't dream. His sleep is too deep for that.

But an image nonetheless makes its way into his consciousness. Now, as his brain finally relaxes, the memories are loosened up and that thing that kept bugging him gradually floats to the surface and materializes.

It's a cat. A black cat.

"Whiskers," Dan breathes, not waking up, but turning his head jerkily from side to side. "It was the cat ..."

A part of Dan's subconscious recognizes the message, and it tries waking up Dan, but his body is simply too exhausted to obey. Instead, he slips further down, his muscles relaxing, and his sleep turns calm again.

TWENTY-THREE

Paul is jerked awake abruptly. He blinks and looks around in the darkness. It takes him a few seconds to remember where he is and what woke him up. Did someone call his name? Or was that just a dream?

"Paul …"

The voice is Irene's. She's lying next to him, her blanket halfway on the floor, her skin glistening with sweat. She's frowning and turning her head. "Paul, watch out …"

"Irene," he croaks. "You're dreaming, sweetheart."

His wife doesn't wake up, but keeps whispering incoherently in her sleep. He reaches over and shakes her gently. Still, she doesn't awaken. Her skin is flaming hot. Could it be a fever?

Paul sits up with a sigh. It's stifling hot in the bedroom, even though the window is open all the way. The summer sure is merciless this year. But this night feels even hotter than the many previous ones. Paul gets the silly notion that it's Irene giving off heat and raising the temperature in the room even further. Ridiculous, of course.

"Please, watch out, Paul," she whimpers.

He sits up and looks over at her nightstand. The pills are right next to a glass of water, but he remembers her taking them before they went to sleep, so it can't be the chemo bothering her. They've had many sleepless nights since she started the second round of treatment, but fever has never been one of the things tormenting her. He reaches over and takes the glass.

"Irene, drink some water, you'll feel better."

He tries putting the glass to her lip, but she thrusts her head sideways, hitting the glass with her chin and causing him to spill most of the water over her neck and chest.

"Ah, goddamnit," he moans.

To his astonishment, though, the splashing water doesn't wake up his wife.

He notices her hand, lying restlessly on her stomach. It's swollen like a rubber glove full of air, the fingers thick as hot dogs, and—doesn't the skin look weird? It's hard to tell in the darkness, and Paul isn't wearing his glasses, but he's pretty sure Irene's hand is greenish.

His eyes fall on the Band-Aid a few inches above her wrist.

What did she say happened? Whiskers scratched her, I think.

That stupid cat. Paul has never trusted it. Had it been up to him, that cat would have been put down a long time ago. He would even have been happy to do it himself, using his old hunting rifle. But Irene loved that arrogant little beast, so ...

He recalls her complaining about the scratch marks itching before they went to bed. She cleaned it thoroughly using hydrogen peroxide, like she used to do back when the kids were small and would fall and scrape their knees. So the scratch marks couldn't have been infected—could they? Maybe some resistant bacteria got in when Whiskers scratched her. God only knows what that nasty animal might have had its claws in. A dead bird, probably.

The Band-Aid seems to be bulging a little. Paul grabs her twitching arm and pulls off the Band-Aid carefully. He lets out a gasp as he looks at what is no longer a harmless scratch, but a throbbing, oozing boil.

"Bloody hell," he snarls, jumping out of bed. "Wake up, Irene! We gotta get you to the ER!"

"No, Paul," she whispers, and for a moment he thinks she's awake, but when he looks at her face, her eyes are still closed. Her demeanor is calmer now, like she's falling into a deeper sleep. "Watch out, Paul," is the last thing she says, before falling silent.

He stands there, looking at her for a moment. He's not sure why, but he's struck by a sense of grief. The thought of everything she's been through this past year. First it was the cancer, and now this traumatic experience with the policeman sawing off his own leg right outside in their shack. The thought that Irene had to see that ... It took the police most of the evening to get everything cleaned up, after they had taken pictures and done tests and whatnot. Paul is not sure he'll ever be able to go in to the shack again without thinking about that.

And now this ... some infection in her hand which probably got a hold of her because her immune system is already weakened by the cancer treatment.

Paul turns and strides into the living room, looking for his phone. But he can't find it anywhere. Then he remembers he brought it into the bedroom. He usually never does that, but he wanted to be sure he heard it in case the police called them.

He walks back through the house, brooding. The thought of going to the ER in the middle of the night doesn't exactly make him ecstatic, but he doesn't want to take any risks concerning Irene's health, so they have to—

He stops abruptly as he almost bumps into Irene, who is standing in the open bedroom door, her eyes closed, her body swaying uncertainly.

"Irene?" he asks. "I think you're sleepwalking, dear. Come back to bed, all right? You need to sit down."

He takes her by the shoulders. As their skin touch, he's surprised to feel how cold she is. The heat has completely left her body within a few minutes.

Then, just as he's about to turn her around, Irene opens her eyes wide, and Paul can immediately tell there's nothing left in those eyes of that woman whom he's known and loved for most of his life. He just has time to think one last amazed thought: She's dead.

Then Irene lunges at him.

DAY 3

The following takes place on
Monday, July 28

ONE

William puts on the headphones as soon as the doors to the elevator close.

He's strictly speaking not allowed to listen to music at work, but come on—how else is he supposed to make it through his shift? Besides, the basement is usually empty, except for the other porters, but none of them will tell on him. Well, maybe Thorsten, that old, grumpy bastard.

William turns up the volume as the tunes of Custard Pie fill his ears. The doors open and he pushes the stand down the deserted hallway, smiling to himself as he drums the rhythm on the stand. He's in an awful good mood today, despite the fact that today is a Monday.

He spins the stand around on its wheels, causing him to overlook the jumping handle on the door as he passes it.

He's had the job a couple of months now. It was only supposed to be a summer gig, but the pay is decent, so he might stick around a little while longer than planned. Also, he actually enjoys the work. Most of the time he's left to his own, pushing stands and beds and wheelchairs back and forth, going up and down the elevators.

It might not be the coolest thing in the world—being twenty-four and still having no education. But he doesn't want an education. His plan is to go to the States and get an apprenticeship with a tattoo artist, then come back and open his own parlor. He already visited Miami once, that's where he got most of his right arm done.

He reaches the laundry and leaves the stand, grabbing an empty one on his way back. This time, as he passes the door with the jumping handle, he notices the movement out of the corner of his eye.

What the hell …?

He stops and stares at the handle. It's not moving anymore. He decides he probably imagined it and is about to move on, when the handle jumps again.

William pulls off the headphones to listen. From the other side of the door he can hear scraping noises. Like someone is fumbling around a dark room trying to get out. As far as he knows it's just an equipment locker.

His first thought is that some poor sick dude has strayed down here and locked himself inside by accident. Maybe one of the dementia patients.

"Hang on," he calls out, pulling the key chain from his belt. "I'll get you out."

He sticks in the key and turns. He pushes the door open cautiously, not wanting to knock down whoever is on the other side. To his surprise, the lights are on in the room. A foul, metallic stench rolls out at him, the unmistakable smell of blood has filled the small room, mixed with something sour and salty; sweat and fever, William guesses.

But what he sees instantly causes him to forget about the smells.

At the center of the room is lying a guy his own age, dressed in a hospital gown and entangled in a tipped-over wheelchair. Both his wrists appear to be tied to the chair, making him unable to get to his feet. Instead, he twists and turns, apparently trying to get free. His head is turned away, and the floor around him is stained with blood.

"Holy fuck," William whispers and is just about to step inside the room to help. Something terrible obviously went down in here. The guy didn't just wander down here on his own; someone tied him up and tortured him.

But some deeper instinct holds William back. Perhaps it's his brain recalling at the last second the jumping handle.

And then the girl steps out from behind the door.

A few years younger than him, she might once have been quite pretty, but now she's a terrible sight. Her skin is greenish and her eyes have neither pupils nor irises. Most of the fingers on her right hand are missing, turned into a mess of knobby bones and black, dried-up blood. It's almost as if the girl wants to show him her damaged hand, because she reaches it out at him, while showing a row of perfect white teeth in a hungry snarl and comes towards him.

William yells out and flings his fist at her. He doesn't have time to think, he's acting out of pure reflex from his boxing practice. His knuckles connect with the girl's cheek, giving off a loud smack and sending her tumbling backwards.

She hits the guy in the wheelchair, but he doesn't seem to notice. He just keeps struggling to get free, turning his head and growling at William, revealing a face as terrible as the girl's, but with the added effect of a lot of dried blood around his mouth.

William's brain adds up everything in a flash. The guy bit off the girl's fingers. The blood on the floor is from her. She must have brought him here and tied him up for some reason, but got too close. Then, while bleeding profusely, she tried to unlock the door, but couldn't do it because of her busted hand.

During those three endless seconds William spends rooted to the floor in the open door, the girl meticulously gets back up and starts staggering towards him, one cheek visibly marked by his punch, but she shows no sign of pain.

William reaches in, grabs the door, slams it shut, and turns the key. A second later, the girl starts once again fumbling with the handle.

William breathes rapidly and stares down the hallway in both directions, making sure he's alone. There's no trace of doubt in his mind as to what he just saw: the girl and the guy in the equipment room are zombies. He has played with the thought of what he would do in this situation a hundred times, and now he's actually here. The most terrifying fantasy has come true.

The zombies are coming!

TWO

Even though it's only eight o'clock, the sun is already up and doing its worst. The air conditioner is blasting away, and still the temperature inside the bus is too high. Mille is sweating.

She's nevertheless looking forward to the trip. Just the fact that she gets away from home for a week, gets to see new things and experience new places. Of course, the heat wave has hit most of Europe, including Prague, so the awful warm weather won't be any different, but still—

A paper airplane hits her chest.

"Hey!" she yells out and looks up.

No one really seems to hear her. Everyone is busy chatting, listening to music or messing with their phones.

"It was Mads," Krista says, pointing. "I saw him throw it."

Mille looks in the direction and sees the culprit four rows ahead. Mads sends her an air kiss. Mille flips him off. Mads laughs and signals for her to open the paper airplane.

Mille sighs but unfolds it. Mads has written a message in red.

Do you want to go out with me?

YES

YES

DOUBLE YES

(you may tick off more than one)

Mille can't help but smile, but makes sure Mads doesn't see. She finds a pen from her bag.

"What did he write?" Krista asks, leaning in.

"He's just trying to be funny," Mille says, adding another option to the list.

WOULD RATHER DIE FROM HERPES

She puts an X next to the line, crumbles up the paper and throws it back at Mads. The paper ball doesn't quite reach him, so he scrambles to pick it up from the floor. He laughs out loud when he unfolds it and reads her answer.

"He's coming on a little too hard," Krista remarks.

"I don't think he's being serious."

Krista raises her eyebrows. "Really? He's been mad about you since freshman year."

"What about Pernille?"

"He just dated her because he couldn't get you."

Mille glances over at Mads, who has turned around and is now talking with the boys sitting in front of him.

"Did Selina text you?" Krista asks, finding her phone. "She didn't answer any of mine."

"Nah, I haven't heard from her. She's probably ill."

"That's like the worst timing ever, falling ill today of all days! Hey, isn't it somewhere out here she lives?"

Mille looks out at the fields gliding by. "I have no idea."

"Yeah, I think it is. She moved with her dad recently, because he found a new wife, remember? I was there Saturday before we went out partying." Krista's eyes grow big. "Hey, did you hear? She made out with that electrician?"

"Who now?"

"Jonas Jorgensen."

"Never heard of him."

"Well, he's a bit older and quite good looking."

"Huh." Mille honestly couldn't care less about who Selina did or didn't make out with. She's got nothing against Selina, they're just not that close, like Selina and Krista are. Also, Mille knows Krista is only sitting with her because Selina isn't here.

"Of course, she pretended like it never happened," Krista goes on, smiling wryly. "But I saw them, and I—"

She's cut off as the bus abruptly makes a stop, causing everyone to be thrust forward in their seats and bags to fall to the floor. Her classmates let out indignant cries.

"What the fuck was that about?"

"Get a grip, man!"

"Is he drunk up there?"

"Why did we stop?"

The driver—a middle-aged, obese guy with greasy hair—honks the horn aggressively.

"What's he doing?" Krista says, stretching her neck like everybody else. "Is someone blocking the way?"

Mille also tries to see, but she and Krista are sitting almost all the way in the back, so there's no way of getting a glimpse of what's going on up front. But they've stopped in the middle of a desolate highway, open fields to one side, a forest to the other, so Mille can't really imagine who would be blocking the way. Except a dog, maybe. Or a deer, perhaps. It could have wandered out from the trees.

Then she hears someone up front exclaim: "There's a lady out there!"

Mille gets a glimpse of the driver getting up and pushing the button to open the door. He looks worried as he trudges down the steps and leaves the bus.

"Jeez, what happened to her?" someone calls out.

"She must've been in an accident," someone else answers.

Mads has gotten up from his seat and walked halfway up through the bus. He's peering out the front window. Then, suddenly, he shouts: "No, don't go over there! Come back inside, man! That's a fucking zombie!"

A few of the boys break into nervous laughter, not sure whether Mads is joking or not. And it would be typical of him to make a joke like that. But Mille can hear something in his voice which gives her the chills.

"What's going on?" Krista asks again, grabbing Mille by the arm. "What's happening up there?"

"I can't see. I think—"

Something outside the window catches Mille's eyes. She looks out to see an elderly man come staggering out of the forest. He's dressed in his underwear, the pale, veiny legs visible. His wifebeater, which might once have been white, is now mostly brown due to the dried-up blood that seems to have spurted from the open crater in his neck. The man trudges resolutely across the road, headed for the bus.

He turns his head slightly up, and Mille sees his face, feeling a jolt of icy fear run through her body. The man's eyes are empty and milky white. If Mads hadn't just yelled out the word "zombie," she might not have been able to find a fitting description for the person passing her window and steering for the front door of the bus.

One of the girls starts screaming up front. More of the students get up and start shoving each other to get to the front. Commotion ensues. The noise level rises. Confusion and fear start to set in.

Mille, once when she was very young, accidentally locked herself in her playhouse, and she panicked when she couldn't get the door open. That same feeling of claustrophobia creeps over her once again in this moment, as she stares at her classmates tumbling over each other to get out of the bus and away from whatever is going on outside.

Got to get out of here. Right now.

No one came to help her back when she was trapped in the playhouse; she had to literally kick the door open. Surprisingly, the panic gave her strength, and she almost kicked it off the hinges.

No one is going to help her now, either, so she looks up and sees the emergency hammer. She tears it free of the holder and slams it against the window. The glass shatters but requires a few more hits before it loosens enough for Mille to push it out. Then, she drops the hammer and turns to Krista. "Come on, we have to go!"

Her voice almost drowns in the yells and the screams.

Krista doesn't seem to hear her. She just sits in her seat, staring ahead. Mille briefly follows her gaze and sees the lady who has now made her way up into the bus. At first, Mille actually takes her for a man, since her head is completely bald, but the bloody night dress turns the picture around. The lady throws herself at the nearest student—Signe, as far as Mille can tell—who's squeezing helplessly up against the window, screaming and trying to get away. Just as the lady sinks her teeth into the cheek of Signe, the man comes into the bus. He immediately bends down over Rasmus, who has fallen down in the aisle. He screams in pain as the man bites the back of his neck.

Then Mille can't see anymore, as everything disappears into complete mayhem.

She grabs Krista by the arm and drags her along as she steps up onto her seat and leaps out the window. She lands on the steaming asphalt, breaking the fall with her hands. She turns to look up at Krista staring down at her.

"Come on! Jump!"

Krista makes a clumsy hop and Mille halfway catches her.

"We gotta go," Mille says, pulling her along, but is surprised to feel Krista resist.

"We can't," she says, her eyes big and terrified. "What about the others?"

Mille looks up at the bus, the inside now turned into a living inferno, students screaming, desperately climbing over the seats, banging on the windows, spurts of blood staining the glass.

"We can't do anything now," Mille hears herself say, amazed at how firm her voice sounds. "We'll only put ourselves in danger too." She tightens her grip around Krista's wrist and tugs her hard. After a few yards, Krista stops resisting and starts running along.

Behind them, the screams from their dying classmates grow only very slowly distant.

Mille pulls out her phone and dials those famous three numbers.

THREE

William just stands there for almost an entire minute, frozen to the spot in front of the locked door. His brain is racing away, trying to decide what to do, the music is still pumping from the headphones around his neck.

He's most of all trying to discern the extent of the situation. If this really is the end of the world, why hasn't everything turned to chaos? All seemed perfectly ordinary when he came to work less than an hour ago.

Perhaps it's only just begun? Perhaps I'm one of the first to meet the undead?

William takes out his phone and checks Facebook and Twitter. There are no unusual posts, only the typical food and pet photos and people boasting about their boring lives. He also checks the news channels, both the Danish and the international. Nothing out of the ordinary there, either.

He glares at the door in front of him, the handle still jumping now and then whenever the zombie girl on the other side fumbles with it.

William looks up at the ceiling, imagining the many, many floors above him. How many patients are in the building right now? A couple of hundred? Maybe more. How many of them have arrived during the night? He didn't hear anyone talking about a sudden increase in bite wounds when he came in, but then again, he didn't really talk with anyone. Did he notice the place being extra busy? Not particularly, no.

But maybe I just wasn't paying attention. Maybe I was like the guy in that British zombie comedy, just walking right past all the fucking zombies because I was too tired to notice!

The thought of the whole damn place turning into a slaughterhouse right this minute makes a cold shiver run down his spine. He feels a growing panic. He's got to get out of here. Right now. But he hesitates.

Can't just leave them like this. Someone might come down here and open the door.

He takes the marker from his shirt pocket and steps over to the door. Luckily, the door is white, so what he writes becomes clearly visible:

DANGER!
DON'T OPEN!
ZOMBIES!!!

Without really thinking about it, he draws a skull too. He's always been good at drawing, and skulls are kind of his specialty, so it turns out quite vivid. Now the warning should be hard to miss.

He drops the pen and runs back towards the elevator. He hits the button to the ground floor. The door closes. William breathes deeply as the elevator goes up. He gets ready to sprint. He prepares himself mentally for whatever will meet him once the door opens.

The elevator stops. The door takes forever in opening.

When it finally does, William stares out into the hall. Everything is normal. People are coming and going. Calm music is playing over the loudspeakers. At the reception, two women are causally talking.

No blood. No screaming. No panic. And no zombies.

So far.

William walks towards the exit.

"Hey, where do you think you're going?"

William stops and sees Janus, his colleague. He's pushing an empty bed and sends him a knowing smile. "It's not time for your smoking break yet."

"I'm just ... uhm ..."

William blinks and has no idea what to say. Is it wise to tell anyone about the zombies in the basement? He risks creating panic if word gets out. On the other hand, he can't just leave Janus hanging. He's the one who taught William the job, and he really likes him.

"All right, listen," he whispers, grabbing Janus by the arm. "You need to get out of here, right now. Something crazy is going down."

Janus first grins, but then turns serious once he realizes William isn't joking. "What are you talking about?"

"The whole building is in danger."

Janus frowns. "You mean ...?" He lowers his voice. "Terrorism? Is it a bomb?"

William makes sure no one is within earshot, then he breathes: "Some contagious disease. I don't think the doctors know yet, but ... they probably won't be able to stop it. It's deadly."

"Look, man, I'm sure whatever it is, the doctors have it under control."

William shakes his head firmly. "There are already two dead. I've seen them. Get out of here, man. I'm serious." He darts one last urgent look at Janus, then he lets go and walks on briskly towards the exit. He's still wearing work clothes, but the thought of going up to the changing room hasn't even crossed his mind; he's got his phone, car keys and cigarettes. That's all he needs.

The revolving doors let him out into the sunshine. He looks around the parking lot. Everything seems normal.

So far.

He jogs to his car, unlocks it and gets in. He finds his phone and checks it again. Still no alarming news. Maybe the media does know about the threat, but has been ordered by the government not to say anything, so as to not spread a panic.

William just sits there for a moment and thinks. Now that he's outside the hospital, he feels a little less trapped and slightly more calm. He considers who else to warn. He has a few friends in town, but no girlfriend. His only family is his mother, who lives in the Netherlands. And then there's his uncle Holger, of course.

The thought of his mom in Amsterdam gives him an unpleasant idea. What if this thing didn't begin here in Denmark, but someplace else? Perhaps most of Europe is right now under attack from the undead ...

William calls up his mom.

"Well, hello, sweetie," his mom answers in a bright tone of voice. "To what do I owe the honor this early in the day?"

"Uhm, hey, Mom. I just wanted to make sure everything was fine."

"Of course it is. Why wouldn't it be?"

William doesn't really know what to tell her. He can hear voices in the background. His mom is probably at work.

"Did they say anything on the radio?" he asks.

"About what exactly?"

"I don't know ... something about a virus, maybe?"

"No, I didn't hear anything like that. Is there a virus going around?"

"Yeah, uh ... it's just some sort of flu, I think."

"And you got worried about your poor old mom?" She laughs heartedly. "You're such a sweet boy. Don't you worry, I'm just fine."

William feels a bit more relieved. He chats briefly with his mom, then ends the conversation by saying his break is over.

He takes out the packet of cigarettes and shakes out a Kings, lights it up and inhales deeply. He rolls down the window and spends a minute or so brooding.

What does this mean? Why isn't there any panic? Maybe it didn't really start yet. Maybe it can even still be stopped ...?

He looks towards the building and drags thoughtfully on his smoke. What if the two zombies in the basement are the only ones so far? What if there's still time to—

His thoughts are interrupted by the sudden blaring of a siren close by. William turns his head to see the gate of the A&E open, and an ambulance comes out, lights blinking and sirens blaring. Then another one. And another one. And another one.

William feels the goose bumps appear at the base of his neck and then slowly spread out over his entire body. The sight of the ambulances erases the last of his doubt. The catastrophe is real. It has begun.

He puts out the cigarette and calls up Holger. It only rings once before his uncle picks up.

"Well, good morning, Will."

"Hey, Holger," William says. "Listen, I need your help."

"Sure thing! What can I do you for?"

"Do you still have your place?"

Complete silence on the other end.

"Hello, Holger? You still there?"

"Uh-huh," Holger says, but with a completely new tone of voice. "I still have it, all right. But I don't use it anymore. How come you ask?"

William shuts his eyes. "I think it's best if I meet you there. Now. Right away."

He can hear Holger hold his breath for a long moment. "Okay," he finally says, as William opens his eyes again. "But why—"

A movement to the side. A figure comes rushing at the car. William screams.

FOUR

"Mille! Wait up!" Krista grabs her by the arm and forces her to stop. "Look! Someone got out …"

Mille really doesn't want to look back, but she does so anyway. They've run for what feels like half an hour, yet they've only managed to put a couple hundred yards between them and the bus. It gives Mille the sense of being in one of those bad dreams where you run and run and never move.

The bus seems to be alive in the wavy rays of heat coming off the road. At first, she can't see what Krista sees. Then, she notices the figure coming towards them. It could be Mads. Mille doesn't like the way he walks, uncertain and wobbly. Either Mads is badly hurt, or—

Or he's already dead.

"Isn't it Mads?" Krista asks, squinting her eyes. "I think he's seen us, Mille. He's coming this way."

"Come on," Mille mutters, pulling at her friend. "We've got to go."

But Krista pulls back. "We can't just leave him!"

"The ambulance is on its way. I already called—"

"Look, he's waving!"

Mille sees Mads lifting one arm and moving it from side to side. He's still alive.

Krista starts running back. Mille follows her hesitantly. Mads meets them halfway, holding his left arm tightly against his body. His T-shirt is stained with blood all the way down one side.

"You … you all right?" Krista asks, even though the answer is obvious.

Mads stops to catch his breath, swaying, and Krista grabs hold of him.

"It ... it bit me ..." Mads whispers, and Mille can't help but see the gaping hole in his T-shirt. "It bit everyone ... what the ... hell ... happened?" Mads seems confused, his eyes glazed and distant.

"I think you should sit down," Krista says as she starts to sniffle. "The ambulance will be here in a minute. Mille already called it."

"Mille?" Mads repeats dreamily as Krista clumsily helps him sit down by the side of the road. He looks up and focuses for a brief moment on Mille. The smile gliding over his face stings Mille right in the heart. "Hi," he says, sounding pleasantly surprised. Before she can think to answer, he closes his eyes and collapses.

"Mads?" Krista sobs, shaking him gently. "Mads?"

"It bit us all," Mads repeats in a hoarse whisper, not opening his eyes.

Krista shakes her head. "I think he's unconscious. Oh, no, he's bleeding so much ... what should we do, Mille? How do you make it stop?"

Mille doesn't answer. She's not hearing Krista at all. Something else has caught her attention. Over by the bus, another figure has appeared. It's a girl, maybe Renée, judging from the yellow top. She runs stumbling right out onto the wheat field while looking back constantly. Another person emerges from the bus. It's the old guy, the one Mille saw through the window. His scrawny, blood-covered frame is very recognizable, even from this far away. He staggers after Renée who gives a shriek and runs faster once she sees him.

Mille feels her heart beating in her throat. Somewhere, Krista says her name. Mille just stares at Renée, who luckily is increasing the distance from her pursuer—right up until she stumbles and falls over.

The old guy speeds up, like a predator sensing prey, reaching out his thin arms eagerly as he trudges through the knee-high wheat. Renée just manages to get back up, when the zombie grabs her hair and pulls her back down.

Thankfully, Mille can't see what happens next, as both figures disappear into the golden wheat. But she hears Renée's scream.

Krista also hears, because she turns to look back. "What was that? Someone else made it out?"

"No," Mille says.

The sound of a car horn makes her spin around. For a moment, she hopes it's the ambulance, but it's not. A silvery station wagon is approaching them and slows down. A middle-aged Arab sticks his head out the window and asks in broken Danish: "Accident happen? He hurt?"

"Yes!" Krista says. "You need to take him to the hospital ..."

"Hold on," Mille begins, but Krista has already started hauling Mads to his feet, and the Arab parks the car and comes running out to help.

At that moment, Mille sees the next person come out of the bus. It's a boy—Tommy, as far as she can tell. But he's not fleeing, like Renée did. He's just standing still, swaying for a moment. Then he turns his head around and looks directly towards her. He starts staggering this way.

"... Mille! ..."

Behind him, two others emerge—a girl and a boy. The girl stumbles, and the boy tramples right over her, not minding her at all. Then another one comes out. And another one after that. Soon, her classmates are all around the bus, all of them moving in the same, sleepwalker-like manner. At first, they seem to just drift around, but then, one by one they apparently catch a scent, turn in this direction and begin walking.

"... Mille! ..."

Tommy, who's in front, is already halfway there. Mille can now tell he's been bitten in the throat, and some of the tendons must have been severed, because his head is bopping sideways. The blood has gushed down his shirt. His eyes are strangely white, almost like someone rolling their eyes upwards, and now Mille can also make out the sound he's making: a rattling, sticky growl.

"Mille, for God's sake!" Krista grabs her hard by the shoulder. "Come on, will you? We've got to—" She cuts herself off abruptly, as she sees half of the class coming trudging at them. "Oh, my God ..." she breathes. "They're ... they're not ... we have to ... we have to help them ..."

Suddenly, Mille can act again. She pulls Krista towards the car, where Mads is already lying in the backseat. She shoves Krista inside and slams the door, herself getting in the passenger seat. The Arab has also noticed the oncoming army of dead college students and is just standing there, outside the open driver's side door.

"Hey, come on!" Mille shouts. "Get us out of here!"

She honks the horn, and the sound pulls the man out of his stupor. He gets in and fumbles to get the seat belt on.

Mille looks out and sees Tommy—who's dangerously close now—speed up, as he seems to sense his chances for something to eat getting slimmer.

"Just go!" Mille screams.

The Arab forgets about the belt and guns it. He turns the car around in a wild arc, causing them all to be thrown sideways, the tires giving off a short, high-pitched screech against the hot asphalt—not nearly as impressive as tires do in the movies. Tommy's outstretched fingers almost graze the sideview mirror where Mille is sitting, but then they're speeding down the road, leaving him with the smell of burned rubber.

Mille sighs and leans back her head.

The driver keeps checking the rearview mirror while muttering to himself in Arabic.

"The paramedics will help them, right?" Krista sobs from the backseat. "They'll be here any minute now, and then they'll help them all, won't they, Mille? Won't they?"

"Yeah," Mille murmurs. "Sure they will."

Her thoughts are going around and around and can't seem to find a reasonable place to land. Only twenty minutes ago she was reading an immature love letter from Mads. Now her entire class is turned into living dead, and Mads is dying on the backseat. Will he make it? Will they get him to the hospital in time?

Mille turns and looks at him. Krista has placed his head in her lap and is stroking his damp hair. His face is fiery red and oddly swollen. He looks like he's in pain and he's breathing rapidly.

It's only a matter of minutes.

"I think he'll make it," Krista sobs, looking pleadingly at Mille. "He'll make it, right? He'll wake up in just a moment, won't he?"

"Yes," Mille whispers, her throat closing in on itself. One way or another ...

FIVE

William drops the phone, jumps into the air and scrambles halfway across the gear shift, before he realizes the person outside the car is Janus.

"Jesus Christ, dude …"

His colleague tries to open the door, then looks in at William. "Unlock it, will you?"

"Other side," William says, hitting the central lock. As Janus walks around the car, William picks his phone up off the floor. "Holger? … No, nothing happened. I'll call you back, okay?"

He disconnects just as Janus gets in. William locks all the doors again immediately.

"I was just in the A&E," Janus says, his voice tight. "I've never seen anything like it. All four cars were sent out at once. Something about a school bus that was attacked …" Janus glares at him. "What the hell is going on, Will?"

William takes a deep breath, then says it. "Zombies."

"Zombies?" Janus raises his eyebrows. "Stop fucking around, I'm really not in the mood for—"

"I'm not. It's fucking zombies, man. Go to the basement and see for yourself if you don't believe me."

Janus shakes his head slowly. "But … that doesn't make any sense. I mean, how the hell …?" He moans and runs his hands through his hair.

"I know it's completely mental. My head is just as fucked up as yours right now. I only found out like ten minutes ago."

"You think it's got something to do with that patient that went missing last night?"

"What patient?"

"You mean you didn't hear? The whole place was upside down this morning when I got in. Some dude our age had been admitted for blood poisoning or something, and he just suddenly disappeared, like he had literally just got up and left. That's what they think happened, anyway."

William bites his lip, thinking about the zombie tied to the wheelchair. "That could have something to do with it, yeah."

Janus is quiet for a moment, then looks demandingly at William. "Is it like Walking Dead? Will everything collapse?"

"I don't know, man. Honestly. I just called my mom; she lives in the Netherlands. Nothing is going on down there—not as far as she knows, anyway. But maybe that means it hasn't really broken out yet."

Janus leans his head back and closes his eyes. "Fuck! This can't be happening. What the hell are we going to do? I need to call Sofie ... and my dad ... and the rest of my family, and my friends, and—"

"Hold on," William says as Janus goes for his phone. "We need to consider things first."

"What do you mean? What's there to consider? We just need to get the hell away from here, as far as possible! We've got to go to an island or something. Isn't that how Dawn of the Dead ends?"

"Yeah, and how many people you figure saw that movie?"

"Who cares about how many people saw it?"

"I do! Because the islands are going to be flooded by people as soon as everyone begins to realize what's going down. And if just one of them brings the contagion out there, we would be trapped. Besides, food and resources would quickly become an issue. And how would we even get out there? I don't have a boat, and—"

"All right, I get it! Bad idea. What's your plan, then?"

"My uncle lives a few miles outside town. He has a safe place, like, survival-style, with power and water and food and the whole shebang. I just called him, and I'm going to meet him now."

Janus frowns. "Why would he have a place like that? Did he know this was going to happen?"

"He used to suffer from paranoia. Like, for real. He was institutionalized and everything. He would talk about aliens coming to Earth one day to wipe us all out and stuff like that. So, he built this impressive underground safety room, big enough for someone to easily live in for years."

Janus doesn't exactly look impressed. "So that's your plan? Living underground with a crazy uncle for years to come?"

"He's not crazy anymore, he's on medication now. He's been fine for many years now. But yeah, that's my plan for now. If you have a better one, I welcome you to try it, man. I'm simply offering you to come with me if you want."

Janus seems to mull it over. His gaze drifts across the parking lot, where everything looks completely normal. He bursts into joyless laughter. "Come on, this isn't really happening, dude."

"If you need proof, it's right in there." William nods towards the building. "But I'm going now. You coming?" He turns the key and starts the engine. The radio, which as always is tuned in on a rock station, begins playing.

"What about Sofie?" Janus asks. "Can I bring her?"

William bites his lip. "All right, but only her. I think four people is the limit—at least if we're going to have to stay for a while."

"Great, I'll call her. You mind turning that down a bit?"

William turns down the music, and Janus makes the call. William drives slowly out of the parking lot, scanning the surroundings. None of the people he sees look ill or injured.

Yet.

SIX

As they cross the town limit a few minutes later, Mads has gone quiet.

"I think he's better now," Krista sniffles.

Mille turns to look at him. His expression is no longer contorted in pain, and his face is less swollen. However, almost all blood seems to have left him, because he has taken on an unhealthy greyish hue.

"Where hospital?" the Arab asks. "I don't know town."

"Take a left here," Mille says, pointing.

The Arab stops at the red light.

"No, go!" Mille demands. "Just go!"

"Light red," the man says.

"Yes, but this is an emergency!" She scans the dashboard and hits the button for the hazard flashers. "Go now!"

The Arab rolls out into the intersection. The oncoming cars slow down as they notice, and the Arab makes a left turn.

"Oh, no!" Krista exclaims. "Mille? I think he stopped breathing ..."

Mille turns. Mads's chest isn't rising or falling anymore. His cheeks have sunk into his face and his whole body seems lax. The skin is even more grey now than only a moment ago. In fact, it appears to have turned slightly green, too.

It's happening.

"Pull over," Mille hears herself says.

The Arab looks at her uncertainly. "Hospital here?"

"No. Just pull over."

"We've got to help him, Mille," Krista whines. "How do you do it ...?" She bends over, and for a crazy second Mille thinks she's attempting to kiss him back to life, like Snow White in the fairy tale. Then Krista starts blowing into his mouth.

"Stop that, Krista," Mille says, unbuckling her seat belt.

"I think it helps," Krista cries and blows helplessly into Mads's mouth.

The car has stopped.

"Krista, stop that! Get out of the car!" Mille opens her door and jumps out. She runs around the car and is just about to open the back door, when her gaze falls on Mads's face through the window. At that exact moment, he opens his eyes.

It's no longer Mads's warm, friendly, hazel eyes with that stupidly charming glare. It's no longer anybody's eyes. They're blank, white, dead.

What happens next plays out in slow motion.

Krista bends down once again to blow into Mads's mouth, but then gives off a noise of surprise and says: "My gosh, it worked!"

Those are the last discernable words out of Krista.

Mads sits up abruptly and sinks his teeth into her chin. Krista screams and tries to push him off, but he's clamping on like a Rottweiler and buries his fingers in her hair, pulling her down farther. Then he makes a violent tug with his head, ripping off most of the skin from Krista's chin. The lower lip tears in two, exposing the teeth in a gruesome smile. The blood gushes out and Krista screams shrilly in pain. It only takes Mads a few seconds to gobble down the chunk of skin, then he shoots up again, this time biting into the soft tissue of Krista's throat, turning her scream into a croak.

Mille doesn't see any more than that. She doesn't hear anything either; not her own drumming pulse, not the Arab's panicked yells, not even the blaring of the car horns as she staggers backwards out into the road. She simply turns her eyes to the sky and faints.

SEVEN

"Fuck, why doesn't she answer?" Janus lowers the phone and looks in at the supermarket as they pass by.

William stops at the red light and looks at him. "She at work?"

"Yeah. Do you mind pulling over?"

William puffs out his cheeks. "I don't know, man. I don't think it's a good idea. Time's running."

"Five minutes, tops."

"All right. But you go in alone, I'll stay here in the car."

"Fair enough. You mind turning that off?" He nods at the radio.

"Why? I already turned it down."

"It's distracting."

"I find it calming." Still, William turns it off, interrupting Axl Rose who is singing about a lovely place with green grass and pretty girls.

The lights shift and William is just about to go, when a silvery station wagon cuts out in front of him. Its hazard flashers are on, so William hits the brake.

"What do you think happened there?" Janus asks, following the station wagon with his eyes as it passes by in front of them.

William gets a glimpse of a Middle eastern man behind the wheel and a teenage girl on the passenger seat. "No idea," he mutters. "But I guess they're headed for the hospital."

He makes a U-turn and is just about to pull into the parking lot of the supermarket, when he notices the station wagon stopping abruptly a little farther ahead. The passenger door is opened, and the girl comes out. She runs to the opposite back door, then stops dead, as though she sees something terrible inside the car.

"What are you waiting for, man?" Janus asks.

William realizes he has stopped in the middle of the road. "Something is going on over there," he mutters and points.

Through the back window of the station wagon, he sees the driver turning his head and yelling something. Two figures on the backseat seem to be wrestling.

The girl is still standing there, one hand to her mouth, and now she starts walking backwards, right out into the road, her legs looking wobbly. An oncoming car honks at her, but she doesn't even flinch; she just collapses, as though the horn blew her over.

"Fuck!" Janus exclaims. "What happened to her?"

William is pretty sure he knows what's going on inside the station wagon, and he also knows the girl on the asphalt only has a few minutes—maybe seconds to live—before someone runs her over. He pulls over, yanks the hand brake and jumps out. He runs to the girl, just as the Arab guy comes tumbling out of the car and opens the back door. He yells something which sounds like: "Stop that! Stop that!" and reaches in with both arms, but pulls them quickly back out with a roar of pain, clutching his right hand, where two of the fingers are clearly missing.

William reaches the car and looks inside. The sight is even more awful than he anticipated—no wonder the girl fainted. Everything is drenched in blood. Most of it seems to come from the girl, who's lying splayed out on her back, arms and legs twitching. Her throat looks like chopped tomatoes and she's either dead or a few seconds away from dead. Above her sits a young guy in a bloody T-shirt with his face buried in the crater that is the girl's throat.

Apparently sensing new prey, the zombie turns its eyes up, fixing them on William. They look exactly as dead and inhuman as the eyes of the girl William met in the basement of the hospital. The guy's face is shiny red from fresh blood.

William grabs the door and slams it. But one of the girl's legs gets in the way, preventing the door from closing all the way. William is not about to begin shuffling her around, so he abandons the effort and steps back, looking around for the Arab guy, who's nowhere in sight. Instead, he sees Janus, who's come to pick up the girl and is now bringing her around the station wagon.

"She hurt?" William asks. "You see any bite marks on her?"

"No, I think she's fine," Janus says. "Let's get her to the car."

"What the hell's going on?" someone shouts, and William darts a brief look around to see another car pulling over, the driver sticking his bald head out of the window and staring in amazement at the scene.

"Get out of here!" William shouts at him, just as the zombie boy comes tumbling out of the car. Behind him, inside the car, the girl sits up.

"Holy shit!" the bald guy shouts and speeds off.

Finally someone with a rational response, William thinks, turning around to run after Janus, who has reached William's car. William opens the door, and they help each other place the girl on the backseat.

"Oh, fuck!" Janus exclaims, alarm in his voice.

William spins around expecting to find both zombies coming at them. Instead, he sees them staggering towards the entrance of the supermarket. Apparently, they've sensed a much larger selection of prey, and the glass doors open to invite them in.

"Sofie!" Janus roars and grabs William. "Come on, we've got to help her!"

William pulls free. "No, it's too dangerous!"

"Too dangerous?!" Janus glares at him, aghast. "Sofie is fucking in there!"

"And in two minutes the whole building will be crawling with zombies! You saw how quickly the girl woke up."

"You fucking coward," Janus sneers and runs towards the entrance.

"I'll wait for you!" William calls after him. "But only two minutes!"

Janus doesn't answer, he just runs into the supermarket.

EIGHT

The air is cooler inside the store, and pop music is playing over the speakers. Luckily, not many people seem to have gone shopping this Monday morning.

By the register is a young, pimply kid scanning an older lady's groceries. Only a few yards away from them is the zombie girl. She's eagerly trying to get to them, but is held back by a metal bar.

"You can't get in that way," the cashier says sleepily, not even bothering to look up at the girl. "You'll need to go through the store."

The girl just keeps shoving to get past the obstacle, and her efforts cause her to tip over, producing half a somersault over the metal bar.

"Hey, what the hell …?" the cashier exclaims.

"Look out!" Janus yells.

Both the cashier and the old lady are now staring in silent amazement at the tumbled over girl who's getting clumsily back up on her feet and is starting to growl.

"Get away!" Janus shouts. "She's dangerous!"

"Oh, fuck me," the cashier exclaims as he gets a look at the girl's face and apparently recognizes the danger. Without a second glance, he turns on his heels and sprints off down the store.

The old lady, on the other hand, is still just standing there, frozen to the spot, holding her purse, mouth open.

"Run away!" Janus warns her once again, and she looks as though she tries to oblige him, at least her feet shuffle a few inches backwards, but the sight of the bloody girl has paralyzed her. Janus can't do anything but look as the zombie lunges at her, quickly wrestling her to the ground.

His stomach churns and he forces himself to look away, to focus on what he came for. He turns and runs down through the store. Somewhere down the back is a muffled scream.

Janus checks every aisle, looking out both for Sofie and the zombie boy, but he only meets a few early shoppers with puzzled looks on their faces. One of them is a young, blonde mom with her two young boys.

"What's going on?" she asks Janus as he passes by them, reaching out in a protective manner for her sons. "Who was that screaming just before?"

"Get out of the building," Janus just tells her and moves on. "Sofie? Sofie, it's me! Where are you?"

He reaches the end of the store and stops by the dairy cabinets. Still, no trace of Sofie.

Maybe she's out back ...

He's headed for the door to the employee's area, when suddenly, Sofie appears from behind a meat dish. She's wearing gloves and blows away a strand of hair.

"Sofie!"

"Janus?" she smiles as she sees him. "What are you doing here? Shouldn't you be at work?"

Janus goes to her and sighs with relief. "You're all right ..."

"Of course I am." She frowns. "Is something wrong? Listen, did you hear someone yell out just a minute ago? I was listening to my iPod, so I'm not sure, but—"

Janus can tell Sofie sees something behind him, because her expression changes from mild confusion to utter terror in half a second. Then she opens her mouth and screams.

Janus darts a look over his shoulder just as a bloody hand grabs him. The boy has crept up on him completely noiselessly. Janus attempts a sideway reflex jump, but the kid has too firm of a grip on his shirt. He pulls Janus back and sinks his teeth into Janus's shoulder blade. The pain is intense. Janus screams and swings at the attacker, connecting with his elbow right under the chin, sending him sprawling.

"Fuck!" he hisses, hunching over in pain.

Sofie comes closer, her eyes large and terrified. "Oh my God ... are you ... are you all right, babe?"

"Get away!" Janus yells, trying to reach the spot where the boy bit him. To his dread he feels the warm blood already soaking the back of his T-shirt. "Fuck!" he repeats, his voice breaking, glaring at Sofie with a pleading look. "Get out of here, Sofie! Get as far away as you can! You got it? Just run!"

But Sofie never runs anywhere. She tries, though, managing a few, tentative steps backwards while she stares at Janus with a perfect mixture of fright and amazement. Then, the girl steps out from one of the aisles, throwing herself at Sofie and wrestling her to the floor. It happens so fast Janus only has time to blink once. Then he gives off a roar and is about to lunge forward when a couple of hands grab his ankles, causing him to fall flat on his stomach, knocking his lungs clean out of air. The boy pulls Janus's left leg closer and bites down hard on the bared shin. The pain is even worse this time.

Then, Janus blacks out. He's screaming but not aware of it. He rips his leg free, losing a large chunk of skin, but no longer feeling the pain. He gets to his feet and begins kicking the boy violently in the face, harder and harder, then he's stomping, driving his heel down with all his force, over and over, hammering the boy's head into the vinyl floor until he hears a distinct crunching sound and the boy stops scrambling.

Janus heaves for breath and turns around, suddenly only able to move in slow motion. He sees Sofie lying there, the girl crouching over her. He sees that it's too late. The floor has already turned red, and the girl is visibly losing interest in Sofie, standing up and sniffing the air greedily, sensing still-alive prey nearby.

Janus just stands there, panting, his mind completely blank, as the girl turns around and growls at him, her face and neck and upper chest all covered in Sofie's blood.

And as the zombie comes at him, Janus still doesn't move.

NINE

William stays by the car for what feels like a very long time, but in reality is probably only a few minutes.

He keeps looking in every direction, making sure no one is sneaking up on him. He's ready to go at any moment, fighting the urge to throw himself in the car and get the hell out of Dodge. He also keeps an eye on the entrance to the supermarket and the girl on the backseat, who's still unconscious.

"Come on, dude," he whispers.

He could really use a Kings right now, but he doesn't want to slack his attention even for a second, in case Janus and Sofie come running out, a mob of zombies at their heels.

From inside the car, Dave Grohl is singing about aviation lessons, and William is not aware that he's humming along tonelessly. One half of him feels like a coward for letting Janus go in there all by himself. The other half, though, feels like he made the right choice by not leaving the car.

The traffic goes by at a normal, lazy pace. Several of the drivers dart him concerned looks, and one of them—an obese lady—pulls over and rolls down her window. "Hi there! You need help?"

"No, thank you," William murmurs, realizing how on edge he must look, pacing back and forth, looking all paranoid. He tries to manage a confident smile at the lady, which feels more like an odd grimace. "I'm just waiting for a friend."

The woman nods, not looking particularly convinced, but seems to accept his explanation.

At that moment, the doors to the supermarket open up, and for a second, William imagines Janus coming out of the store, carrying Sofie in his arms like a superhero. And he's right: It is Janus coming out. But he's not carrying Sofie, and he doesn't look at all like a superhero. In fact, he's walking in a very weird and unsteady way, his head tilting back and forth like on a toddler who just learned to walk.

William stares at his friend and colleague, at the white hospital shirt which is no longer white, but red from blood.

Maybe he just fell, a single, stupid thought yells out in William's mind, desperately wanting to cling on to the hope that Janus might be okay. Maybe it's not even his own blood.

But it's nonsense, of course. And the last grain of hope is brushed aside when Janus turns to reveal his left side, where both his T-shirt and skin are reduced to bloody shreds. Underneath can be seen a gaping hole with a couple of ivory colored ribs protruding from the red flesh.

There are also the eyes—Janus's eyes aren't human anymore, not by any means; they're milky white, cloudy and dead. And they're fixing right on William, as Janus starts to stagger in his direction.

"My goodness!" a voice exclaims from behind William, pulling him out of his trance. "Poor guy, what happened to him?"

The heavyset woman has pulled the hand brake and is now fumbling to get her seat belt open.

"No!" William says, going to her car. "You get away from here! He's dangerous."

The woman eyes him like he just spoke Chinese. "What are you talking about? He's bleeding! He's obviously—"

"He's a fucking zombie!" William shouts, shoving the door shut as the woman opens it and tries to get out. She stares at him, blinking in surprise. "Unless you want to get eaten alive, I suggest you get the hell out of here—right now!"

William turns his back to the woman and runs to his own car, not looking back to check if she got the message. If she didn't, it's on her. He's not going to play hero for the sake of some dense middle-aged hag.

William throws himself behind the wheel, just as he catches a glimpse of Janus out of the corner of his eye. His friend has crossed the parking lot and almost reached the street. Exactly what he's aiming for is hard to judge, because he keeps changing direction, as though the passing cars all tempt him and he can't decide which one to go for.

Like a kid in a candy store.

William pulls the car into first gear and checks the traffic before turning out onto the road. He notices the doors to the supermarket open once more, and he forgets everything else for a moment, as he stares at the group of undeads who come staggering out into the parking lot.

He knows the girl who died on the backseat of the station wagon. And Sofie, even though half her face is missing. The others are unfamiliar to him. There's an old lady, her bloody handbag miraculously still dangling from her shoulder; a younger woman dragging one chewed-up leg behind her; a pimply teenager whose clothing reveals that he used to work in the store; and two small boys, whom William feels genuinely sick just looking at.

His gut clenches up as the zombies spread out into all directions. If he'd still had a frail hope that the catastrophe could be somehow stopped, it dies in this moment.

He jerks the wheel and pulls out into the lane, causing the car coming up behind him to slam on its brakes and honk its horn. William barely notices. His eye catches Janus, who's walking right out onto the road. A yellow van swerves to avoid him, but it's too late. There's a loud bang, and Janus is thrown several yards, tumbling round and round like a rag doll.

"Fucking hell," William whimpers as he guns it and heads down the road. He doesn't want to look in the rear mirror, but he can't help it.

He sees the traffic jamming up around the accident.

He sees the zombies all headed for the concerned drivers getting out of their cars to stare at the poor young man who just got run over.

And he sees Janus, who laboriously gets up without any signs of pain or discomfort and attacks the driver of the van, who has come rushing to help him.

TEN

William keeps darting glances at the girl on the backseat, even though she makes no sounds and doesn't move. As far as he can tell, she wasn't hurt before she passed out—but she was in a car with a zombie, so William can't be sure she's not infected.

Perhaps I ought to check her for any scratches ... or simply kick her out ...

He looks again at her in the mirror, but the mere thought of undressing her while she's unconscious makes him feel dirty. And to put her out on the sidewalk and just leave her to whoever finds her, dead or alive ... well, he's not willing to go that far just yet. So, he has no choice but to wait until she wakes up.

He arrives at a new intersection, stopping at the red light. Next to him, in the other lane, a city bus is also waiting. William glances up and sees an elderly lady staring blankly out the window.

She has no idea what's going down. As far as she knows, it's just a regular fucking Monday.

The thought makes him shiver. A woman in runner's clothes comes jogging by, a yellow Lab running next to her on a leash. The sight of the dog produces a jolt in William's stomach.

"Oh, fuck! How could I forget him?"

The thought of Ozzy alone in the apartment makes his heart race. He looks up at the light, still red, as his thoughts start churning faster and faster. If he makes a right here, he could reach the apartment in a couple of minutes. But that will bring him back towards the hospital.

He squeezes the wheel, breathing heavy through his nose. He can't leave his buddy, but he can't risk his own life, either.

In the movies, zombies usually aren't interested in dogs—and besides, the front door is locked, which means Ozzy probably isn't in any immediate danger. He's got food and water enough for tomorrow evening. But maybe William won't get a chance to go get him before then. Maybe the town will be shut down completely within hours. This could be his last chance.

You can't do it, a rational thought urges him. You can't risk your life for a dog.

He would do it for you without blinking, says another—and a lot less rational—thought.

William bites down hard. The light switches to yellow just as another song begins on the radio. It's Iron Man.

William glares at it, muttering: "If that's not a sign, I don't know what is …"

And when the light turns green in the next second, William waits for the bus to go forward, clearing the way for him to turn right. But the bus only moves a few feet before the driver stops and hits the horn.

William stretches his neck to see what's going on in front of the bus. He gets a glimpse of a middle-aged man trudging out into the road. His skin has the unmistakable greenish hue, and from a crater in his belly dangles what looks like threads of oversized spaghetti. The man's shorts, which once were probably beige, are now soaked with blood and have traveled down to his knees, revealing his undies and causing him to walk in an almost comical, duck-like fashion, small steps, bopping from side to side. He stops in front of the bus and reaches up his hands, leaving bloody stains on the front shield. He morbidly reminds William of a giant baby who wants his parent to lift him up.

The bus driver gets out.

"No, no, no!" William slams the horn and fumbles for the button to roll down the window. "No, stay away from him! He's—"

But it's too late. The zombie has already lunged at the driver and wrestled him to the ground.

A car suddenly honks impatiently behind William, the driver probably annoyed at the unexplained hold in traffic, completely unaware of what's going on in front of the bus. Another driver from the opposite side has stopped his car and comes rushing to help. He grabs the zombie to drag him away from the driver, but only manages to get himself bitten at the wrist.

As William stares at the scene, his head is suddenly drained of all thought. He can only sit there and glare in dumb amazement and horror. He realizes just how fast this thing will spread. How soon everything will turn to chaos. He had somehow naively figured that zombies had by now become a known phenomenon; that regular people would recognize the danger, that they had watched at least a few fucking episodes of Walking Dead. Afterall, it only took him a split second to react when he faced the girl in the basement of the hospital. But apparently, not all modern people.

Maybe it's a cultural thing, William muses as he still just sits there, staring at more cars stopping. Maybe, if this had been happening in the United States, it would have been different. But most modern Danes, with their down-to-earth, no-nonsense take on life, don't seem to acknowledge the undead when they see them.

The car behind him honks again, jerking William awake. The intersection has almost been blocked now, and in a matter of seconds, he will be caught in a jam. So, William decides not to give a fuck about traffic laws and floors the gas pedal, racing forward, then twisting the wheel to the right. The shorts-wearing zombie has lost interest in the bus driver and is now getting up to go after the unlucky Samaritan who's standing there, clutching his bleeding wrist.

William sees the shot, and before he has time to think about it, he jerks the wheel and catches the zombie with the corner of the front bumper, sending it flying across the sidewalk.

William doesn't slow down, but races out of the intersection and down the street, his heart thumping in his chest and a sudden burst of energy bubbles up through his throat.

"Fuck you, you piece of shit!" he yells at the rear mirror. "The living finally scores a point!"

William turns up the radio and Ozzy Osbourne.

ELEVEN

When he drives into the parking lot in front of his block three minutes later, the adrenaline has run its course, Iron Man has caused death and destruction, and William has turned down the music.

He cruises around the lot a few times as he peers out, checking every direction, before stopping by the door to his stairway. No zombies in sight, only a couple of kids playing at the playground on the lawn next to the parking lot.

William pulls the hand brake but leaves the engine running and unbuckles the seat belt. He just sits there for a moment, considering. The girl on the backseat hasn't stirred the slightest; she's still just breathing calmly.

Right, you can do this. It's only three floors. You'll be gone less than two minutes.

He takes a deep breath. Then he turns the key and pulls it from the ignition. Silence descends immediately as the engine dies. Only the happy cries from the boys and the distant background noise of the town can be heard.

William gets out and jogs to the door. Upon entering the empty stairway, he stops and listens for a second, then he begins the climb three steps at a time. Panting and heart thumping, he stops in front of the door to his apartment.

He rattles the key and says in a low voice: "It's me." Then, he unlocks the door.

Ozzy, who was sitting perched right on the other side, licks his hand in a happy greeting. Had the German shepherd not heard the keys and William's voice, the welcome would have been quite different. William has been training Ozzy with a retired police dog handler.

"We gotta hurry," he says, squeezing past the dog in the narrow hallway. "We're going for a ride."

Those last four words cause Ozzy to become even more excited, and he immediately jumps up to snag his leash from the nail next to the door. William goes to the kitchen and grabs the bag of dog food. He looks at the fridge, feeling his stomach rumble. It's almost noon, and breakfast feels like a very long time ago.

He puts down the bag and throws together a couple of sandwiches. He also grabs four canned beers and stuffs everything in a plastic bag. He brings it and the dog food back out to the hallway, where Ozzy is sitting with his leash in his mouth, tail wagging.

"Good boy," William says, taking the leash from him. "Let's go."

Ozzy slips out onto the landing, and William locks the door behind them. They hurry downstairs and out into the sunshine and the merciless heat. The parking lot is still empty, the boys are still playing, the girl is still sleeping on the backseat.

William throws the bag of dogfood into the trunk. "Now you, buddy. Up!"

The German shepherd jumps up and sits down.

"Good boy," William says. He's just about to close the trunk, when something catches his eye. From the other side of the playground a lone figure comes walking across the lawn. Even this far away William can see the outstretched arms and the head which is bopping from side to side. A woman, judging from the hair. And she's headed straight for the boys.

"Oh, fuck me …" William runs across the parking lot. "Hey! You guys!"

The boys, who are in the business of throwing handfuls of sand up the slide, turn quickly and look at him guiltily, both of them instinctively hiding their hands behind their backs. They can't be more than eight, maybe nine years of age.

"We weren't doing anything," one of them blurts out.

William stops in front of them and points to the zombie. "You see that woman over there? She's a zombie."

One of the boys gasp out loud. "Wow, that's crazy! A real zombie!"

"You've got to get home right away, all right?" William goes on, talking fast. "Right this minute. Tell your parents to lock the doors and turn on the news. You got that?"

The boys stare from him to the woman, who's already reached the playground and now staggers into the sandpit. The soft ground doesn't seem to make it easier for her to walk, but she steers adamantly towards the boys.

William is just about to shout at them to get them moving, but luckily, the boys already seem to have caught on, as they're backing away.

"Go!" William tells them. "Get out of here! Run!"

One of the boys turns and runs towards the apartments. The other sends William an uncertain look. "But ... my parents aren't at home," he says, his voice shaky.

"Then go home with your friend! Hurry!"

The zombie woman is wobbling her way past the sand, closing in, less than ten yards away now. She snarls and opens her fingers in an eager gesture. Most of the back of her neck is missing, and her hair has been almost pulled from the skull.

The boy finally turns to run, but smashes directly into the swing set, giving off a cry and falling down.

William, who already turned to run himself, stops abruptly. "Fucking hell ..." He sprints over to the boy, grabs him by the arm and tries to pull him to his legs, but the boy is hazy after the collision, so William ends up dragging him along through the sand.

The zombie woman snarls even louder, upping her speed, like she's sensing the opportunity. She's gaining on them. William can't drag the boy fast enough, and there's no time to pick him up. Instead, he shouts pointlessly at the woman. "Stay the fuck away!"

The zombie bends over to grab the boy's sprawling legs, misses and takes another few steps, misses again, narrowly, almost losing balance but stays on her feet, going for a third try. William gives one last hard tug at the boy's arm, hoping to get him out of reach of the zombie—but he loses his grip, and they both fall down.

For one long, terrifying moment, William realizes there's only one outcome left. The boy can't make it up in time. The zombie is already bending down, grabbing his foot. The boy screams as her mouth descends upon his bare leg.

Then, everything speeds up, as something big and brown comes flying in from the side, hitting the woman and knocking her sideways.

William glares dumbly at Ozzy, who's sunk his teeth deep into the lower arm of the zombie, ripping and tearing at it like he's trying to pop it right out of the socket. The woman barely seems to notice the dog, she simply tries to get back to the boy, still clutching his shoe in one hand, but now she's being dragged the opposite direction in a series of violent tugs from Ozzy.

Holy shit, he's stronger than me, William thinks in amazement, still not able to act.

The boy, who's begun bawling, gets up and makes a clumsy one-shoed run for the apartments. William jumps to his feet and runs to the car, glancing back at Ozzy who's still holding onto the zombie.

When he reaches the open trunk, he sticks two fingers in his mouth and gives a short, loud whistle. "Release, Ozzy! Heel!"

The dog immediately lets go of the woman's torn-up arm and sprints to him.

"Up!" William says. Ozzy obeys and jumps into the trunk, even though he keeps darting eager glances back at the zombie woman, who's taken up pursuit. "Good boy," William says, slamming the trunk.

He rushes to the driver's door and throws himself behind the wheel. From the trunk, Ozzy has started whimpering uneasily, as he stares out at the woman approaching the car.

"It's okay," William says, turning the key. "Calm down, Ozzy, we're leaving." He's mostly talking to calm down himself. His whole body is trembling from adrenaline, cold sweat is running down his back, like a junkie doing a cold turkey. He slams the car into gear and guns it.

As they leave the parking lot, he sees the zombie in the rearview mirror, following the car another few yards. Then, she slows down, apparently losing interest, before turning away and heading towards the apartments, obviously sensing more accessible prey.

"Hope she can't get the front doors open," William mutters to himself, wiping a flood of sweat from his forehead.

He thinks about the boys and how surprisingly fast they got the message. As soon as he said the word "zombie," they knew exactly how dangerous the woman was. The term obviously wasn't new to them; they'd probably blown out several zombie brains playing computer games.

Long live the youth, William thinks, reaching into the bag for a beer. They just might have a chance of surviving this ...

TWELVE

Thorsten curses to himself in a low voice as he glares up at the red numbers of the elevator slowly counting down.

Goddamned punks. You just can't count on young people nowadays ...

Thorsten is only three years from retirement—actually, he's too old to still be working as a porter, but he's been taking good care of himself, minding his back and not overworking himself, so he's still feeling in pretty good shape.

Still, it pisses him off to have to run double speed because two of the younger porters decide to just leave in the middle of a very busy day.

Normally, Thorsten never would work in the basement, but someone needs to do the work left by the two deserters. At least until they get hold of a replacement.

If those punks don't get the slip for this, I'll make sure they at least get a talking to they'll never forget.

The elevator stops and the doors slide open, revealing the basement, and Thorsten strides down the hall. He's worked at this place for ages, and he knows the building better than his own home, so he doesn't need to—

Thorsten stops abruptly as he notices the writing on the door. It's done with black marker in a quick handwriting.

"What the hell is this now?"

He steps closer, frowning. It's got to be a joke. Some kid must have snuck down here ... except for the fact that the text is placed too high for a child to have done it. Could it be someone from personnel, then? Who on earth would do such a thing? The young porters might not be the most well adjusted, but Thorsten still has a hard time imagining one of them doing this.

The handle suddenly jumps twice, causing Thorsten to jerk backwards. He didn't expect anybody to be in the room. He grabs for his keys, but then hesitates.

Either it's a distasteful joke, and someone is waiting to surprise him—or it could be something more serious. Perhaps someone got locked in against their will.

"Hello?" he asks loudly. "Who's in there?"

No answer from the room, except for another jerk of the handle.

"I'm going to unlock the door now!" he calls out. "But I'm not in the mood for any surprises, you got that?"

Still, no answer.

Thorsten puts in the key and turns it. He pushes down the handle and opens the door.

The girl immediately steps forward. Thorsten lets out a gasp and steps back. He had mentally prepared himself for a surprise, maybe even an unpleasant one, but not this. The stench comes rolling at him like an avalanche, causing him to gasp for breath.

Thorsten has seen a lot of sick and wounded people in his life, but this girl takes the prize. Something is obviously very wrong with her, and yet she's still, amazingly, able to walk. She comes at him in a staggering pace, reaching out her arms, and Thorsten notices the missing fingers, probably torn off in some sort of accident.

He backs up and instinctively reaches out to grab her hands, catching her by the wrists and trying to hold her back—he wants to help her, but he doesn't want her to come any closer.

"It's all right, take it easy now," he says in the most calming voice he can muster. "We'll get you help. We just—"

He's interrupted as the girl's head jerks forward and bites down hard on his wrist.

"Ouch, goddamnit!" Thorsten roars and pulls back his hand. The girl immediately goes for the other one, so he lets go and steps back farther. "You stop that, you hear me?" The girl doesn't seem to hear him at all; she's only interested in taking another bite, so Thorsten takes yet another step back and meets the wall, clutching his bleeding wrist. "Now you listen to me. You need to lie down and ..."

That's all he has time to say before the girl lunges at him. This time, he's somewhat ready for it and manages to avoid her snapping teeth. Instead, he shoves her backwards, causing her almost to tumble over.

He stares from his throbbing wrist to the girl. What the hell is wrong with her? Must be rabies or something ...

He decides to abandon any attempt to help out the girl and instead go get help. He jogs back towards the elevator, squeezing hard on the wrist, trying to stop the blood, which finds its way out through his fingers in thin trickles, leaving a bloody trail down the hall.

The elevator has gone back up, so Thorsten hits the button. He hears steps behind him and turns around.

The girl has followed him, her arms outstretched, as though longing to hug him. Thorsten never had any kids himself, but he used to be married to a woman who had a teenage daughter—Camilla was her name—and Thorsten developed a pretty good relationship with his stepdaughter. Thorsten and the woman separated, and it's been almost four years since he's seen Camilla, but for one fleeting glimpse, he sees her face on the sick girl in front of him, and it makes him hesitate.

Jesus Christ, that's someone's daughter ...

The eyes of the girl are so unlike anything he's ever seen—if he didn't know any better, judging from the eyes alone, he would have thought the girl was already dead. Except she's clearly not, coming at him eagerly, looking an awful lot like Camilla.

"You ... you stay away from me," he croaks, trying to make it sound like a demand, yet it comes out a plea.

The girl doesn't pay any attention either way. She's only a few steps away, when the doors finally open behind him, and Thorsten is able to move again. He steps inside and hits the button for the ground floor. Then, he backs towards the back wall, staring at the girl who's about to enter the elevator, as the doors begin to close.

"Stop!" he shouts, suddenly finding his voice again. "You stay there! You hear me?"

The doors close less than half a second too late. The girl is in. Thorsten begins shouting.

As the elevator reaches the entrance hall less than one minute later, Thorsten is dead.

The girl, whose name was once Selina, is busy eating his liver. Sensing new, living prey, she turns her head, licking the dark brown blood from her lips.

In front of her, just about to step inside the elevator, stands a young man with a cup of coffee and a look of stunned terror on his face, frozen to the spot. He became a father for the first time just this morning, and he only came down here to get the coffee. Now, he's headed back up to the maternity ward to be with his wife and their newly born. He never gets to see any of them again, though.

Three minutes later, the entrance hall has turned to chaos.

THIRTEEN

Finn is sweating profusely under the scorching high noon sun and his lower back is starting to complain. But he's almost done trimming the hedge, so he pushes on.

A movement makes him turn his head to see his wife crossing the lawn carrying a beer can and a shallow dish. "Cool refreshments for my gardener," she says, handing him the beer.

"Thanks, hon," he groans, wiping the sweat from his brow. "You want me to drink it out of that?"

"This is not for you," she tells him, putting the dish down in the shade of the hedge. Finn notices it's full of water. "It's for the poor hedgehogs. They suffer terribly in this heat, I'm sure."

"They're not the only ones," Finn mutters, opening the can and gulping down half of it. He's become a little too skilled at drinking beer after his retirement last year. It's just such a wonderful pastime—whenever the garden doesn't demand his attention.

"I don't get why you don't just wait till sundown," Lone says. "This is no weather to be working in."

"Thought I'd finish before it got too bad. Overestimated myself, I guess. But I'm almost done now, so—"

A loud, shattering bang from the other side of the hedge is followed by the sound of glass. Finn instantly knows the source of the noise and stretches his neck in order to see the neighbor's greenhouse. Probably Olsen's grandchildren at play. Finn has often had to throw back their soccer ball when they've accidentally kicked it over the hedge.

But he can see neither kids nor ball anywhere. Instead, he sees a man wobbling along the side of the greenhouse, apparently struggling to stay on his feet. He's Middle Eastern or maybe Arabic.

"What's going on over there?" Lone asks, as she's not tall enough to peer over the hedge.

Finn's first thought is that the man has been breaking in at Olsen's—he certainly looks like someone out on shady business, the way he keeps darting nervous glances in all directions. He probably ran into the greenhouse by accident.

"Go inside," Finn tells his wife and grabs the rake.

"What's going on, Finn?" she demands.

The answer to her question comes barging through the hedge at that exact moment. The Arab stumbles and falls onto the lawn.

Lone gives off a shriek of surprise, and Finn steps quickly forward, holding the rake ready. "Whaddya think you're doing?" he asks loudly. "Whaddya doing on my property, huh?"

The man looks up, bewildered, blinking and focusing on Finn. And when Finn looks back at him, he sees the man's face properly for the first time, and he feels an unexpected pang of sympathy. The guy is obviously scared out of his wits; his golden skin is pale and sweaty. He mutters something in Arabic and holds up one hand.

"Christ," Finn groans when he sees the missing fingers in the bloody mess.

"God Almighty," Lone whispers behind him. "Finn, he's really hurt!"

"Call an ambulance," Finn says, dropping the rake, as Lone turns to run back to the house. "Here, let me help you ..." He kneels and tries to pull the man to his feet, careful not to touch the wounded hand. The man clings to Finn and keeps jabbering incomprehensibly.

He's going into shock.

Finn has seen worse things when he served in the military during the Balkans, and that's probably what enables him to think clearly in this situation.

"We gotta get you inside, away from the sun," he says, not sure whether the man understands him, but still he wants to reassure him with a calming voice, so he goes on: "The ambulance is on its way. We'll clean the wound in the meantime. You'll be fine."

Finn supports the man across the lawn. It's heavy work, since the guy can barely stay on his feet, and Finn has to almost carry him.

I'll feel this in my back tomorrow, he thinks to himself and grinds his teeth.

FOURTEEN

Dan sits bolt upright in bed. Sweat is pouring from him, the air is stiflingly warm, and for a terrifying moment, he's sure he's back in the basement of the old lady's house.

Then, he blinks and comes to. He's in his room. The heat is from the sunlight streaming in through the window. He's not in danger. There are no more zombies.

Dan sighs and wipes the sweat from his eyes, swings his leg out over the side of the bed and gets up. His stomach feels like a big, empty hole, and his body is sore in several places—especially around the ankle.

He's instantly reminded of Jennie and Thomas, and it feels like his insides take a dive into a very deep well. He staggers out into the bathroom, gushes cold water on his face and drinks greedily until his throat hurts.

He glares at himself in the mirror for a moment. The sight isn't exactly a cheery one; he might have survived the zombies, but he sure looks like one anyway: pale, weak and dark half-circles under his eyes.

A cat. I dreamt about a cat.

The thought leaps through his head apropos of nothing. He's not sure why, but somehow, he gets the sense his mind is pointing to something important. He's still too groggy to think clearly, though, so he shoves the feeling aside and goes to the kitchen.

His mom is sitting at the dining table, staring blankly out into the back garden, her eyes red from crying. His grandma is making coffee. "Oh, hi, Dan," she says, shuffling over to embrace him. "I'm so glad you're okay."

Dan smiles weakly and glances at his mom. "Where's Dad?"

"He just went for a drive," his grandma says, turning rather abruptly away from him to concentrate on the coffee. "He had to ... take care of something."

"Your father is at the mortician," his mom says without moving, her voice completely emotionless. "He's picking out a coffin for Jennie."

Dan sees the pill bottle on the table next to his mom. She suffered a breakdown from stress a few years back, and the doctor gave her anxiety drugs. Even though she's better nowadays, she still keeps the pills and takes one whenever she feels stressed out. Dan remembers all too clearly how drowsy she gets from the drugs, and it makes him sad to see her like this. Not so much the fact that she's drugged, but how she can't seem to handle difficult situations anymore.

Grandma brings the coffee. "You must be starving, Dan. You want me to make you something? How about oatmeal porridge? I know you love oatmeal porridge."

"I'm not really hungry," Dan mutters and sits down next to his mom.

From the living room he can see the television is on without sound, showing some stupid afternoon show. Outside, in the garden, the sun is shining like it's been doing for the past weeks. From the looks of it, everything seems normal. Except nothing is normal today.

"Mom," Dan says cautiously. "I'm sorry about what happened ... I really tried to help her."

"It's not your fault," his mom says, still not looking at him, still the dead voice. "It's nobody's fault."

Dan squeezes his lips together. He had hoped she would say something which could alleviate his guilt just a little. He knows logically that Jennie's death wasn't his fault, and yet he still feels like it was.

They sit for a while in silence. His grandma brings him a big bowl of porridge, and when Dan smells the food, he suddenly becomes extremely hungry and wolfs down the entire serving.

Afterwards, with his stomach full, he feels a little better. He wants to say something else to his mom, but decides not to. It won't do any good as long as she's like this. Instead, he gets up and goes to the living room. He's about to throw himself on the couch, when he notices what's happening on the television.

It's a news report—live, apparently—and they're sending from somewhere in this town. Dan recognizes the hospital where he passed by himself just a few hours ago. Now, police cars are parked all over the place, and officers with dogs and guns dressed in riot gear are running into the building. The picture moves as the cameraman steps closer, and Dan catches a glimpse of something through the glass doors which makes his stomach clench up.

Inside the entrance hall, a chaotic scene is playing out. A lot of people seem to be fighting with the police, and wounded persons are lying everywhere on the floor. A figure staggers by, glancing out through the glass for a brief second, and Dan recognizes her.

"Selina!" he breathes, his mouth opening wide.

They go back to the studio where a reporter with a very grave expression is talking under the headlines: Breaking! Bloody riots at local hospital!

"How … how can it …? I don't get it … she killed him … she said she killed him …"

"What's that, Dan?" his grandma asks from someplace very far away.

The pieces fall into place with dull, heavy thuds in Dan's mind.

Jonas wasn't properly dead. That's the only explanation. Or maybe … maybe Selina got a scratch she hadn't noticed.

Either way, it doesn't really matter. What matters is that the catastrophe Dan was sure they had successfully avoided, is now unfolding in front of his eyes.

The reporter touches his ear like someone is talking in his earpiece. Dan looks around for the remote, finds it and unmutes.

"… that no more than a few hours ago, a similar attack went down just miles outside the same town. Our intel is still sparse, but apparently, the target was a school bus, and an elderly couple is said to have been involved. We're trying as we speak to find out more …"

"Elderly couple," Dan whispers. "Outside town …"

More pieces clamber into place. Something from his dream. Something about a cat.

The cat! … Holy hell, it was the cat! It stepped in the blood and then it scratched the lady … She got infected, just like Thomas did from the broken glass …

And suddenly, the picture is completed, and Dan sees everything clearly. How the disaster is not averted, how, in fact, it's been growing while he slept, expanding into catastrophic proportions, and now it's probably too late to stop. Unless the police are quick and effective.

But do they even know what they're fighting? And do they have the resources?

"What's this now?" His grandma is standing next to him. "My goodness! That's not here in town, is it?"

The picture has changed back to the scene by the hospital.

"Listen, Grandma," Dan says, turning to face her. "We need to leave town, right now. It's not over. What happened to Jennie is happening to many others. It's only a matter of time before the entire town ..."

"Easy, Dan, calm down."

"... will be taken over! It's not safe to be here. We need to ..."

"Take a deep breath, Dan. You're not making sense."

Dan turns and runs to the kitchen. "Mom!"

His mom looks at him sleepily. "What?"

"You need to listen to me. We're in danger here. We need to leave, right now."

An expression of mild irritation passes over his mom's face, but she doesn't reply, simply turns her head to stare out into the garden again.

"Mom!" Dan shouts and grabs her shoulders. "Will you listen to me, please!"

His mom shrugs him off with a grumpy groan. She looks like she's about to say something, but then her face crumbles up and she starts to cry.

Dan steps back. "I'm sorry, Mom, I didn't mean to ..."

His grandma places a hand on his shoulder. "Leave your mom be, Dan. She's already struggling."

Dan's ears pick up a sound which he at first takes to come from the television: the sound of sirens. But the sound intensifies, and Dan runs to the kitchen window facing the driveway.

An ambulance comes into sight, stopping by the curb. Two paramedics wearing yellow vests jump out and run into number 18.

FIFTEEN

"What the heck is taking them so long?"

Lone is pacing back and forth across the kitchen as she keeps darting glances out the windows.

"Take a seat," Finn mutters. "Or at least stop moving about. They'll be here as soon as they can."

He's sitting on a chair in the kitchen, keeping an eye on the Arab, who's lying on the couch in the living room. The injured hand is resting on his chest, wrapped in a fairly decent bandage which Finn was able to make thanks to the first aid kit still open on the coffee table. Next to it is a glass of water which Finn attempted—unsuccessfully—to get the guy to drink. He just thrusted his head back and forth and kept mumbling deliriously.

"At least he settled down now," Lone says, an unmistakable tone of relief in her voice. "I guess that's a good sign, right?"

"I would think so," Finn says, emptying the third can of beer before getting to his feet.

"What are you doing?" Lone asks at once.

"I'm just going to check on him." Finn walks into the living room. As soon as he gets close to the couch, he senses the smell of something sour. It could just be sweat, but it reminds him of fever.

He looks down at the Arab's wet face and can tell right away that his condition has actually taken a turn for the worse. While it's true he's not thrashing about anymore, and has stopped muttering incoherently, his brown skin has taken on a greyish hue which Finn finds very alarming.

"God damnit," he groans, kneeling down.

"Is something wrong?" Lone calls from the kitchen.

Finn ignores her and takes a closer look at the bandage. It's dark red from dried up blood, but the skin right next to it has turned almost green.

Blood poisoning. But how the hell could it have come on so fast? Poor guy must have been infected before he cut himself on the glass.

Finn stares at the bandage and recalls the sight of the wounded hand. The stump where the fingers had been was bloody and all torn up. Not exactly an injury you would attribute to the clean cut of broken glass. In fact, the hand looked more like the guy had stuck it in a blender.

Maybe something bit him ... maybe he got into a fight with a big dog.

If that's the case, what's happening to the guy could be rabies or something similarly aggressive. Finn puts his palm on the Arab's forehead, feeling to his surprise how cold the skin is.

Huh! The fever must have broken.

Normally, Finn would take that as a good sign; however, in this case, he's pretty sure it's quite the opposite. The Arab's body seems to be giving up the fight against whatever is attacking it. His breathing has turned short and shallow.

If they're not here within minutes, he'll go into cardiac arrest.

Finn closes his eyes and breathes heavily for a moment. What a day this has turned out to be. Not half an hour ago he was out in the garden trimming hedges, his only worry was the ache in his back. Now he's sitting with a dying man.

Lone calls from the kitchen: "They're here! Finn, they're here!"

Finn notices the sirens. He gets to his feet and goes to the kitchen. He sees the ambulance come to a halt and two paramedics jump out.

"Go and see to him," he says, starting for the entrance hall. He opens the front door just as the paramedics come running. "It's in here! Hurry up, he's not doing very well. In the living room!"

The two men squeeze past him without any questions and head for the living room.

"Finn!" Lone calls from the living room, her voice shrill. "Finn, come look at this!"

Finn strides back into the room, almost bumping into the paramedics, who have stopped dead in the doorway. When he sees what they're seeing, he too stops abruptly.

Lone is standing next to the couch. The Arab is sitting bolt upright, his mouth slowly opens and closes, a stream of drool running from his lower lip. But Finn only sees the man's eyes. They're wide open, staring at nothing, and both pupil and iris are completely gone. Looking at the guy, Finn is reminded of those fish that live deep down near the bottom of the ocean, their eyes blind from living in eternal darkness.

Lone is the first one to speak. "I ... I think he ..."

She's interrupted as the Arab suddenly moves with striking speed. He twists to the side, reaches out his arms, grabs Lone's blouse, pulls her down, opens his mouth and bites down hard on the side of her neck.

Lone screams shrilly, more surprise than pain, and the paramedics jump back to life.

Finn, however, finds himself utterly unable to move. It's like someone pulled the plug on his old body, and he can only stand there and watch everything that happens in front of him through a veil of shock.

The living room turns into a tangle of flailing arms and snapping teeth. The paramedics manage in a joined effort to wrench the Arab free of Lone, but he comes away with a massive chunk from her neck, and the blood immediately starts gushing. A second later the Arab has instead clamped down on one of the paramedics' shoulder, causing him to yell out and stumble over his own feet, reaching out and grabbing hold of the other paramedic in an effort not to fall down, but only managing to pull his colleague down with him.

The noises only come through to Finn in a muffled drone. The shouts of the paramedics, Lone's screaming, the animal-like growl of the Arab, the crash of the coffee table being flipped on its side as the paramedics scramble frantically to hold down the Arab while simultaneously not being bitten—which proves impossible, as both of them quickly suffer bloody wounds as the Arab's teeth tear through their uniforms.

Lone is the last person standing, but only for a few seconds, as she tries in vain to stop the blood from pouring out of her neck, her tiny, shaking hands getting soiled in no time. Her eyes sweep the room, distant and dreamy, and for a moment they connect with Finn's. Later, he will swear that he saw her smile; that his beloved wife of almost fifty years summoned her last effort of will to send him one last smile. Then, she collapses and disappears from view behind the couch.

Finn blinks hazily and turns his gaze back to the Arab, who's now on top of one of the paramedics, the poor guy screaming and fighting to get him off, while the other paramedic is rolling around the floor, clutching his jaw, which is missing most of the skin. The Arab is the only one who hasn't slowed down; he's still biting at everything within reach, desperate like a predator who has gone hungry for weeks.

So, this is how it ends, Finn thinks very soberly. Part of his brain is trying to convince him it's all just a bad dream, but the more rational part knows better. It knows Lone is dead and he himself will be joining her on the way to heaven in only a few moments, as soon as the Arab loses interest in the already dead-or-very-close-to-it paramedics and turns to see Finn just standing there. He ought to run, of course, but his body is still completely unresponsive, and besides—what would be the point? Lone is gone, so he might as well go too. He only hopes it'll be over quick and not—

"Finn!"

Someone shouts his name very close by. Finn turns his head to see a boy he knows. It's Dan, the boy from across the street. Dan stares at him with eyes large and scared—but also, surprisingly, somehow determined.

"Come ... with ... me," Dan says, the words finding their way to Finn's ears as distant echoes. "We ... gotta ... get ... out ... of here ..."

Dan pulls him by the arm, hard, and Finn is surprised to find himself moving along. His eyes are reluctant to obey, though, and his neck turns to get one last glimpse of Lone.

Just as Dan drags him out of the living room, Finn actually sees part of his wife: her hand is sticking out from behind the couch. The skin is greenish. The fingers twitch a few times. Lone is waking up again.

SIXTEEN

Dan hauls Finn out the front door and only lets go of him once he's sure the old guy will stay on his feet and not collapse.

"Finn?" he says, attempting to catch the swimmy, grey eyes. "Where's the key?"

Finn blinks dazedly. "The key …?"

"Yeah, the key to the house. Do you have it? Where is it?"

The words don't really seem to resonate, and Dan is about to abandon his effort, when Finn suddenly goes to the pockets of his shorts. "I don't … have it on me," he murmurs. "It's probably hanging on the nail."

"What nail?" Dan demands. "Where's the nail, Finn?"

"In the front hall."

"Right. Stay here for a moment, okay?"

Dan steps back into the house and looks around. From the living room the screams and bangs have died out—instead he hears the unmistakable sound of someone chewing noisily and wetly on something. Dan doesn't have to look in order to guess who won the fight. In a matter of minutes, there'll be three new zombies in the house. That's why he needs to lock the front door …

His eyes catch the nail in the wall next to the coat stand, and he grabs the key, slips out into the baking sunshine once more, slams the door and locks it.

"Right," he says to Finn, who's still standing there, an expression of not-quite-sure-what's-happening on his face. "They can't get out."

"Get out?" Finn repeats in a murmur. "But Lone … Lone is in there …"

The emotion flickering across Finn's face as he turns to look at the house sends a jolt of empathy through Dan's heart. The experience of losing a loved one is still all too familiar to Dan, and he sees

Jennie's face before him. He forcefully pushes the image aside—and is surprised to find he can actually do it. "Come with me, Finn," he says gently. "There's nothing more you can do for her."

"But ... but I ..."

Dan takes hold of his arm and leads him down the garden path. Finn struggles weakly for a moment, then follows along. They cross the street and are met in the driveway by Dan's grandma, her eyes wide. "Where did you go, Dan? Why would you run out the door like that?"

"Help me out here," Dan says, avoiding the questions. "He's unharmed, but I think he's in shock."

Grandma takes Finn's other arm, her eyes ping-ponging between Finn, Dan and the house across the street. "What happened over there, Dan? Where are the paramedics?"

"They ... they are still in the house," Dan mutters, helping Finn inside.

"But why aren't they helping Finn? And who was that screaming just a minute ago? We heard it all the way over here. I was afraid you—"

Dan suddenly stops listening. Something has struck him with the force of a brick to the back of the head.

The garden door!

"I need to fix something, Grandma," he says, letting go of Finn and stepping back outside. "I'll be back in a second!"

"No, Dan! You stay here!"

Dan runs out the driveway. He doesn't pause to check for any traffic and is almost hit by a station wagon. It honks its horn at him. The window rolls down, and his dad sticks out his head. "What the hell are you doing, Dan? Why are you running around out here?"

"Dad! ... I ... it's ..." Dan has no idea how to explain the situation in a short amount of time. He looks to Finn and Lone's house, and at that moment, he sees Lone, as she comes staggering around the corner of the house. Her head is bobbing around on her shoulders, due to the fact that the tendons in her neck have been severed, and still-shiny blood has drenched her flowery summer shirt.

Too late ... she already found the way out ...

"Come on, let's get inside," his dad says. He hasn't seen Lone yet, and he rolls the car into the driveway before Dan can say any more.

Dan follows the car, not taking his eyes off Lone, who is headed this way.

The car's engine shuts off, and Dad gets out. He sees Lone. "Oh, hi, Lone! We're not really—" He interrupts himself as he gets a closer look at the neighbor. "What the hell ...?"

Dan finally gets his tongue working. "Watch out, Dad! She's turned into a zombie!"

Dad looks briefly at Dan, then back at Lone, looking as though he's not really sure what to believe. Some sort of instinct seems to be telling him Lone is dangerous, while another, rational part of his brain can see she's obviously hurt and wants to help her.

Dan has told the police about the zombies, has explained it all to the shrink and to his parents, has been going over the events of the past couple of days what seems like a thousand times—yet none of them believed him, and Dan couldn't very well blame them. His dad, though, was the only one who actually seemed to consider the legitimacy of what Dan was saying—although he didn't say it outright. But right now, his dad seems to reconsider if maybe the horrible creatures Dan has described might have been real—and that one of them might be headed for them right now.

Dan doesn't wait for his dad to decide, but runs over and grabs his wrist. "Come on, Dad! We need to get inside! She's dangerous! She wants to eat us!"

"Eat us?" his dad repeats. "Honestly, Dan ..."

But he never finishes the sentence, because now Lone has crossed the street and is coming up the driveway, and she's close enough for Dad to see that something is completely off—her always warm and friendly old-lady eyes are now empty, white balls rolling around blindly in their sockets, yet somehow still seeing.

Dad shoves Dan towards the door. "Hurry up, get inside."

Dan runs to the door, just as Finn pops back outside. Dan's grandma is trying to pull him back, but Finn has already seen his dead wife, and his expression turns blank as he mutters: "Lone?"

Dan pushes him back as he tries to go to her.

"No, get inside! Grandma, help me get him back inside!"

His grandma is already tugging at Finn, but he's surprisingly strong for an old guy, and for a second all three of them are caught in a deadly stalemate right on the doorstep, Finn repeating his wife's name. "Lone ... Lone, I'm right here ... I'm right here, Lone ... I'll help you ..."

Dan is gripped by panic. "Get in, get in!" He shoves Finn in the chest hard enough to cause him to stumble backwards and would have fallen on his ass, if Dan's grandma hadn't been there to catch him.

"Dan, she's coming!" his dad calls from behind him.

Dan turns to see Lone lunge at his dad.

"Dad, no!"

His dad catches Lone's wrists a split-second before her long nails can scratch his face. He forces her arms back, but Lone in response flings her head forward, snapping wildly at his face and throat, her tiny teeth clapping just inches away from Dad's skin. Surprisingly, his dad doesn't seem to panic, but holds on to Lone firmly, keeping her at a safe distance. Dan just stares at his dad for a second, amazed and impressed.

"Get inside, now, damnit!" Dad roars over his shoulder. "And get that door closed!"

Grandma is still struggling to hold back Finn. Dan hesitates a moment longer, staring indecisively back and forth. He can't just leave his dad out here, but he can't really do anything to help him either.

Then he sees the paramedics—it's a wonder he hasn't seen them before now, really, since one of them is already halfway up the driveway. Dad is still wrestling with Lone, still shouting for them to get in and close the door, and he hasn't noticed the newcomers.

"Watch out, Dad! Behind you!"

Just as Dan shouts, his dad shoves Lone away hard. She tumbles over and slams her head into the pavement with a sickening thud. She blinks, groans and flails her arms, trying to get back up, but seemingly unable to, as her brain just took a hit hard enough to knock a living person unconscious.

The quickest of the paramedics steps forward and plants his teeth right in Dad's shoulder. He roars out in pain. The sound is mixed with Dan's anguished scream. Then Dan's body takes over. He jumps right into the action, grabs hold of the paramedic's blood-stained shirt and yanks him backwards just as he's about to bite down on Dad's shoulder a second time. The zombie has caught hold of Dad's shirt in return and holds on tightly, not intending on being dragged away from its first meal. But the short break gives Dad a second to react, and he doesn't waste time; he turns halfway around, almost tearing his shirt, and starts bashing the zombie with both hands. A clenched fist right between its eyes causes it to let go and stagger backwards—but the other paramedic has now joined the fun and goes directly for Dan's dad, who pulls back, clutching his shoulder, a look of terror on his face.

Everything slows down for a heartbeat, and Dan sees everything like from very far away. He sees paramedic number two lunge at Dad, who no longer has the strength to fight back. He sees the zombie sink its teeth in his neck, the blood spurting out, Dad screaming in pain.

And things might have played out just like that—had it not been for Lone, who at that exact moment, in an effort to get back up, rolls clumsily to the side. The paramedic doesn't see her, trips over her legs and falls down face-first. Dan hears a couple of sharp snaps, and when the zombie a moment later cranes its neck back to look up at them, most of its teeth rattle out onto the pavement.

Paramedic number two is a bit more capable, as it manages to step past Lone, who's still struggling to get up, and now the paramedic is blocking Dan and his dad from the doorway.

Dad sneers, holding a hand to his shoulder. His shirt has been torn, but Dan can't see any blood—at least not yet. Maybe, just maybe, his dad was lucky enough that the zombie's teeth didn't break the skin. But with the amount of luck Dan has had lately, he doesn't get his hopes up. And bleeding or not, his dad is obviously in pain.

"You stay back!" he shouts, kicking out at the paramedic. The zombie doesn't seem to heed the warning; in fact, it sees the kicking leg more as an invitation and grabs at it eagerly, missing it by inches.

Dan and his dad back up farther, coming closer together. Soon they'll be caught in the carport with nowhere to go. Then it happens again: Dan reacts before he knows it. He pulls sideways, away from his dad, and runs in an arc past the paramedic, headed for the street. The zombie turns and follows him.

"Dan! What are you doing?"

"I'll lure them away from the house! Get inside!"

"You're coming with us!"

"I'll draw them down the street, then I'll come back!" Dad is about to say something else, but Dan cuts him off: "It's okay, Dad, I can outrun them! Just please go inside the house!"

Dan doesn't wait for an answer. He runs out the driveway, passing the toothless paramedic and Lone, who both have gotten back up. As he reaches the street, Dan looks back up to see his dad run inside the house, shoving Finn back and out of sight, and Dan feels a jolt of relief.

The paramedic without teeth and Lone come staggering at Dan, but the other one is headed for the front door. Dad sticks out his head and darts one last look in Dan's direction, their eyes catching each other, but there's no time to say anything, and his dad slams the door right in the face of the zombie, who immediately starts clawing at the woodwork.

Dan turns and jogs down the sidewalk. His plan is to draw the zombies down the street, just far enough for him to run back. As he looks over his shoulder to make sure the zombies are following him, his foot catches a crack in the pavement and he tumbles over, just managing to break his fall in the last second, resulting in a bad bruise on his palm.

A loud scream from down the street makes him forget the pain immediately. He looks up and sees the Arab from Finn and Lone's house attacking a woman on a bicycle. He turns his head and looks back. The paramedic is still in pursuit, but Lone has lost interest and is instead headed across the street where one of the neighbors—John, a big fat man wearing no shirt—has popped out to see what the noise is about.

Dan wants to yell out to warn him, but his voice doesn't seem to work, and besides, he's got his own problems. The paramedic is just a few yards away now, eagerly picking up speed and reaching out to grab Dan. Dan scrambles to get to his feet, when suddenly he hears the angry roar of an engine. The car swerves right in front of Dan, crashing into the paramedic with a loud bang, sending the body flying through a hedge. The car comes to a halt halfway up the sidewalk. The front door is pushed open, and a young guy with tattoos all the way up his arm stares out at him. "You been bit?"

Dan just glares dumbly at the question. From the trunk of the car a big German shepherd is barking furiously.

"Have you been bit?" the driver shouts.

"N... no," Dan manages.

"Then get in!"

And he doesn't really seem to have a choice. At that moment, John cries out as Lone attacks him, and on the other side of the hedge, the paramedic has gotten back up, wobbling uncertainly on a pair of thigh bones obviously shattered, but nonetheless headed stubbornly back out towards Dan.

"Come on, goddamnit!" the guy in the car shouts. "If you don't get in, I'll go without you!"

Dan gets to his feet and staggers around the back of the car. He darts a glance down the street and sees the Arab getting up from the woman, who's already dead and has lost her appeal, as the man heads for the nearest driveway, drawn by the scent of fresh, living meat.

Then Dan opens the car door and gets in.

The guy has already put it in reverse and now backs down from the sidewalk. He stops in the middle of the street, blocking the nonexistent traffic.

"Buckle up," he says through gritted teeth. "Seems like he didn't get the message the first time."

The dog in the trunk has stopped barking, but is now panting and whining impatiently, as though it knows what's going to happen.

Dan, however, is a little slower in catching up. Only when he sees the paramedic come barging through the hedge does he guess the driver's plan, and he quickly grabs the seat belt and fastens it.

The driver floors the accelerator just as the zombie wobbles onto the street. The sound of the collision is even louder from inside the car, and this time the zombie is thrown under the tires. Dan feels the bumps in the seat, and they remind him of the little girl he and Linda ran over in the courtyard of the old lady's house.

"Sorry about that," the driver says as he speeds down the street. "I know that was gross, but I'd like to take out a few of them if possible. You know, weed out the herd a little."

"It's all right," Dan mutters, and, before he can think, adds: "It's not the first zombie I've run over."

He notices the guy sending him a look. Then he smiles.

SEVENTEEN

"My name's William and the dog is called Ozzy."
"I'm Dan."
William points a thumb over his shoulder. "I don't know her name, but she'll probably tell us once she wakes up."
Dan turns his head to see the girl lying in the backseat, surprised that he didn't notice her before. "Is she asleep?" he asks.
"Unconscious."
"Did she ...?"
"Don't worry, she's clean," William says, immediately guessing the question. "I picked her up shortly before I found you." He makes a right turn, coming out into the main street, where the traffic looks pretty normal for a Monday afternoon.
"Thank you for picking me up," Dan mutters. "But I'd like to go back home now."
William looks at him briefly. "You mean back from where you just came? Didn't you notice the zombies attacking everyone?"
"Yeah, but ... I need to get back. My mom and dad—"
"I'm sure your mom and dad will be fine without you for now," William says, not slowing down. "As long as they don't open the front door, of course."
"I'd still like to go back," Dan says, shifting his weight uneasily in the seat.
"Listen, Dan, you're a lot safer with me right now. I'm going to—"
"Drive me back!"
Dan surprises himself by almost shouting.
The girl on the backseat grunts, but doesn't wake up.
William pulls over and stops the car. "Fine, get out then."
"I ... I can't walk home from here," Dan says, looking out nervously.

"I'm not going back," William says. "It's way too dangerous. That street is crawling with zombies by now. For every minute we spend here in town, we increase the risk of getting eaten."

Dan looks hesitantly from William to the street outside. No zombies in sight right now, but that might change any moment.

"My uncle has a safe place just outside town," William goes on, his voice softer now. "There's a spot open, if you want to come. Personally, I think it's a hell of an offer, but of course you're free to get out and walk back home."

Dan's phone rings in his pocket. He finds it and looks at the display. "It's … it's my dad."

"Before you answer it, please tell me if you're coming or not? 'Cause I'm about to go."

"Could you wait just one minute?" Dan pleads. "I'll just make sure they're okay."

William pushes his tongue into his cheek and scans the street. "One minute," he says.

Dan answers the call. "Dad?"

"Dan, where are you?"

"I'm in a car. A guy picked me up."

"You all right? Are you hurt?"

"I'm fine, Dad. How about you?"

Dad gives off a sigh of relief. "Good, that's great to hear. We're also fine. Finn has calmed down now that he can't see Lone anymore."

"What about your shoulder?"

"Don't worry about me."

"But Dad," Dan says, lowering his voice. "Did you … did you get …?"

He can't get the question out, but he can tell from the silence his dad guesses it.

"It hurts a little, but I don't think the skin is broken."

Dan feels a glimmer of hope. "So, no blood?"

"No, but I'll probably get a bruise."

"I think that's okay. As long as you're not bleeding."

Dan senses William sending him a sharp look.

"Perhaps," Dad mutters. "Guess I'll just have to wait and see, because I won't be going to the ER anytime soon … the street is riddled with them."

"Make sure you close all the windows," Dan says, feeling a drop of sweat making its way down his back. "Don't give them any chance to get inside."

"I already checked all the windows." Dad is quiet for a moment, then he says: "I'm sorry we didn't believe you, Dan."

"That's all right. I get it, Dad." But he still feels a great amount of relief, despite the circumstances. It feels like a great burden has been lifted from him; as if it isn't only the zombies his dad is acknowledging, but also the fact that Dan had no fault in what happened to Jennie.

William clears his throat and points to his wrist.

"Listen, Dad, I don't think I'll be able to come home right now," Dan says.

"Who picked you up? Was it someone you know?"

"No." Dan turns discretely away from William. "He … he says he knows a safe place outside town."

A couple of seconds before his dad replies: "Does he strike you as someone you can trust?"

"Yes," Dan says without really considering the question.

"Then go with him, Dan."

"But are you guys—"

"Don't worry about us. It's way too dangerous for you to come back right now. The whole street has turned into chaos. I can see it from the living room window. Some of the neighbors have come out to try and help, and they … oh, Christ …" Dad is quiet for another moment, and Dan thinks he can hear a distant scream. "Don't come home yet, Dan," Dad says, even more firmly. "We need to wait till it's safe."

"All right," Dan mutters.

"What's it gonna be?" William asks.

Dan glances at him. "I'm coming with you," he says.

William doesn't waste any time, but immediately slams the accelerator and pulls back out into traffic.

"I need to go, Dan," Dad says. "Your grandma needs help with Finn, he's become restless again. Call me once you get to the place, okay?"

"I will."

"Right. Talk to you soon, son."

Dan disconnects and puts the phone away.

William turns left at an intersection and speeds up. "Your old man sounds like a reasonable guy."

"Could you hear what he said?" Dan asks, feeling a little awkward.

"Yeah." William sends him a brief smile before looking out into the street again. "This part of town looks okay. At least for now."

"It only just started," Dan mutters, almost to himself.

William looks at him again. "You don't seem like you had the best day."

"I didn't."

"What happened? You said something about running over a zombie?"

"It's a long story."

William sneers at him. "Dude, cut out those movie lines and tell me what happened. We've got plenty of time."

Dan breathes in a couple of times, then he begins talking. "I wasn't the one driving, but I was in the passenger seat. It was a little girl. We had to do it. She was—"

"Sorry, shut up for a moment," William interrupts, turning up the radio, which Dan only now realizes has been on at very low volume the whole time.

"... latest reports from local police indicates some sort of terrorist attack, possibly involving biological weapons. Our current intel puts the number of wounded at thirty people, but many more are ..."

"Goddamnit," William murmurs, turning down the radio again. "Biological weapons? They have no idea what's going on."

"They'll find out soon enough," Dan says quietly. When he senses William looking at him, he goes on: "I saw how it began. I tried to stop it."

William is trying to look simultaneously at the road and Dan, as Dan begins to tell his story. He lays it out as briefly and concisely as he can. How he, Jennie and Thomas arrived at the old lady's house. How they discovered she had tried to resurrect her dead grandchild, inadvertently creating the first zombie who then killed her and her son second. He also tells the story of how he and Linda escaped the house, and how he later would go chasing a zombie cop with a girl named Selina.

"Last I heard from her, she had killed Jonas at the hospital," he closes. "And I thought this time it was really over." He sighs heavily, shaking his head. "Something must have gone wrong, because I saw her in a news report from the hospital ... as a zombie. They also said something about a bus outside town that got attacked by an elderly couple. I'll bet you it was the old woman, the one who lived in the woods. She got infected from her cat after it stepped in the officer's blood."

William is quiet for a while after Dan stops talking. They're almost out of town now, and the traffic is sparse.

"It all makes sense," William finally says. "It all began here. Right here, right in the middle of fucking Denmark, and not even in Copenhagen, oh no, it began all the way out here in our tiny shithole of a town. Right here!" He stabs the steering wheel with a finger, as if to emphasize his point. "What are the fucking odds, man? Of all the places ..."

"I know."

"And it's only here," William goes on. "Right? Isn't that what you're telling me?"

"As far as I know."

"Yeah, it has to be. Since it started with that voodoo-shit. Holy crap, I always imagined it would be some kind of top-secret military project with genetically modified super soldiers or, or maybe a radioactive release or some shit—didn't you think so? I mean, that's always how it goes in the movies."

"I ... I didn't really think about it," Dan mutters.

"You seriously never contemplated how the apocalypse would go down?" Williams asks, giving him a critical look. "Come on, everybody has!"

"How about you?" Dan asks, conveniently switching the subject. "When did you find out?"

"I was at the hospital right before it went crazy."

"You were?"

"Yeah, man. I work there—or worked, now that the world is ending. You thought these were my regular clothes?"

Dan hadn't really noticed it before, but William is wearing what looks like the white shirt and pants that hospital staff usually wear.

"I think I saw that girl you mentioned," William goes on. "Selina."

Dan stares at him. "You did?"

William nods and swallows something, but doesn't say anymore. Dan eyes him for a moment, surprised to see his driver hesitate for the first time. William strikes him as the type of person with tons of confidence; the suntanned skin, tattoos and the latest haircut.

"I think it's your turn to tell your story," Dan says, just as they cross the town border and continue out onto the open road stretching far ahead between the open fields.

EIGHTEEN

She's floating somewhere between wakefulness and unconsciousness. Unpleasant images keep flickering by. Mads sitting up, his eyes all wrong. Krista screaming her heart out as Mads bites down on her chin. The sound of the skin ripping.

"Krista!" she tries to shout, but the word won't come out. She tries instead to call for help, but that doesn't work, either. When she turns to look down the street, all the cars are suddenly gone. Instead, an army of living dead comes marching at her.

Mille screams and opens her eyes. The scream catches in her throat, only producing a hoarse whimper. She stares around bewildered, blinking the stinging sweat from her eyes and trying to comprehend what she's seeing.

She's lying on the backseat of a car, but not the same as before. Krista isn't here, and neither is Mads nor the Arab. Instead she can hear unfamiliar voices talking together.

"... in a way it's my fault; I guess I should have called the police instead of just bailing."

"They probably wouldn't have believed you anyway."

"No, and I thought it was too late anyway. You know, that it had begun in other places, too."

"It had. At that time the bus must have already been attacked."

"Yeah, and you know I wrote a warning on the door, but I guess someone must've opened it anyway ..."

Mille sits up with a strained groan. Her head is spinning, and a stinging pain is throbbing just behind her forehead. Something sniffs the back of her head, and she spins around with a whine of surprise to see a large dog look curiously at her.

"Oh, hey! You're awake."

She turns around again. A boy is in the passenger seat and guy a little older than her is behind the wheel. They're both looking back at her.

"Who are you?" Mille murmurs, rubbing her forehead.

"I'm William and this is Dan. I picked you up back in town—you remember?"

Mille moans. "I don't know ... I remember Krista, she ... oh, no ... what happened to her? What happened to Krista?"

The guy behind the wheel sends her an apologetic look in the mirror. "If you're talking about the girl who was with you in the car—I'm sorry, but she's dead."

Mille lowers her head and feels like crying. She's not sure whether it's mostly due to grief or shock or confusion, as all of them fight inside her. "My head's all ... did I pass out?"

"Yeah."

"And where are we going?" She looks out at the fields gliding by.

"We're going to my uncle's place, where we'll be safe for now."

Mille's brain is slowly clearing up, and her memory starts throwing up fragments from what she thought was only bad dreams. Her classmates screaming inside the bus, Mads dying on the backseat of the car, Krista trying helplessly to perform CPR on him ... it all spins into an awful cocktail, faster and faster.

"Are you all right?" the boy in the passenger seat asks, eyeing her closely. "You're turning pale."

"I ... I think I'm going to throw up," Mille croaks.

"Hold on," William says, hitting the brakes. "Keep it in just a second longer."

Mille feels the sick come rolling up her throat, and she swallows it convulsively back down. As soon as the car comes to a stop, she opens the door, tumbles out on the burning asphalt and pukes into the dried-out grass of the roadside. It's been a few hours since she ate, so only a handful of oatmeal comes up. She spits and wipes her mouth with her sleeve. She straightens up and looks around. Except for a few farms in the distance, the area is completely desolate.

When she turns to the car, both boys have gotten out and are now looking at her with something Mille at first interprets as concern.

"I'm okay," she assures them. "I feel better now."

She goes to get back in, but William steps carefully in front of her. "Hold on," he says. "Are you, uhm ... are you sure you feel better?"

"Sure," Mille says. "I mean, it's the worst day of my life, but other than that, I'm fine. I won't throw up in your car, I promise."

"That's not what I'm worried about," he says, finding a packet of cigarettes from his pocket. Mille notices he's dressed in what looks like a hospital staff uniform. "Do you have any wounds?"

Mille looks down and shakes her head. "No."

"No tiny scratches or anything?"

"No, I tell you!" She's starting to feel annoyed, mostly because she's afraid. Afraid because part of her already knows what he's driving at. "I think I'd notice if I was bitten."

"You don't need to get bitten," Dan says in a grave voice, stepping slightly forward. He can't be more than fourteen, although his face looks twenty-five. He's obviously tired, ragged and scared, all at once. "You don't even need to have been in direct contact with one of them. If you cut yourself on anything with their blood on ... I've seen it happen."

Mille breathes deeply, making an effort to get her emotions under control, although everything is firing inside of her. She looks down again. Her clothes are a little messed up—probably from when she collapsed in the middle of the road—but she can't see any blood. She shrugs. "Look, I don't know what you want from me. You want me to strip down so you can check me?"

"I thought you'd prefer doing it yourself," William says, without the faintest smile. "We'll look away."

Mille gapes at him. "You can't be serious. Do you know what I've been through today? I have ... I have been almost ... almost ..." Her body is shaking so violently that her throat closes up. Rage and sorrow are choking her and she blinks furiously to keep back the tears as she glowers at William. "Who the hell ... do you think ... you are?"

He doesn't answer.

She steps towards the car, expecting for them to grab her and hold her back, but they simply step aside and let her pass. Mille goes to open the car door, but the lock snaps shut.

She turns and stares at William who has the key in his hand. He lights his cigarette in an infuriatingly nonchalant way, as though he's Bruce Willis in some stupid action movie.

"Drive me home!" she demands. "Drive me back into town!"

"I think you'll regret that if I do," he says calmly blowing out smoke. "But if you really want it, I'll drive you back. I just can't let you inside my car before you've checked yourself. It's nothing personal, really, but I saw you inside the car with a zombie, and I have no way of knowing what happened to you."

Mille takes in air to scream at William, when Dan suddenly steps forward and takes hold of her arm.

"I've seen it happen twice before," he says, fixing her eyes with his. "My friend died because he stepped on a piece of broken glass, and an elderly lady got scratched by a cat that had stepped in infected blood. I'm sorry, but I can't risk it happening again."

Mille is struck by the amount of pain she sees in his large, blue eyes, and suddenly it feels like she's imploding. The rage seeps out in a long, shivering breath. She shrugs. "Look, I really don't think I have any scratches. Honestly. I don't feel pain anywhere."

"We just need to be completely sure," William says, spitting.

Mille checks herself for any scratch wounds. She doesn't strip down, but she rolls up her sleeves and pulls out her shirt and shorts. The boys watch her silently.

"There," she says. "All done."

William looks down. "What about under your feet?"

Mille takes off her sandals and checks the soles of her feet. "Nothing."

"Can I check the back of your neck, please?" Dan asks carefully, and Mille pulls her hair aside, letting him check her skin. "It looks fine," he says.

"Congratulations!" William says, smiling at her in a way Mille finds both really annoying and annoyingly charming, as he drops the cigarette on the asphalt and steps on it. "You've made it through round one."

NINETEEN

"This is it," William announces as he sees Holger's place coming up ahead.

The house is lying atop a small hill a couple hundred yards off the road, making it visible from far away, a single windmill right next to it, whirling lazily in the hot summer air. William slows down the car and turns onto the gravel road winding its way up to the house.

"Does your uncle know we're coming?" Dan asks.

"Sure, I spoke with him on the phone earlier," William says, darting a glance in the rearview mirror. "Speaking of, don't you have anybody to call? Like your parents, perhaps?"

To his surprise Mille just shakes her head, not even looking at him.

"Really? Is there no one who needs to know where you are? Or maybe someone you'd like to warn about what's going to happen?"

"No," Mille says, still glancing out of the window. "All of my friends died on that bus."

William can still picture the scene, even though Mille only described it briefly and with very little detail. She's obviously traumatized, and it's no wonder.

"Then how about your fami—"

"I don't have a family," she cuts him off, a sudden fierceness in her voice.

"Okay," William says, sending Dan a look.

Dan returns the look and shakes his head discretely, as though to say: "Stop digging."

William changes the subject. "Right, there's a few things you need to know about my uncle. He's been battling some mental stuff, but he's on medication now, so he's perfectly functional. He might seem a little suspicious, but don't take it personal, he's just like that with people he doesn't know. And he doesn't like being touched, so don't shake his hand or anything like that." He looks at Mille in the mirror; she's looking back at him with an expression of growing skepticism. "Now, it's his place, so if he doesn't want you there for some reason, I'll have to take you back to town. But I don't think it'll be a problem."

"Is this really the best place to be?" Mille asks. "At a mentally ill person's house, far away from anyone else?"

"Wait until you see the place," William says. "I think you'll understand once you do."

They reach the courtyard, and William brings the car to a halt. Seen from the outside, Holger's house looks like any other house you'd expect to find out here; there's a garage and an outside boiler-room beside the residential building.

Holger comes walking around the garage, eyeing the car suspiciously. It's been a few years since William saw his uncle. Holger gained a couple of pounds and his hairline has receded a bit farther back—other than that, he looks like William remembers him, dressed in way too warm cargo pants and a worn shirt with rolled-up sleeves. His round face is glistening with sweat, and his hands are black from dirt and oil.

"Is that him?" Dan asks.

"That's him," William says, adding quickly as Dan unbuckles: "I think it's better I talk to him first."

Ozzy whines from the trunk, impatient to go say hello to Holger, whom he apparently recognizes even though he only saw him once.

William opens the door and steps out into the warm afternoon air. "Hey, Holger. Long time no see."

Holger stops a few yards distance from the car, and William notices a tiny shovel in his hand. "Hello, William," he says with a bated smile. The tiny eyes seem even more squinted because of Holger's heavy forehead, but they're also alert, and right now they're darting back and forth between William and the car. "Who's that you've brought?"

"Just a couple of friends. I think I might have promised them a spot here at your place."

Holger's gaze stops ping-ponging and fastens on William. "Is it because of what they're saying on the radio?"

William nods.

Holger breathes deeply through his nose and exhales heavily. He looks somehow both scared and relieved at the same time, and

William gets why. Holger has been living for twenty years with paranoia, the last ten a little less bad due to the medication, and yet William knows his uncle never really let go of his nagging suspicion that the world would one day soon come to an end, and that belief has made him isolated and a cast-out. Even William's mom, Holger's own sister, has had a hard time dealing with her brother, and William still suspects it was part of the reason why she moved to Holland after William left home.

William himself is probably the closest family member Holger has left, quite simply because William is the only one who never judged him for his paranoid thoughts, and today William feels particularly grateful that's the case.

"How bad is it?" Holger asks, his voice grave.

"Pretty bad. I think it might be the end of society as we know it, but ... maybe the authorities can still stop it."

"The authorities," Holger sneers, showing his tiny teeth in a humorless grin. "They're probably the ones who started it."

"Nope," William says, and when Holger looks surprised, he adds: "You'll get the story later."

Holger eyes him. "So, is it ... zombies?"

"Yeah."

"Are they acting like in the movies?"

"As far as I can tell."

Holger nods slowly. "I thought it sounded like zombies from what they're saying on the radio. Of course they didn't use that word. And I wasn't really paying attention, 'cause I've been busy harvesting vegetables." He holds up the shovel, as though to prove what he's saying. "I got to it right after you called me. It's a lucky time of year, you know, 'cause there'll be lots to eat the coming months. We can store the potatoes and the onions for weeks, and that way we'll get fresh vitamins every day. As long as we just—"

"Holger," William says, holding up a hand. "That's all great, it really is. But let's wait and see, all right? Maybe it doesn't need to go that far. For now, we'll just have to take one day at a time. That sound fair?"

Holger studies him for a moment, as though he just said something rather crazy. Then, he nods. "All right. But I already prepared everything."

"Awesome. I'm really happy you're willing to help out." He gestures towards the car. "So, is it cool with you if Dan and Mille stay too?" He quickly adds: "They might be going back home soon, depending on how things unfold."

Holger looks to the car, then back to William. "Are they trustworthy?" he asks, lowering his voice.

"To be honest, I don't know them very well. But they've both been in contact with the zombies, so they might have—"

"They been in contact with them?" Holger exclaims, stepping backwards.

"Easy, Holger!" William says, realizing his mistake. "I've checked them for any wounds or scratches. All three of us. We're all clean, I promise."

Holger looks like he seriously considers turning on his heel and sprinting out of the courtyard, but he forces himself to stay. "If we let them in and one of them becomes sick …"

"Then we'll throw them back out," William says immediately. "We all agree on that. And same goes for me, of course." Holger lifts his eyebrows, and William goes on: "I didn't touch any zombies, I'm just saying."

Holger takes a few deep breaths, scratches his neck and glances at the car. Two white butterflies whirl across the courtyard in a carefree dance, and William is reminded how surreal the situation is. It might look like an ordinary summer's day, but nothing might ever be ordinary again.

"All right," Holger finally mutters. "They can stay for now."

"Thank you, Holger," William smiles.

"Shall we go inside?" Holger suggests, nodding towards the house. "I could really use something to drink."

TWENTY

They enter what seems at first glance like a pretty normal home. But Dan already notices the subtle signs in the hallway. The front door, for instance, is reinforced on the inside with a heavy iron grid and has three large sliding latches. He looks up and sees a camera in the ceiling, staring down at them.

Holger kicks off his shoes in the corner before going into the kitchen. "You guys just wait in the living room," he calls back.

Dan and Mille both look to William, and he waves them discretely into the adjacent room. Ozzy follows close to William while sniffing the air curiously.

The living room is pretty big, but it seems smaller due to all the stuff taking up every available surface. Shelves, chairs, windowsills, the couch, even the floor is crammed with all kinds of stuff, not to mention the dining table in the middle of the room, which is covered in book piles and cardboard boxes reaching almost to the ceiling. Holger has collected all kinds of things, tools, accessories, electronic devices, and objects Dan can't even identify. There are also quite a few plates and cups strewn about, and flies are buzzing in the air. It smells like it's been weeks since a window was opened. Holger is pretty obviously a bachelor.

But there are no apparent signs that Holger's home should be the zombie-proof fortification William hinted at. The only form of protection Dan can see is the metal grids barring the windows and making him feel like he's in prison. Oh, and more cameras in the ceiling.

He begins to seriously consider if he made a mistake going with William. Maybe he should have taken the chance when William offered to drop him off.

"Sorry for the mess," Holger calls from the kitchen. "Try to find a place to sit down. Just don't break anything."

William clears a couple of chairs and offers Mille one of them. Dan moves a tower of books off the couch's armrest and sits down.

Holger brings in a large pitcher of red lemonade and takes a glass from a cupboard which he fills and chucks down in one go. He burps and pours himself another glass before sitting down at the corner of the coffee table.

"You know, I always knew this day would come," he mutters into the glass before taking another big swig—the sight of the lemonade has suddenly reminded Dan how thirsty he is, but Holger doesn't seem intent on offering any of his guests something to drink. "It was only a matter of time."

"Yeah, you were right all along," William says, getting up. He takes three glasses from the cupboard and hands them to Dan and Mille, before he takes the pitcher from Holger, who barely seems to notice.

"Now I guess they wish they'd listened," he says, staring into the floor.

William pours lemonade for the three of them, and Dan immediately gulps down the sweet, synthetic-tasting liquid. Then he licks his lips and stares longingly at the pitcher, which William hands back to Holger, who pours himself a third helping.

"Cheers," William says, raising his glass, looking around at them with a pale smile. "To the end of the world."

"Cheers," Holger mutters, as though not really listening.

Dan glances at Mille, who has found her phone and is checking something on it. She sips her glass but doesn't seem to like the taste. Ozzy is slinking around sniffing the surroundings.

"Well," William says, going to the window. It's not easy getting a clear view, because the curtain is hanging down on one side, and the other is blocked by more books. "This is like the beginning of a disaster movie. Four people and a dog hobbled together in a fight for survival. Now all we need is the zombies."

Dan can tell William is trying to make a joke out of it, but he doesn't really feel like laughing.

"Excuse me," Mille says. William turns to her, and Dan can see how Mille strains to talk calmly. "I'm glad you helped me. I think you saved my life."

"I think so too," William says, neither shame nor pride in his voice.

"But," Mille goes on, "I really don't see how we're anymore safe out here than at our own homes. Is it just because we're outside town or what? Because if the whole world is going to end, like you say it is, then the zombies will probably come out here too at some point. And if I had to choose, I think I'd rather be somewhere I know."

"It's not just because we're outside town," William says, finding his cigarettes. "Okay if I smoke in here, Holger?"

"Please don't. It's unhealthy."

"I know," William sighs, putting the pack back into his pocket. "But why stop now?"

"Then how are we more protected out here?" Mille exclaims, throwing out her arms. "As far as I can tell, this is just a regular house with barred windows." She glances at Holger. "No offense. It's nice of you to … let us stay here." Those last words sound like they don't want to come out.

Holger avoids her gaze and says nothing.

William empties his glass, wipes his mouth and gets up. "What do you say we show them the place, Holger?"

Holger looks around at them uncertainly, then he nods and gets to his feet. "Follow me. We'll take the entrance in the bedroom."

"The entrance?" Mille repeats, but since neither William nor Holger replies, she looks to Dan. Dan simply shrugs, gets up and follows them into the next room.

Holger's bedroom is dimly lit and smells even more stuffy than the living room. His bedsheets visibly need a changing, and dark blinds keeps out most of the daylight. Dan notices the bed is placed at an odd angle, and he realizes why as Holger kneels down and pulls aside an old, worn-down rug, revealing a hatch in the wooden floor. He opens it and reaches down to pull up a flashlight.

"Follow me," he says, placing the flashlight in his belt. Then, he climbs down a ladder fastened to the inside of the hole in the floor.

"Ozzy, stay," William says, following his uncle. The German shepherd sits down and watches his owner disappear out of sight.

Dan glances at Mille, who's staring at the hole with a highly skeptical look.

"Is that like a hidden basement or what?" she whispers.

"I have no idea," Dan admits. "Do you want to go first?"

Mille steps back and waves him forward.

Dan takes a deep breath before he sits down and climbs down the rusty steps. The descent is longer than he anticipated, maybe twelve feet before he finally feels solid ground underfoot. He turns and is blinded by the flashlight.

"Where's the girl?" Holger's voice asks.

Dan is too stunned to answer right away. He looks around to see not a basement but a long, narrow corridor stretching as far as the light reaches. The ground is dirt, but the walls are made of planks and wooden boards. The ceiling is just high enough for Holger and Dan to be standing upright, but William has to crane his neck slightly.

"Holy shit," Dan whispers.

William sends him one of his crooked smiles. "Wait till you see what's at the end." He looks up through the hole. "You coming, Mille?"

No answer, but after a short while the steps creak, and Mille comes climbing down very carefully. She looks around, appearing just as surprised as Dan. "What is this place?" she asks, stroking her arm.

"That's a good question," William says, looking at his uncle. "What do you call it, Holger?"

Holger shakes his head. "I don't call it anything."

"Well, let's name it … Fort Holger!"

Holger bares his baby teeth in a silent grin. Then, he turns and paces down through the corridor, bringing the flashlight and causing the rest of them to follow along quickly so as to not be left in the dark.

The corridor goes on for what feels like a hundred yards with no turns or forks. Finally they reach a door with no visible lock but only a small panel of numbered buttons. Holger glances briefly over his shoulder before typing the code. The lock beeps and the door can be opened.

Holger steps through it, and an automated light turns on on the other side.

"You first," William says smiling and stepping aside. "I've seen it before. Mind the step."

Dan squeezes past him, steps down a single step onto a vinyl floor and sees a surprisingly large room. He stops in the doorway and stares around at what looks most of all like a pretty regular apartment. If it hadn't been for the lack of windows and the big, heavy wooden beams supporting the ceiling, Dan would never have guessed they were still underground.

There's a kitchen area with a stove and two large refrigerators, a dining area with a table big enough for four people, an old couch with a flat screen TV and a bookcase stuffed with books, and a home office with three laptops. The shelves in the kitchen are stuffed with cans and jars and something that looks like dried herbs and fruits.

But this is where the similarities to a normal home end.

Next to the dining table is what looks to Dan like a mini hospital, complete with a full array of surgical instruments, pill bottles and even an operating table hinged to the wall. On the opposite end of the room are two large metal cabinets with heavy padlocks, clearly marked with the next: FIREARMS, KNIVES & MACHETTES, EXPLOSIVES.

Holger has gone to the office area and activated one of the laptops. The screen shows eight live feeds from around the property, both inside and out—and the purpose of all the cameras suddenly becomes clear to Dan.

"This is insane," he mutters as Mille steps past him, glaring around in stunned silence.

The fact that Holger built a big underground room is impressive enough. It must have taken him years—not to mention the structural knowledge and skills it would take—but that he also turned it into a seemingly perfect survival place with everything you would need to outlast a minor nuclear war ...

"You haven't seen it all yet," William says, putting a hand on his shoulder, pointing to a door Dan didn't notice until now. "Come on, I'll show you the other rooms ..."

TWENTY-ONE

Finn is staring blankly at the plate in front of him. The lasagna has gone cold but still it smells good. He just doesn't have any appetite. That's an understatement, really; appetite is no longer a feeling Finn understands. Food is an unknown concept to him.

The only thing still present in him is the thought of Lone. That she's walking around out there right now with all the other lost souls. So many people dead all at once; it's unfathomable. And yet, Finn really doesn't care about all the rest of them. He has no relatives, no kids or siblings, so why would other people's fate matter to him? All he cares about—all he ever really cared about—is Lone. And Lone is dead.

"Try to eat something, Finn."

The voice causes him to lift his head and blink sleepily. Henrik is looking at him with an expression of warm concern.

"You'll feel better if you eat," the neighbor says, pointing to the plate.

Finn lets his eyes wander around the table. He has actually forgotten where he is and who else is present. There's Trine, of course, Henrik's wife. And Trine's mother—Finn can't recall her name, he's not even sure she told him. Trine's mom, who's around Finn's own age, is eating her lasagna neatly using both knife and fork, while trying to look as though everything is normal. Still she can't help but dart a look towards the windows every time there's a screech of fingernails scraping the outside of the glass. The windows are carefully blocked off with towels and blankets in the hope that those outside would stop trying to get in once they couldn't see them anymore.

But they didn't stop. Apparently, they don't need to see them to know they are there. They can probably smell them. Like sharks, who can pick up on the smell of a single drop of blood at a distance of several miles. Finn saw that once in a documentary.

There's also another reason why Henrik and his mother-in-law took great care to seal off every window in the house. They didn't say it, but Finn knows it's because they don't want him to see—

"Finn?"

Henrik's voice pulls him back once again.

"How're you feeling? Have the pills started working?"

"The pills?" Finn repeats.

"I gave you a couple of Trine's sedatives, remember?"

"Oh, right," Finn mutters. "Yeah, I—I think they're doing the job."

"That's good. I still think you should get some food, though."

Finn picks up the fork and looks at it like it's some sort of advanced piece of equipment he never operated before. He scoops up some lasagna and transports it to his mouth, chews it, swallows.

Henrik smiles at him. Then he goes on eating.

It's warm and stuffy in the living room, since they can't air out and because the evening sun is still baking away outside. He should have been sitting at the terrace right now, a cold beer in his hand and Lone by his side while she did her crosswords.

Finn forces down another bite and looks at Trine. She is the only one present who looks like Finn feels. Her eyes are red and distant, her lasagna untouched. She prods it with her fork now and then, only to put it down again.

"You too, honey," Henrik says. "Try to—"

"Mind your own business," Trine sneers, not looking up.

Henrik sighs. "I know it's a terrible situation, but ... I'm sure Dan is fine, and he'll come home."

Trine shakes her head slowly. "He's not. You told him yourself to stay away."

"Only because it's not safe around here right now. You can hear them outside, can't you?" Henrik gestures towards the window. "Would you really want Dan to come home while they're still out there?"

Trine lets out a long, trembling breath, and Finn can see her eyes turn moist. "I've lost my daughter," she whispers, "and now you've sent off my son to die ..."

"Honey, please," Henrik says, reaching for her hand.

She draws it away hissing: "Don't touch me."

Henrik looks to his mother-in-law. "Kirsten, would you ...?"

Kirsten nods, puts down her knife and fork and dabs her mouth with the napkin. "Listen to me," she says, turning to her daughter. "Henrik did the right thing. I'm sure Dan is safe."

"How would you know?" Trine asks as she begins stabbing the lasagna with her fork. "You don't know the people he's with."

"As soon as the police get this under control, we'll go and get Dan," Kirsten goes on.

"We can't," Trine says, raising her voice. "'Cause we don't know where he is! And he's not answering his phone ... do you think that's a good sign, huh, Mom? Or do you think he might be dead somewhere, just like Jennie, just like my girl ... my girl ... my little girl ... oh God ..." Trine bursts into tears, and Henrik and Kirsten get up in unison.

"Let me take her," Kirsten says, glancing at Finn. "Maybe he could use some sleep."

Henrik nods and turns to Finn, while Kirsten helps her daughter to the couch.

"Would you like a nap, Finn?" Henrik asks.

Finn agrees without really thinking. Henrik helps him to his feet. They leave the living room and the sound of Trine's sobbing cries, and they go down the hallway to a room slightly cooler, even though the window here is also blocked by a blanket.

"Is this ... is this Jennie's room?" Finn asks absentmindedly, looking at the posters of singers.

"It was," Henrik murmurs. "Until yesterday."

"Until yesterday?" Finn parrots, not understanding.

"Jennie's dead, Finn."

"Oh, right."

"Come on, lie down."

Finn lies down on the neatly made bed, folding his hands on his stomach. He stares up to the ceiling, where Jennie did a collage of photos of her and her friends having fun.

Henrik glances up at the pictures and swallows audibly. "Try to get some rest," he says. "You just call me if you need anything, okay?"

"Okay. Thank you, Henrik."

Henrik leaves the room, closing the door almost all the way.

Finn just lies there for a while, studying the photos without really seeing them. His eyelids are growing heavy when someone suddenly scrapes on the window.

Finn sits up and looks at the blanket. He can make out a low figure on the other side, hands groping the glass and the person uttering a low, almost pained moaning.

Could that be her?

Finn's breathing automatically speeds up a notch. The silhouette could very well be Lone—but then again, what would the odds be? Henrik said earlier there must already be hundreds of them out there, so it could be anyone outside the window. Perhaps another one of the residents of the street. Perhaps a total stranger.

Perhaps ... Lone.

Finn gets up and steps carefully closer. The tuneless groans from the figure grow slightly louder, the hands start fumbling more eagerly, as though the person feels him approaching.

The blanket is attached all the way around with tacks. Finn picks one of them out and gently moves the blanket a little aside, allowing him to peek out.

A strong dropping sensation in his lower belly almost makes him stagger.

Lone's face is staring at him through the glass. Her mouth is open, and there's dried blood on her chin and down her throat. Her glasses are gone, and her hair is messy and lumpy with more dried blood. The eyes aren't the grey, loving eyes he remembers, but dull and white, empty and without a trace of anything human.

Or—are they? Are her eyes really completely empty?

The more Finn stares into Lone's face, the more he begins to sense a remnant of her old self. She, on the other hand, doesn't seem to recognize him, as she just keeps running her hands over the glass and growling at him.

But maybe ... maybe that's her way of communicating? Maybe she can't talk or move normally anymore, but who's to say she's not still in there? After all, how else would she have found him, if she wasn't at least partly herself still? Maybe she could even be cured!

She shouldn't be out there with all the rest of them.

The thought awakens a new feeling in Finn: fear. If he just leaves Lone on her own, who knows what might happen to her? She could be run over by a car or shot by the police. He can't risk that. He can't risk losing her for good.

So, Finn begins picking out more tacks. The blanket falls to the floor, exposing the view completely and letting the evening light pour into the room. Finn doesn't notice, though; he just stares at his wife, who has by now greased up most of the window with her hands.

"Lone," he whispers, placing a hand on the glass.

She eagerly tries to kiss his palm, and it causes Finn to tear up.

"I knew you were still in there somewhere," he says, choking up. His hand goes for the hasp. A tiny voice at the back of his head shouts to him, telling him he's making a big mistake, that Lone can't be saved, that she's dangerous and wants to hurt him.

But Finn can't believe that voice. He can only believe what he sees, and knows Lone's eyes seem even more human than just a moment ago, as though simply seeing him has cured her a little. If he lets her inside the room, she'll probably become completely herself once more.

"I'll help you, dear," he whispers hoarsely, as the tears pour down his cheeks. "I can't live without you, you know that."

His hand unlocks the hasp.

No! the voice shouts.

"Yes," Finn croaks, smiling as he opens the window.

TWENTY-TWO

Mille pulls her legs up and wraps her arms around her knees. She's sitting in the window looking out over Holger's back garden, where the last of the sunlight is coloring the grass orange.

It's almost eleven o'clock, and even though this has by far been the longest day of her life, she barely feels tired. Her body is exhausted, of course, but her eyes don't feel like closing.

She can still taste curry from the stew Holger served. To her surprise she found herself ravenous and she cleaned off her plate in no time. After all, she hadn't eaten anything since breakfast that morning.

Her brain is still fighting to keep up. It feels like it can't really update its software, like it doesn't want to compute how everything has changed. She should have been in Prague right now, she and Krista should have been lying in bed next to each other in a hotel room with two other girls from the class. They should have been complaining about the long, warm bus ride and talking about what sights they were going to see tomorrow morning.

Instead, Krista is dead, just like Mads and the rest of the class. Same probably goes for most of everyone else she knows. And she herself is sitting here, in a guy's house with two other strangers and a German shepherd, as they simply wait for the world to end.

She looks around at the others. Dan is huddled in one corner of the couch, sleeping with a thin blanket wrapped around him. William is sitting on a chair, elbows resting on his knees, staring at the television, where the sound is turned down to a whisper. He looks like a soccer fan intensely watching a game which he bet a lot of money on—except it isn't soccer on the screen, but a news report. They keep showing footage from the air and video recordings from cell phones. A lot of it is censored, and the reporters warn again and again about "strong imagery."

The dog is lying faithfully right next to William, halfway dozing, but raising its head now and then, as though constantly listening for something no one else can hear. Holger is the only one missing; he's down in the bunker to prepare something or other—he has barely taken a rest since they came here.

Mille didn't understand half of what William told them during the tour of the bunker. All the technical stuff about how the generator produces power from the windmill and the solar panels, how the rainwater is cleaned and filtered, and how the security systems work went right past her. All she knows is that Holger obviously thought of every tiny detail when he built this place, and that you could probably live down there for years.

But who would want that?

She gets an image of herself four years from now, pale and long hair, not having stepped outside the bunker for even a second, the only company has been her three involuntary roommates, the rest of the earth's population dead and the zombies are the only ones wandering around.

What would she have to live for in a scenario like that? Survival, and nothing else. Mille gets the chills.

It probably won't come to that. They still have time to stop it.

But the news reports don't seem great. Mille has also checked social media on her phone now and then. At first, she mostly read grieving posts from the relatives of those who died on the bus, and other people offering their condolences. Then, other kinds of tweets began ticking in, like:

WTF is going on in this town?? Anybody know anything?

And more and more started replying and giving their two cents worth, even though none of them seemed to know what was really happening. Mille read creative guesses like terrorism or natural disasters. One guy even suggested the whole thing was a giant prank, put up by a television network.

But as the evening progressed, the tweets became more and more grave.

Why aren't the police doing anything?

and

One of them just walked by my window!

and

Just drove by the library—serious, stay away from there, folks! Not a sight anybody needs to see!

Slowly people began catching on to the seriousness of the situation, even though many were still utterly confused. But more and more often, Mille would see the magic word.

Zombies.

People began posting videos from their phones, either filmed from their windows or cars. Some more gory than others. Mille didn't feel like watching any of them. A video from a press release also went viral, where a spokesman of the police told people to remain indoors and avoid physical contact with anybody until further notice.

"They're declaring a state of emergency," William mutters.

Mille looks at the television and sees the prime minister talking to the camera with a very grave expression, her lips quivering slightly.

"The whole town is being shut off," William says. "About damn time."

Dan stirs from the couch, and the dog lifts its head.

"How many dead?" Mille asks.

"They aren't giving any numbers anymore," William replies, not taking his eyes from the screen, which is now showing a live feed from a helicopter somewhere over town. Three figures are staggering down the street, empty cars are left everywhere, and even from this distance and in the dying daylight, Mille can make out several dark bulges on the asphalt. "It must be in the hundreds, maybe even thousands by now," William goes on.

"So, Holger's calculations will prove true," Dan says, rubbing his eyes, then gesturing to the whiteboard on the wall, where Holger drew a graph and wrote a lot of numbers. "Tomorrow evening, there will be no one alive in the town."

"Not if they get their act together and send in the military, like I've been trying to tell them," William says, obviously frustrated. He's been calling the police several times, trying to convey to them the scope of the situation. Mille can't blame whoever was on the other end of the line—probably some young on-duty cop—for having a hard time believing it.

"I promised to call my dad by now," Dan murmurs and finds his phone. "Oh, shoot, it's out of power. Does Holger have a charger, William?"

"Check the bedroom."

Dan gets up and goes to the bedroom.

William finds his own phone. "I'd probably better call my mom too. How about you, you're not going to—" He stops as he apparently remembers something, then he just shakes his head. "Sorry, none of my business." He gets up and goes to the kitchen. A moment later, Mille can hear him talking to his mom.

Mille checks her phone and the seven unanswered calls. Most of them are from private numbers, and she's pretty sure it's the police who have been trying to get to her to make sure she is okay, like they probably did with everyone aboard the bus whom they couldn't find right away.

But there's also a single call from a number she knows. A single call she didn't expect at all.

Helle, the display says.

Forty-five minutes ago. Mille saw the call coming, but she just stared at the silent phone. She didn't try calling back, and Helle hasn't tried calling again.

Mille didn't pick up, because she had no idea what to say. What do you say after three years?

Suddenly, she wants to call back, but the thought immediately makes her uncomfortable. There are too many questions. How will the voice sound? Like she remembers or completely changed? Older? Weaker? More loving? Maybe even concerned?

Mille is just not sure she would know how to handle it. Yet her finger moves closer to the Call button, hovering there for several seconds.

Then she sees something out of the corner of her eye and turns her head. Far away over the field, she can make out a wobbling figure in the twilight. No, not one—two. No, three. More and more are appearing. There are over twenty in total, and still more are coming.

Her throat constricts and it's suddenly difficult to breathe.

The living dead aren't walking in any particular formation, they don't even seem to be walking together. But they're all nonetheless headed in the same direction. They're all aiming directly for Holger's house on top of the hill.

At that moment, Dan comes back into the room. "I found a charger," he says, but his expression changes once he sees Mille's face. "What is it?" he asks in alarm.

Before she can answer, there's a loud bang from the bedroom, and Dan whirls around. William's dog comes barging in from the kitchen, barking at the noise.

But it's only Holger, who slammed open the hatch in the floor, and now comes tumbling into the living room, his expression wild.

"Shut up, Ozzy!" William commands, as he joins them from the kitchen, phone pressed to his chest. "What's going on, Holger?"

Holger looks like he wants to run someplace but can't decide where that place is, so he ends up just standing there. "I saw them," he pants. "I saw them on the screens. They're coming."

The words leave a chill silence in the living room.

"How ... how many?" William croaks.

"Many," Mille says, surprised to hear her own voice. All three of them turn to look at her. She points out the window.

William is instantly by her side. "Oh, fuck me," he mutters and steps back. He looks from Mille to Dan and then to Holger. There's a special glow in his eyes—it could be fear, yet to Mille it looks almost like wild excitement—as he says: "Here we go ..."

***

Find out how it all began.
Get the free prequel, Day 0, only available at
nick-clausen.com/day0

Or, continue to the next book at
nick-clausen.com/day456

Printed in Great Britain
by Amazon